7 W9-BZP-401

NO USE DYING OVER SPILLED MILK

Also by Tamar Myers

Too Many Crooks Spoil the Broth
Parsley, Sage, Rosemary, and Crime

NO USE DYING OVER SPILLED MILK

A PENNSYLVANIA DUTCH MYSTERY

WITH RECIPES

✦

TAMAR MYERS

A DUTTON BOOK

DUTTON
Published by the Penguin Group
Penguin Books USA Inc., 375 Hudson Street,
New York, New York 10014, U.S.A.
Penguin Books Ltd, 27 Wrights Lane,
London W8 5TZ, England
Penguin Books Australia Ltd, Ringwood,
Victoria, Australia
Penguin Books Canada Ltd, 10 Alcorn Avenue,
Toronto, Ontario, Canada M4V 3B2
Penguin Books (N.Z.) Ltd, 182–190 Wairau Road,
Auckland 10, New Zealand

Penguin Books Ltd, Registered Offices:
Harmondsworth, Middlesex, England

First published by Dutton, an imprint of Dutton Signet,
a division of Penguin Books USA Inc.
Distributed in Canada by McClelland & Stewart Inc.

First Printing, April, 1996
10 9 8 7 6 5 4 3 2 1

 REGISTERED TRADEMARK—MARCA REGISTRADA

LIBRARY OF CONGRESS CATALOGING-IN-PUBLICATION DATA:

Myers, Tamar.
No use dying over spilled milk : a Pennsylvania Dutch mystery with recipes / Tamar Myers.
    p. cm.
    ISBN 0-525-94099-5 (acid-free)
    1. Women detectives—Pennsylvania—Fiction 2. Hotelkeepers—Pennsylvania—
Fiction. 3. Mennonites—Pennsylvania—Fiction. 4. Pennsylvania Dutch—Fiction.
I. Title.
PS3563.Y475N6 1996
813'.54—dc20   95-20505
                                                                    CIP

Printed in the United States of America
Set in Plantin
Designed by Leonard Telesca

To the Source of all my inspiration

ACKNOWLEDGMENTS

I would like to acknowledge Joseph Pittman, Senior Editor at Dutton Signet, for his faith in me, and his excellent advice. Thank you, Joe. And thank you, Nancy Yost of Lowenstein Associates Inc., for being such a super agent.

As always I would like to acknowledge my Number One Fan (of twenty-five years), Jeffrey Charles Myers. As for those two aging half-Siamese cats, Dori and Gray, who wander across my keyboard at inconvenient times, I have a question. Which one of you is responsible for that hair ball in my new laser printer?

One

Yost Yoder drowned in a tank of unpasteurized milk. He was naked. It happened on Valentine's Day.

From the very beginning I suspected there might have been foul play involved. Amish men don't often go swimming in milk, without their clothes—especially in February. Therefore, for my own sake, as well as yours, I faithfully recorded all the details as they happened, beginning with the phone call that woke me up while I was sleeping on the wrong side of my bed.

"PennDutch Inn," I answered automatically.

"Magdalena?"

"That depends. Who's calling?"

"Magdalena, is that you?"

"Maybe, maybe not. Who wants to know?" There are few things I dislike more than rude callers who won't identify themselves from the get-go.

"It's me."

"It is? I thought it was me." Perhaps I was a little sarcastic, but last I heard there were over eight billion "me"s in the world. This one sounded a little like Barbra Streisand, but Babs never calls me before eight in the morning.

"Magdalena! I know that's you. This is Annie Stutzman over in Farmersburg, Ohio. I'm your father's cousin—I mean, I was."

"Oh." Papa was dead. He and Mama died in a car wreck twelve years ago. Every now and then one of their far-flung kin, whom I haven't seen since before my parents' deaths, calls or drops by. This always makes me uncomfortable.

"You are Magdalena, Amos Yoder's daughter, aren't you?"

"Well, even if I am, my parents' will was airtight."

"So it is you!"

"Rumors of my death may have been exaggerated," I said. If it was good enough for Mark Twain, it would have to do.

"Are you done wasting my time now, Magdalena? This call is costing me a pretty penny."

The woman was definitely my dead papa's cousin. "It's your dime, dear," I said agreeably. "Talk as long as you want."

The silence on the other end was just long enough to make me nervous.

"Spill it, Annie. There's still a half hour until my alarm goes off."

"Well, I never! And at a time like this, too!"

"The time here is six-thirty a.m., Annie. What time is it in Ohio?"

"Yost Yoder drowned this morning," said Annie, getting right to the point. "Will you and Freni be coming out for the funeral?"

I racked my sleep-dulled brain for a clue as to who she was talking about. Yost Yoder is a common name among Amish, and those Mennonites of Amish origin. There were five Yost Yoders alone in the small town of Hernia, Pennsylvania, where I lived. There was no telling how many Yost

Yoders had been living in a place as big as Farmersburg, Ohio. I would have to do a little fishing. "Didn't Aunt Lydia's youngest marry a boy by that name?"

Annie's barklike laugh did not travel well over the wires. "That was Noah Yoder. Yost was your second cousin twice removed, and my second cousin once removed. He was also Freni's first cousin. Double, in fact."

Believe it or not, this made perfect sense to me. My family tree is so intertwined that it is a veritable thicket. I am, in fact, my own cousin—well, if not, almost. The point is I can have a family reunion when there is no one else present but me, and still manage to have several generations in attendance. I knew exactly what Annie was talking about, even if I didn't know who she was talking about.

"Oh, I'm so sorry," I said, trying to find the right tone for a cousin I didn't remember ever having. "Did it happen at the Y?"

"Goodness no!" Annie barked. "Yost was Amish, and a good Amish man wouldn't be caught dead at the Y. He drowned in his milk."

I digested that information. "Falling asleep in your porridge must be a terrible way to go, dear."

"Magdalena! You are every bit as dense as your father was! Yost didn't die in his breakfast bowl. He drowned in the milk holding tank on his farm."

I decided it was best to hold my tongue until I had more information. A lot more.

"It happened this morning—sometime before five. Yost got up to do the milking at the usual time, and when he was late for breakfast, Sarah—that's his wife—went to fetch him. That's when she found him floating in the milk tank."

"Oh my!" It is hard to respond creatively at a time like that.

"But that's not all!"

"Do tell." However, if there was cereal somehow involved in the story, I didn't want to know before breakfast.

"He was naked, Magdalena!"

I made her repeat it.

"Naked, I tell you! As naked as the day he was born."

That only temporarily threw me. I have long since given up on the idea that babies come into this world in cute little layette sets. That idea was put to rest once and for all last year when a girl named Heather had a baby right before my eyes, in my very own barn. At any rate, when it finally sank in that the man we were talking about was found floating in a tank of milk, and without any clothes, I was speechless. There is, after all, a first time for everything.

"The funeral is the day after tomorrow, at the farm, of course. Burial will be at the Amish cemetery off Hershberger Lane. That's provided there isn't an investigation," said Annie matter-of-factly. "Will you and Freni be able to make it to the funeral, or just the burial?"

"Well—"

"Then tell Freni the funeral will start about nine. Since you're just going to the burial, I suggest you be at the cemetery no later than noon."

She hung up before I got a chance to ask her how to find Hershberger Lane. Not that I had decided to go, mind you. One needs at least a little time to sort things out, and at the rate things were moving up in Farmersburg, Yost might well be compost before I could properly catch my breath. The poor man had only been officially dead for an hour and a half, and already distant cousins were being called on to commit. Those Ohio folks had always been a little too fast for my blood.

On the other hand, I could always use a change of scenery. Hernia, especially in the winter, can get on one's nerves if one doesn't get out now and then. Of course, I could go only if I found someone to run the PennDutch Inn for me during my absence. Too bad that person couldn't be Freni. Despite the fact that Freni Hostetler is the most cantankerous woman I have ever known—Grandma Yoder excepted—she is, in her own grudging way, quite competent.

But if anyone from Hernia ought to go to Ohio for the funeral, it was Freni Hostetler. She was, after all, a double first cousin to the deceased. Reluctantly, I decided to do the right thing and tell Freni that our cousin had died.

She took it calmly. Then fainted.

TWO

Mose, Freni's husband, and I carried Freni to the Victorian sofa in the parlor. My sister Susannah merely watched.

Fortunately there was a spring loose in the sofa, so Freni didn't stay out long. *"Ach du lieber!"* she said, sitting bolt upright. "Somebody get the biscuits before they burn!"

Freni is the cook at my inn. She's seventy-five, or thereabouts. I don't know exactly because the number she quotes keeps changing. Personally, I think Freni pads her age in a misguided attempt to gain more respect. No one over thirty could do all the things Freni does and still have enough energy left over to hate her daughter-in-law.

"The biscuits are fine," I assured her. It was a white lie about to turn black. Already I could smell the smoke.

"Would you like a glass of water?" Mose asked his wife. He has never seen a TV show in his life, which proves that some behaviors are indeed instinctive.

"Better to throw the water on the biscuits," Freni said. She made an attempt to stand, but Mose and I restrained her.

"Should I call Doc Shafor?" asked Susannah with surprising sensibleness. Doc Shafor is a veterinarian, not a people doctor. But anybody in Hernia with a lick of sense prefers him over Harold P. Smith III, our resident M.D. We are, after all, God-fearing, and Harold is idolatry personified. The M.D. in his case stands for Male Divinity—at least that's what he seems to think.

"I'll be fine," said Freni, "but those biscuits won't." She made a move to stand up again, and this time we let her. Both Amish and Mennonites are pacifists, but Freni has been known to bite, and despite her advanced age, her teeth are all her own.

"I'll call Doc," said Susannah feebly. Clearly she was reluctant to let go of one of her few good ideas.

"You will not!" Freni said. By then she was on her feet and headed toward the kitchen door.

"Are you all right?" Mose and I chorused.

"I'm fine!"

"What about the funeral?" I would need time to find a replacement for her.

"I'll go, of course," she said, without even looking over her shoulder.

There was no "of course" to it. Freni was Amish—albeit Church Amish—and she didn't even ride in a car on a regular basis, much less own one. Freni and Mose relied on Sadie, their horse, and Sadie's black buggy for all but their longest trips. Neither did the two of them own a telephone, or a credit card, for that matter. By and large when an emergency happened the Amish folk of Freni and Mose's ilk relied on the good graces of their Mennonite and "English" neighbors. In this case, I was certain Freni was going to rely on me.

I am a Mennonite. I am one of those Mennonites whose ancestors were at one time Amish, from Switzerland—as opposed to those other Mennonites whose forebears were never Amish and originated in Holland or Germany. Nonetheless, in Freni's eyes I am just one step away from being "English," or of the world. The same cannot be said of my sister, Susannah. In her case, the apple not only fell from the tree, but rolled out of the orchard as well.

Susannah Yoder Entwhistle is ten years my junior. She is everything I am not, and a good deal more. Don't get me wrong, I love my sister—but Susannah not only has no use for her heritage, but for her the term "family values" refers only to the financial assets our parents left us when they died.

How else can one explain the fact that Susannah married a Presbyterian, and then divorced him as well? Or that she dyes her hair, paints her nails, smokes cigarettes, and sometimes stays out all night with men? Somewhere along the line some very strong "English" genes had found their way into the family tree and mutated one of the limbs into a thorn branch. If I had to pick just three words to describe my sister, they would be "slothful," "slovenly," and "slutty." I know, that is a terrible thing to say about one's own flesh and blood, but even our parents must have seen it coming.

A year or so before they died, Mama and Papa wrote a new will which named me executrix and temporary custodian of their estate. The temporary aspect of the latter was discretionary on my part. In other words, I was to decide when it was that Susannah had matured enough to participate in the decision-making. That day has yet to come.

In the meantime I sold off all but two of the cows, and most of the chickens, and turned my parents' dairy farm into a bed and breakfast (plus lunch and dinner) establishment. I'm not supposed to believe in luck, but it appeared to be with me nonetheless. Almost immediately the PennDutch Inn received a rave review from a yuppie reporter, and the rest is history. Since then I have jacked up my prices seven times, and my waiting list keeps getting longer. Even insisting that my guests clean their rooms and do their own laundry has only helped the flow of cash into my coffer. After all, you'd be surprised how much abuse people will put up with if they can view it as a cultural experience.

But back to the problem at hand. Someone would have to drive Freni Hostetler to Farmersburg, Ohio. And since Susannah didn't have a car and I wasn't about to lend her mine, it would have to be me.

"Who will run the inn?" I asked, thinking aloud. "I need someone capable who knows the ropes."

Surprisingly, Susannah was miffed. "What am I, liver pudding?"

"You might ask Doc Shafor," said Mose, heading me off. "He's a good cook, and I can help him."

That wasn't a bad idea. Doc Shafor is in his eighties, but he deals with the English on a regular basis—something Mose is not at all comfortable doing. With Mose working quietly in the background, and Doc up front with the guests, the two old geezers just might be able to pull it off. Of course, I would instruct Susannah to help them, for all the good that would do.

"I'll give him a call."

Susannah perked up. "Good, so I'm going with you, right, Mags?"

"Over my dead body," I said with sisterly sweetness.

"What's-his-name was my cousin too," she sniffed.

"You didn't go to Aunt Pearl's funeral two years ago," I reminded her.

"But the Ohio men are so cute!" she wailed.

"I'm sure you can vouch for most of them, dear."

"Of course, I could stay and throw a big party. Two of our guests are super-hunky, and one of them has already—"

"Only one small suitcase, dear. We're not going to be gone that long." To be truthful, I was hoping the luggage limitation would make her think things over a bit more carefully. Susannah dresses in a style that calls for voluminous amounts of flowing fabric. Since just one of her outfits can clothe a small Third World country, I knew that one small suitcase would be totally out of the question for her.

But much to my surprise, baby sister began jumping up and down for joy, and I feared for her dog, Shnookums. The mutt is one of those rat-sized dogs, and since Susannah has been cursed with a concave bosom, she often carries her pet around in her bra to act as ballast. Of course, I'm not exactly blessed in that department either, but at least I have the decency to use tissues. At any rate, Shnookums had begun to howl mournfully, and although I am no great fan of his, I will not tolerate cruelty to animals.

"Stop jumping, and start packing. I want to get to Ohio before dark."

"Aye, aye, sir." Susannah mockingly saluted me and then swirled out of the room before I could issue further instructions.

"And the dog stays!" I shouted. I'm sure she didn't hear me, but it didn't matter. I'd frisk my sister before I let her put so much as one toe inside my car. If need be, I would even bring myself to look into her purse. Believe me, there are things in there that would make the whore of Babylon blush, but it is another of Shnookum's haunts. There was no way I was going to drive the two hundred miles to Farmersburg with Freni Hostetler, Susannah Yoder Entwhistle, and that mangy mongoose for company. A gal has to put her foot down sometimes, and with size eleven shoes, that's easy to do.

Three

I had done my own packing and was about to check on the others when the doorbell rang. Since the front door of the inn is always unlocked during daylight hours, I knew at once that I had another salesman on my hands. When will those people ever learn? Well, perhaps they have. It used to be that they called, instead of coming over in person.

"PennDutch," I would say cheerfully into the phone.

"Good morning, ma'am. I'm LeRoy Tibbs, from Tibbs Heating and Cooling. What kind of furnace are you using in your establishment?"

I'd quickly pick from my repertoire of fake accents. "Yah mon, dis here is de Jamaican PennDutch Inn. We have no furnace, mon." Click.

That wasn't a lie, mind you. Lies are told for nefarious purposes. I simply mean to decline in an entertaining way. If I were to really lie, Mama would turn over in her grave, and even the folks out in L.A. could tell I had fibbed by the tremors.

Now that the sellers come right to my door, dealing with them is even more of a challenge. I felt my pulse race as my brain strained to lock in on a persona. I decided to be a missionary just returned from Fiji.

"Greetings," I said in my meekest voice.

"Greetings right back at you, Magdalena."

I looked up to see Aaron Miller's sinfully handsome blue eyes fixed on me. I wished then that I was a missionary—still in Fiji. Certainly it couldn't have felt any warmer over there.

"Are you going to let me in, Magdalena, or are you coming outside?"

I stared stupidly at him. I've known Aaron for a few months, or a lifetime, depending on how you choose to look at it. We spent our childhoods on neighboring farms, and then Aaron left to escape the draft. It was the height of the Vietnam War. We did not see each other again until last summer, when, on a beautiful cloudless day, he pushed me into his father's pond (that is how I remember it). The important detail is that I fell head over heels in love for the first time in my life. And although he won't come right out and admit it, Aaron fell in love too. With me, if you can imagine that!

"Magdalena," he said gently, and then touched me with a finger the temperature of molten steel.

I jumped wordlessly aside. No male has ever made me feel like Aaron makes me feel. Surely it is a sin to feel this way outside the bonds of marriage. I will tell you, as proudly as my faith permits, that I have never known a man—not in the Biblical sense. I am forty-four years old and still a virgin. I have no experience in the ways of the flesh. And no—that time I sat on the washing machine during the spin cycle does not count! My point is that Aaron Miller makes my entire body burn, in a delicious sort of way, but I am not comfortable with the feeling.

"You look flushed, Magdalena."

"I've been packing."

"Going somewhere?"

"No, I'm just practicing in case I do."

Just then Susannah came into the room dragging a suitcase large enough to have its own zip code. When she saw Aaron she all but squealed with delight.

"Aaron!"

He glanced at her just long enough to see the suitcase. "Your sister must need to practice more than you do."

I think Susannah might have said something then, but I don't recall what it was. When Aaron's in the room it's hard to concentrate on anyone but him.

"So, where are you off to, Magdalena? Is Susannah going with you?"

I told him about cousin Yost's death, and the need to take Freni to the funeral. I told him that Susannah had insisted on accompanying us, and about the arrangements I had made for the inn.

"Not to worry," Aaron said. He put a muscular arm around my shoulder. "I'll help Mose and Doc as much as I can. You just concentrate on getting to Ohio and back safely."

Silly man. If my shoulder didn't stop smoldering I wasn't going to make it out of the driveway, much less to Ohio. I forced myself to think of practical things.

"All right, Susannah, it's time to dump that dinky dog of yours."

Susannah smiled sweetly. "Why, whatever do you mean?"

"Hand over your coat, dear," I said. "You can take my old one." Susannah's coat is really a cape with a catacomb of pockets sewn into it. It would take a week to search it thoroughly, by which time her crafty canine could croak. Leaving it behind was the humane thing to do.

My sister parted with her wrap far too easily. When she threw it on the floor and did a quick tap dance, I knew it was time to start searching elsewhere.

"Okay. Hands above your head." It was time to frisk her again.

Susannah smoothed her silken swirls and smirked. "No Shnookums, see? Or in my suitcase, either. Check it, for all I care."

I did. Besides clothes, there were enough electrical gadgets in there to stock two hardware stores, but no dog. I would have pursued the matter further, but just then Freni came bustling in. It was time to go. Quite sensibly, she had only one small black fabric bag. The sight of it should have shamed Susannah, but of course it didn't.

"Slumming it, are we?" she quipped.

Freni frowned. "This is a funeral we're going to, Susannah, not an English party."

"Well excuuuse me!" Susannah flounced off to the car, without a coat, leaving her luggage behind.

Aaron gallantly carried all our bags to the car. As I was about to climb in, he grabbed me gently by the arm. He might as well have been using heated tongs.

"There's something I just have to say before I let you go, Magdalena."

I closed my eyes, straining to hear the sound of wedding bells. "Say it," I murmured.

"Check your water and oil before you start back. That heap of yours has seen a lot of wear."

I opened one eye. "Anything else?"

He released my arm. "As a matter of fact, yes. Stay out of trouble when you get there."

I opened the other eye. "I don't know what you mean, Aaron Miller."

He smiled, revealing those perfect white teeth. Who would have thought that molars could be mesmerizing? "You're attracted to trouble like ants to a picnic. And I have a hunch that your cousin was in a whole lot of trouble before he took that milk bath."

"I'll be careful," I promised. I pursed my lips slightly on the off chance that Aaron would kiss me.

He did not. Mennonites are not big on public displays of affection. Instead he pulled a huge white handkerchief out of his pocket and proceeded to blow his nose. You would have thought a flock of geese had swooped down on the PennDutch.

That was my last view of Aaron that morning, but I cherished it nonetheless. Even with a handkerchief in front of his face, Aaron Miller was the most handsome man I have ever laid eyes on.

We had just passed through the Allegheny Tunnel (where Mama and Papa were killed) when I heard a strange, high-pitched noise. My first thought was that Susannah was crying. She may not be a sensible gal, but my sister is at times sensitive. What else would explain the similar noises I heard the last time I caught Susannah entertaining a boyfriend in her room? His mother had just died, and she was crying on his behalf, she said. Somehow it sounded plausible at the time.

"Enough," Freni said, after I had ignored the sobs for almost a mile. "If Susannah wants to sit up front that bad I'll change seats."

"I don't want to sit up front," Susannah almost shouted. "What I want to do is sing. How about we all take turns singing our favorite hymns?"

Immediately I slowed down and pulled over. Something was rotten in Denmark, and my sister was speaking Danish. I turned in my seat and inspected her. She hadn't been crying at all.

"Okay, what gives?" I asked calmly.

Susannah's an expert at giving blank looks, and gave me a doozy.

"Susannah, I don't have time for—" Suddenly a heart-rending sob filled the air, although Susannah's lips remained as tightly closed as a clam at low tide.

Sometimes I'm slow on the uptake, but just one more sob was all it took for me to deduce that my sister had somehow managed to convey her canine to the car and had stashed the stowaway in the trunk. And sure enough, I found the pitiful pooch, along with a pile of poop, in Freni's black bag.

"*Ach du Heimer!*" my elderly cousin exclaimed. Literally that means you are a hammer, and that's as bad as Freni can curse.

I will admit that I had a few choice words myself, but of course nothing quite that strong. Mama had washed out my mouth with soap enough times to ensure that I stuck to clean speech for life.

I suppose we presented quite a sight there by the road— one Amish woman, one Mennonite woman, and fifteen feet of flowing fabric, all gesticulating as if we were engaged in an animated game of charades—but I didn't especially care what others thought. The people in the cars whizzing by were not without their own dramas, and I was sure that our little scene was tame compared to some of them.

In the end, Susannah promised to do Freni's laundry, and Shnookums was liberated from Freni's bag, but only to be detained in Susannah's bra. Since I didn't relish driving through the tunnel two more times, there was nothing to do but press on. But can you blame me for arriving in Farmersburg with a splitting headache? Perhaps if I'd only felt better I wouldn't have gotten into all that trouble Aaron had warned me about.

Four

We drove straight to the widow's house. I had no idea how to get there, but I had Freni with me, remember? That woman has a sixth sense for ferreting out relatives. As farfetched as it may sound, I suspect that she might actually be able to smell shared genes.

"That's definitely a Hostetler house," she said, as we neared Farmersburg. "Bloughs live on that farm. Oh, now there's a Mast place if ever I saw one. Ach, look at that Bontrager barn—you wouldn't see one like that back in Hernia. Personally, I think the Troyers have always been a bit vain about their flower beds. You'd think the Stutzmans could plow straighter rows than that. The Shrocks should be ashamed to hang out laundry in need of mending, if you ask me."

So, I was relieved, but not really surprised, when Freni had me turn right on Hershberger Lane and left on Leesburg Lane. Immediately after the second turn we saw the dairy farm owned by the late Yost Yoder and his wife, Sarah. That one even I could identify, although I must confess that the sea of black buggies in the front yard might have been a tip-off. Amish generally don't congregate to party on Tuesday afternoons.

There were a few other cars there, so our arrival did not raise much of a stir. Except for some children who scampered up to stare, no one seemed to notice us—Amish often rely on their more liberal neighbors for long-distance rides.

We got out of the car.

"Is this the Yoder farm?" I asked a towheaded youngster just to be on the safe side.

The girl giggled, and I saw myself when I was three or four. With limited gene pools, one doesn't need photo albums.

Another towhead, about six years old, pushed the girl aside. "Yah, this is the Yoder place," he said. "Who is she?" He pointed at Susannah.

"My name's Susannah. I'm a distant cousin," my sister explained.

"Well, you look like a clown!"

The children all laughed and scampered away, proving that English children don't have a monopoly on bad manners.

"Why I never!" Susannah said.

I patted her arm comfortingly. "It could have been worse, dear. At least they didn't scream."

We made Freni lead the way to the house. Even though her dress differed slightly from that of the Ohio Amish, she was still obviously one of them. Amish houses don't have doorbells, but Freni is a world-class knocker. People with termites should pray Freni doesn't knock on their doors. It would be only a slight exaggeration to say that structurally unsound houses have collapsed under that woman's knuckles.

"Yah?" said a woman who was perhaps in her late thirties. For some reason she looked right over Freni's head and straight at me.

"Sarah Yoder?"

"Yah?"

"I'm Magdalena Yoder from Hernia, Pennsylvania, and this is—"

"Freni!"

Freni and Sarah, Yost's widow, were in each other's arms and talking a mile a minute. Unfortunately for Susannah and me they were speaking in "Pennsylvania Dutch," a form of High German. Outside of a few prayers and harmless expressions, neither Susannah nor I can speak it. At least I can understand it, which is more than can be said for Susannah. Even the King James version of the Bible taxes her linguistic abilities—which might have something to do with why she married a Presbyterian.

Sarah literally pulled Freni into the crowded house. Susannah and I followed anxiously on our own steam. Despite our kinship, and friendship, with Freni, we were entering a world where we were the outsiders. The strange ones. For Susannah that might not have been a first, but for me it most certainly was. I must confess that I was nervous enough to perspire—of course ever so slightly.

At least I had introduced myself to Sarah Yost, whereas poor Susannah had been utterly ignored. To her credit, my baby sister handled this social gaffe with remarkable aplomb. Instead of drawing attention to herself in a negative fashion, Susannah appeared to be content merely rolling her eyes. This action not only speaks louder than words, but substitutes for at least fifty in my sister's vocabulary. Whereas I get the bulk of my exercise from jumping to conclusions, Susannah gets hers from ocular rotation. In our defense, I must state that neither form of exercise requires any special equipment, and both can be performed virtually anywhere.

At any rate, the message was clear. Susannah was bored.

"Ahem," I interrupted. I have learned the hard way that

it is best not to push the limits of Susannah's patience in public.

Freni frowned. "Magdalena, can't you see that our cousin needs comforting?"

I nodded at Susannah, whose eyes were rolling so fast they were a blur of white. The poor girl was going to exhaust herself any second and pass out. Either that or go blind.

"I am touched that you two came," Sarah said graciously. Her English, like that of most of the younger Amish, was flawless. "It means so much to me to have family around at a time like this."

"We're delighted to be here," I said, and then would have kicked myself, had I not been wearing my pointed shoes. "I'm so sorry about Yost's death," I added feebly.

At least Sarah's tears were genuine. "I suppose I'm still in shock. Somehow it doesn't all seem real."

"I know just how you feel," Susannah said. "I felt that way when Bubbles, my goldfish, died."

I am not averse to kicking Susannah with my pointed shoes. "Is there anything we can do?" I asked.

Sarah smiled wanly through her tears. "No. Just your being here is enough."

"Well, maybe we should go find a motel," I offered. Freni had filled me in on a few statistics on the way over. Since Amish traditionally have large families, I was not surprised to learn that Sarah and Yost had ten children, and she was a lot younger than I.

"Ach! How you talk!" Sarah said with sudden vigor. Clearly she and Freni were blood kin somewhere down the line.

"I'm sorry. I didn't mean that I'm anxious to leave. We can look for a motel later."

Sarah wiped her face with a sleeve. "Imagine staying in an English motel when you have family!"

"I only meant—" I gestured helplessly at the crowd.

"Just Freni will be staying here. The two of you will be staying with Samuel and Elizabeth Troyer. Sam is your father's second cousin once and your mother's third cousin twice, and Lizzie is your father's fourth cousin once removed and your mother's double second cousin twice removed. They only have five children—all boys—so there is plenty of room. It has already been arranged."

I was only mildly surprised. If the American people really wanted a balanced budget and a government that ran as efficiently as Swiss trains, they would elect an Amish woman to the Presidency. Of course, no Amish person would be caught dead in the White House. (Although I have yet to convince Susannah that Abe Lincoln wasn't Amish.)

"How old are the Troyer boys?" my sister asked hopefully.

My pointed shoes quickly put an end to that line of questioning. I said a few more words of comfort and whisked Susannah out of speaking range.

"Excuse me, but do you know if Annie Stutzman is here?" I asked a woman who was the spitting image of Mama at her age.

The woman pointed wordlessly at a girl who couldn't have been more than twelve.

"No, I'm sure that's not her. This Annie Stutzman was my father's cousin."

The woman shrugged. "I know eight Annie Stutzmans, dear. Do you want me to point them all out to you?"

I decided to save Annie for later. Anyone who didn't have a phone yet was capable of calling me up at six-thirty in the morning to pass on news she had just heard would manage to get in touch with me before I left the area. Anyway, Annie had said she would see me at the cemetery. If she wanted to talk to me that afternoon, all she had to do was come up to me and open her mouth. Two tall English women, one wearing enough makeup to supply a small suburb of Pittsburgh for a year, could not be that hard to spot in a sea of bobbing bonnets.

For the next several hours we sat around like warts on a pickle, waiting for the Troyers (who were present) to leave. Although all the Amish were extremely cordial, it is sometimes hard to connect with a roomful of strangers, even if half of them are wearing your face. I wasn't particularly interested in learning that Emma Hershberger's bunions were acting up again, or that Milla Kauffman made her broad noodles without any eggs. As for the fact that Amanda Miller was three weeks overdue with her eighth baby, well, in the words of Susannah, "Who cares?"

There were three other English there, but undoubtedly they had been brought up better than Susannah and I. They wore their looks of boredom quite gracefully.

I struck up a conversation with one of them—an ample woman named Harriet. She had driven a carload of Amish over from Goshen, Indiana, but she had done it for money. Harriet had just begun her career as a middle-aged mercenary, driving the devout in dire times, and what she knew about the Amish would fill one page in a doll-sized notebook.

"I think their ancestors were pilgrims," Harriet said. "That's right, the Amish are some kind of modern-day pilgrim, and they believe in dressing up like in the olden days. Which is really kind of silly, when you think about it," she added, "because even the Indians today don't dress like they used to."

"Is that so," I said politely. Susannah, however, smirked.

"Now take the Mennonites," Harriet said knowingly. "They're a queer bunch as well."

"Do tell," I urged.

"They're sort of diluted Amish, if you ask me. They're not as strict, but they're just as clannish. Won't look you straight in the eye if you're not one of them. Did you know that Richard Nixon was a Mennonite?"

I stared at her. "He was a Quaker," I said firmly. "It's not the same thing."

She gave me a pitying glance. "How much were you paid to drive your Amish passengers here, if you don't mind my asking?"

"A thousand dollars." It was a joke said with a straight face—which isn't the same as lying.

Harriet's eyes bulged and she gasped for air. "Well," she said at last, "I'm going to have me a talk with the Berkeys before I drive them home!"

I prayed silently that God and the Berkeys would forgive me. "I suppose the Berkeys told you about the oil wells they have on their farm?"

Harriet shook her head. "Nope, but it doesn't surprise me none. The Amish might look poor—on account of their pilgrim costumes—but they're smart businessmen. The Berkeys said that the Amish man who died was starting up a rival cheese factory. Farmersburg Swiss, you know."

"Yes, the Amish are Swiss." At least she had gotten one fact right.

"No, I meant the cheese. Farmersburg Swiss cheese. Surely you've heard of it."

"Not until now, dear."

Harriet rolled her eyes, giving me a preview of what Susannah might look like twenty years and fifty pounds down the pike. "Farmersburg Swiss is gourmet. Everybody knows that. Even in Goshen, Indiana, people with sophisticated taste eat Farmersburg Swiss."

"You don't say." This from a woman who made "gourmet" rhyme with "your pet"!

"Farmersburg Swiss has a rich, nutty flavor that the other Swisses can't touch. Its firm but creamy texture alone puts it in a class all by itself." She licked her lips and sighed contentedly.

I would have run out right then and bought some, except that something she had said earlier suddenly clicked. "Did you say that Mr. Yoder was starting up a rival cheese factory?" I asked. "Who owns the first, and where is it?"

Harriet shook her head in amazement. "It's hard to believe what people miss out on when they're not paying attention. Daisybell Dairies is by far the largest building in town!"

I confessed that we had taken a back way and avoided town altogether. Mercifully I didn't have to explain how that happened.

"Well, if I were you I'd stop at the factory on my way out of town and buy some of the cheese direct. That's what I plan to do. With the competition dead, prices might soar. You might even want to do a little investing in Daisybell stock, provided it's a public corporation."

I promised to check the cheese stocks in my local paper on my return home. In the meantime I had a little local checking to do. Something was definitely rotten in Denmark, and it was beginning to smell like cheese.

Five

Farmersburg Swiss Cheese
Hors d'Oeuvres

✦

2 tubes crescent roll dough
16 paper-thin slices of Farmersburg Swiss cheese
24 paper-thin slices of hard salami

Preheat oven to 400 degrees. Divide crescent dough along perforated lines into eight rectangles (two triangles each). Pinch seams together.

Cover each rectangle with a slice of Farmersburg Swiss and three overlapping slices of hard salami. Overlay with another slice of Farmersburg Swiss. Roll the rectangles into tight logs, and pinch dough shut along seams. With a sharp knife, slice each log into four even pieces.

Arrange pieces, seam side down, on an ungreased cookie sheet. Bake for ten minutes or until light brown. Serve hot.

This recipe makes enough hors d'oeuvres for eight polite people or two of Susannah's friends.

Note: In the event Farmersburg Swiss is unavailable, any Swiss cheese will do.

Six

Lizzie and Sam were as nice a couple as one could hope to meet. They made us feel instantly at home on their farm, and if they felt uncomfortable having two English women invade their world, they never let on. Unfortunately the same could not be said about their boys.

The children virtually ignored me, but Elias, the baby, cried every time Susannah got within focus. Isaac, the eldest, was the towheaded boy who had called Susannah a clown. Apparently he had been only warming up then. As for the middle boys, Benjamin, Solomon and Peter, they either cried or taunted Susannah, depending on the proximity of their parents.

Poor Susannah. It was the first time in her life that members of the male sex had refused to put her on a pedestal.

"Why don't they like me?" she wailed that evening at supper. To emphasize her anguish, my sister flung out her arms, and the explosion of fabric that followed took several seconds to settle, draping across the adjacent plates like a collapsed parachute.

We were eating supper by the light of a hurricane lamp.

Perhaps the flickering shadows made my sister look particularly ominous, or perhaps it had just been a long day for everyone involved, but even six-year-old Isaac was provoked to tears.

"The English woman scares me!" he sobbed. Much to my relief, he pointed only at Susannah.

"Hush," Lizzie said sternly.

"No dessert for naughty boys," Samuel said, although he looked a little wary of Susannah himself.

But the five little boys could not be quieted. It was as if they took turns sobbing, each one inspiring the next to reach higher pitch and louder volume. In Hernia, when the volunteer fire department rehearses its disaster alarm, we are at least given written notice three days in advance.

The five boys took their turns screeching and howling while their parents sat looking helplessly on. The threat of no dessert had meant nothing. Clearly, the Troyers possessed genes that the Yoders did not. Papa would have sent us straight off to bed, without any supper, and the next day Mama would have made us clean out the chicken coop. In a Yoder house, one did what one was told.

Eventually the boys tired of taking turns and began bellowing in unison. Who knows how long the racket would have lasted had not a sixth voice, even louder and higher-pitched than the others, joined in. Fortunately only Susannah and I picked up on the interloper. Immediately my pointed shoes found a home.

"Well, excuuuse me!" Susannah said, but without need of another hint she left the dinner table and went outside. She should have been grateful, because I know she was dying for a cigarette by then. Undoubtedly Shnookums needed to be fed too, for his stomach couldn't be larger than a thimble.

With Susannah's departure the din dimmed dramatically, and I managed to demonstrate that I was an appreciative guest by consuming a respectable portion of the meager repast Lizzie had provided. Not that there wasn't a lot of food, but canned sardines and bread are not your typical Amish supper. Not being a connoisseur of finned things, I concentrated on the bread and its accouterments. The whimpers and snuffles around me were not enough to deter my appetite.

"This apple butter is the best I've ever eaten," I said, spreading a fourth slice of bread. Truthfully I'd tasted far better, but the good Lord knew my motive for stretching the truth was pure.

Lizzie beamed. "It's the extra cinnamon. And just a pinch of ground cloves."

"And this bread! Even Freni Hostetler can't make a loaf this light."

Lizzie blushed deeply. "It's store-bought. What with the wedding to cook for and Levi passing last week, I didn't have time to bake."

I nodded. Amish weddings, I knew, demanded copious amounts of food. I had no idea who Levi was or what he had passed, but if it was important enough to cause an Amish woman to stop baking, it had to be a matter of consequence.

Suddenly Isaac stopped whimpering. "Is Uncle Levi still dead?" he asked.

Samuel patted his eldest son's head. "Yah, he's sleeping in the ground. But soon he'll be with God."

I carefully swallowed a rather large bite. I had heard nothing at the gathering about a man named Levi dying recently. Of course, I had spent most of the time avoiding conversations, and the gal from Goshen, an outsider like me, was apparently in the dark as well.

Lizzie seemed to sense my curiosity. "They're talking about Levi Mast. Samuel's first cousin. He died last Tuesday. Exactly a week ago."

"Oh, I'm so sorry." I turned and looked sympathetically at Samuel.

"Yah, he was a good man," my kinsman said. He didn't return my glance.

I took another big bite, chewed it slowly, and swallowed. "How did he die?"

The room was suddenly as silent as the cemetery where Levi Mast slept. Seven pairs of eyes, and that included the baby's, were trained on Samuel's face.

It was a rather handsome face, topped by a salad bowl of blond hair and ringed at the bottom by a light brown beard. Like all Amish men, Samuel had no mustache.

"It was a farming accident," he said slowly.

I could tell he was hedging, practically begging for a question or two. "What kind of an accident?"

"Silo," Samuel mumbled.

I nodded. Levi Mast wasn't the first farmer to slip and fall off a silo ladder. Jacob Berkey back in Hernia fell twenty feet from his and would undoubtedly have been transformed into a paraplegic if he hadn't landed on his wife, who had come to call him to dinner. Thank goodness Rachel Berkey had a strong constitution and drank plenty of milk. The clever way she sewed her aprons did a lot to camouflage the fact that her posture was no longer ramrod-straight.

"A tragic thing," Lizzie said. She wiped at least a pint of apple butter off the baby's face and sighed deeply. "On his wedding day a nice young man like that turns into a pretzel."

Suddenly seven pairs of eyes were trained hungrily on her face. It would be vain of me to say Lizzie is attractive, because I think she and I bear a strong family resemblance. Suffice it to say she has the Yoder nose and light brown hair. The Creator neither smiled nor frowned when he made our mold.

"He died on his wedding day?" I blurted out.

"He was supposed to marry Barbara Hooley that morning." Lizzie was suddenly bitter. "It was a very inconvenient time."

The five youngest pairs of eyes now focused on my face. Undoubtedly my mouth was wide open.

"Yah, a terrible thing," Samuel said. "His mother found him when she went to call him in for breakfast. His head had broken open like an egg."

Neither parent seemed at all concerned about discussing gruesome subjects in front of the children. It was the Troyer genes again. Susannah and I had been habitually banished by our parents whenever the table talk strayed from food, farm, or faith. It was no wonder the five little Troyer boys were basket cases.

I picked up a fifth slice of bread and slathered it with the thick red apple butter. "What was he doing on top of the silo, anyway? I mean, on his wedding morning?"

Samuel shrugged. "Who knows? The Masts have always been a little strange, if you ask me. Maybe he was trying to see Barbara's farm from up there. At any rate, it resulted in a tragedy."

"We had all been cooking for a week," Lizzie added peevishly. "Relatives had come from as far away as Iowa and Lancaster, Pennsylvania. There was even a family in from Hernia. Jonas and Lydia Zook. You know them?"

I nodded absently. Of course I knew them. I knew all the Hernia Amish. "What happened to all that food?"

"Ach, the food!" said Lizzie. "That was saved for the funeral meal. What a waste that was. Food tastes better at a wedding, don't you think?"

"I'm sure it does," I said agreeably. Although if it was canned sardines she brought to the wedding, unless she had opened them three days earlier, it probably didn't make any difference.

"My sardine sandwiches were all dried out by then," Lizzie said sadly, "so I had to bring eggs."

"Uncle Levi's head cracked open like a broken egg," Isaac said and giggled. His four brothers giggled along with him.

I cast the urchins a quick, disapproving frown. Clearly, it was possible to be corrupted without the aid of television.

"I suppose there was a thorough investigation," I said.

The parents of the errant boys volleyed glances, but said nothing.

"Well?"

"Yah, the Farmersburg deputy took care of everything. He ruled it an accident, and there was no problem."

"And of course it was an accident, right?"

"Yah," Samuel said, but he refused to look me in the eye.

We ate in silence for a while. There was obviously more to Levi Mast's death than I'd been told. But I knew enough about human nature, if not my kinsmen, to know that I wasn't going to force any more information out of them. When the time was right, one or the other would supply me with all the important details.

"I have a confession to make," Lizzie said suddenly, much to my surprise.

"Yes?" I hoped it didn't sound too eager.

"That isn't apple butter you're eating."

I swallowed quickly. "Oh?"

Lizzie looked away. She was obviously embarrassed. "Our apple crop was miserable last fall. Full of worms, and as coarse as corncobs. I decided to make up a batch of mock apple butter."

I tried to preempt the rest of the confession. "Well, it's just great. Now tell me, who was that pretty young woman with the twin babies I saw this afternoon?"

"Zucchini," Lizzie said.

"I beg your pardon?"

"That's what's in the mock apple butter. Zucchini."

"But it's red!"

Lizzie smiled. "Cherry Kool-Aid."

"You don't say!" I picked up my knife and discreetly scraped off what I could from the bread on my plate.

"Time for dessert!" Lizzie said, getting up, and the boys all smacked their lips and rubbed their hands together in anticipation.

She returned from the kitchen with a huge pan of warm bread pudding, my favorite dessert. It was studded with raisins and smelled delicious, so I decided to risk it. After all, I had just survived a pint of Kool-Aid-flavored zucchini—what possible harm could Lizzie's bread pudding inflict on me? Just to be on the safe side, however, I carefully picked out all the raisins.

Susannah and I and the mangy mutt all shared one double bed. Susannah's snores generally sound like a pig fight at a slop trough, with the occasional snore reminiscent of that time Papa accidentally backed over our prize boar, Samson, with his tractor. Shnookums snores as well, but because of his smaller size, his slumber sounds are softer. Nails raked across a chalkboard seems to describe it about right.

Before you start feeling too sorry for me, I feel obligated to point out that Amish houses don't have central heat. In fact, generally only the ground floor is heated, by a large stove, or sometimes a fireplace. Occasionally kerosene space heaters are placed in upstairs rooms, but not in the Troyer manse. And since it was February, after all, the proximity of another warm body, and a two-pound hair ball, was better than nothing.

Despite the racket next to me, I did eventually fall asleep. But before I did, I replayed the day's events many times over in my mind, and true to form, I generated more questions than a four-year-old is capable of thinking up.

Why hadn't I heard a peep about Levi Mast's death from other Amish that afternoon? Why had Levi Mast climbed to the top of a corn silo on the morning of his February wedding, when it was in the autumn that farmers filled their silos from the top? And why would a strong young man, who had undoubtedly climbed silos many times before, lose his grip on the ladder and split his head open like a cracked egg? And why would Sam and Lizzie Troyer, who were obviously a little cracked themselves, bring the young man's death to my attention? And what were sardine bones doing in the bread pudding?

Seven

Breakfast was toast and sardine omelettes. I was not surprised. The five Troyer boys resumed howling the moment they saw Susannah, and my poor sister was forced to take refuge on the front porch again. I am convinced that the cigarettes she buys are vitamin-enriched, since smoke is about the only thing that passes her gullet on a typical day. If it weren't for all the tar in Susannah's lungs, even just a gentle breeze would inflate those yards of flapping fabric in her frivolous frocks to the extent that she might well float far away. The two pounds of barking ballast in her bra would not be enough to keep her grounded.

During breakfast I tried unsuccessfully to get back on the subject of Levi Mast. It was like trying to get chickens to talk. There was a lot of clucking and a little crowing, but nothing specific said. I had the impression that the couple, especially Sam, regretted having opened up to me the night before. I decided to let the matter roost until later.

After breakfast I helped Lizzie do the dishes. Since the Troyer house does not have electricity, we did it the old-fashioned way by heating water on the stove and washing them in the sink. I washed while Lizzie dried. In fact, I insisted on that, even though the bottom of the omelette pan sported a crust of egg and fish a quarter inch thick. It is my belief that the best way to get people to share their innermost secrets is to perform their hardest chores for them. Guilt and gratitude go a long way toward relaxing even the most restricted larynxes.

"I can certainly understand how frustrating it would be to cook for someone's wedding, and then have him die," I said, holding up the gleaming frying pan.

"A real waste," Lizzie said. She reached for the pan, but I held it just out of reach, a reminder of what I had just done for her.

"You don't suppose that young Levi might have changed his mind about the wedding, and didn't know how to back out gracefully?"

Lizzie stared with her mouth open. Her orthodontia confirmed that we were indeed kin. "Suicide?"

I nodded sympathetically. Per capita, the Amish have an astonishingly high rate of suicide. Like everything else, conformity comes with a price.

"Ach, no," Lizzie nearly shouted. "Levi was very happy. He and Barbara Hooley made a perfect couple. They were so much in love, it was almost shameful. They were like me and Sam in the beginning." She blushed.

"Appearances can be deceiving," I pointed out. "I know of a married man who would much rather spend time with his buddies—one in particular—than with his beautiful wife."

"*Ach du lieber!* Is that how they talk in Hernia? Well, Magdalena Yoder, you should be ashamed of yourself, speaking of the dead that way. Levi Mast had eyes for only Barbara. His death was no suicide! If anything it was pos—" Her jaws clamped shut so hard I could hear her teeth click.

"What did you say?"

"I said that Levi didn't commit suicide."

"That's not all you said."

Poor Lizzie reminded me of the raccoon I once cornered in my henhouse. Had it been able to speak, no doubt it would have denied killing my prize hen, Pertelote, despite the feathers stuck in its teeth. While Lizzie didn't have any feathers in her mouth, it had betrayed her nonetheless. "I am not the person you should be talking to," she said. It was an admission of guilt.

I handed her the gleaming pan. "Oh? Who is then?"

"Stayrook Gerber," she whispered.

By the set of her jaw I knew our conversation was over. Fortunately, after the frying pan, there were no more things to wash.

Susannah and I elected not to attend the funeral itself, because it was in German and would last for several hours. Besides which, at the burial there would be another, much shorter service, and we could just as well pay our respects there. Of course, this meant taking my car, not that there would have been room in the Troyer buggy for Susannah and me and five bawling boys.

It was just as well we took separate vehicles. I needed to make a phone call, and Susannah needed a last puff on a cigarette before we hit the cemetery. It had been hard enough getting my sister to dress appropriately for the funeral. Fortunately Lizzie just happened to have twelve yards of black material, and Susannah, once she had skeptically draped herself in it, decided that she looked like some TV character named Morticia. She thought it was highly appropriate for the occasion, and for once I didn't comment. The real secret of happiness, I've finally discovered, is knowing when you're ahead.

I found a gas station on the way that had a public telephone, and I dialed while Susannah dragged.

"Hello, PennDutch Inn," the voice on the other end said.

I felt my knees go weak, and I clutched at the phone-book shelf for support. "Aaron?"

"Yes. Magdalena, I presume?" He has the only eyes that can twinkle over a phone wire.

I took a deep breath, envying Susannah's ability to inhale. "How are things at the inn?"

"Cozy."

"What?" If there was panic in my voice, it's because one of my guests that week was a leggy blonde who had *man-eater* tattooed on her forehead. I made a mental note to require photos when I took reservations.

"What I mean is that we're snowed in," dear sweet Aaron explained. "Last night we got eighteen inches of snow, and they're predicting another ten inches for today. Didn't you get any snow in Ohio?"

I glanced around at the frozen ground. All I could see was black pavement and brown grass. The late-winter sun shone brightly. "No."

"Well, we sure got it here. I heard on the news this morning that the turnpike is closed. In fact, the governor has declared a state of emergency and asked that all nonessential travel be curtailed. So I guess that includes you, Magdalena. You're just going to have to stay put after the funeral. For a day or two at least."

"But—"

"Hooter Faun went to Pittsburgh for a concert and is now stuck in Somerset," Aaron said, reading my mind. "The Allegheny Tunnel is closed, and we don't expect her back for a day or two either."

"That's a shame," I said in all sincerity. What I meant was that Hooter is a shameful name to call oneself. And no, I don't believe for a minute her parents named her that.

"Yeah, well, anyway," Aaron said, "the two old geezers and I are looking after things just fine, and there's no need for you to worry. So relax and enjoy yourself. Not the funeral, of course, but just being away for a while."

I said goodbye reluctantly. Like most advice, Aaron's was easier said than done. How was I going to survive, much less enjoy myself, when I was billeted with a brood of bawling bread-eaters? How was I going to occupy my time?

Okay, so I would speak to Stayrook Gerber if I could, and maybe learn a little about what really happened the day Levi Mast died, which, it suddenly occurred to me, might somehow be connected to Yost's mysterious death. But I was certainly *not* going to spend my time getting tangled up in a murder investigation. I took a mental breath. I knew from experience that murder and I did not mix well. Twice before, in two separate instances, the murderer read my motive as meddling and minded very much. I wasn't about to make that mistake again.

The Amish cemetery on Hershberger Lane isn't marked, but on that cold February day a blind fool couldn't have gotten lost looking for it. Even Melvin Stoltzfus, my Hernia nemesis, might have found the place. All one had to do was listen to the sound of horse hooves. The cloppity-clop of hundreds of hooves on the highways and byways in the Farmersburg area made the ground vibrate. Since all the hooves were headed to the same place, all one needed was a good ear—and maybe a good nose.

"What goes 'Clop, clop, clop—bang'?" Susannah asked.

"What?" I said absently.

"An Amish drive-by shooting!" My sister howled at her own joke, and Shnookums, always an easy laugh, yowled along with her.

When we got near the cemetery I was pleased to see at least fifty cars caught in the tide of bobbing black buggies. Perhaps some of the former belonged to tourists, or townspeople who had chosen an unlucky route, but I suspected that most of them were there for the funeral. Many upstanding Amish, and Yost was certainly one of them, have admirers among the community at large. Undoubtedly some of the cars were driven by Mennonites, but I suspected that a fair number of English had shown up for the funeral as well.

I parked the car along the edge of a frozen alfalfa field about a quarter of a mile from the cemetery entrance. I was lucky to get that spot.

"You don't expect me to walk that far, do you, Mags?" My sister pointed at her feet. She was wearing a pair of ridiculous platform things, which I refuse to call shoes, and which, while they might make sense in the Mississippi flood basin come spring, were totally inappropriate for Farmersburg in February. I would have made her change back at the Troyers', but she had nothing more sensible to change into, and not even Sam Troyer had feet as large as Susannah's.

"Sorry, sis," I said calmly, "but if I lose this space, we might have to walk twice as far."

"I mean, why don't you drop me off at the cemetery gate, and then find a spot? You don't mind walking a little ways, do you?" Susannah had the audacity to smile at me then and blink her baby blues beseechingly.

I put the key back in the ignition. "Of course I mind. Why don't you stay here and save this spot, and I'll drive on past the cemetery and see what the parking looks like ahead. If it's more promising, I'll come back and pick you up and drop you off at the gate."

"But I'll look like a fool just standing here!"

I bit my tongue and took the key out of the ignition.

"But I'll do it anyway," Susannah said quickly.

"Be here when I get back," I admonished her.

One summer, when Susannah was about twelve, Mama made me drive her to the county fair in Bedford. Apparently even she had gotten tired of Susannah's bored whining and needed a breather. At any rate, I wanted to see the quilt judging, but my sister insisted on attending the 4-H lamb show. There were boys there, she said. Cute boys she knew from school. Non-Mennonites even.

I was twenty-two at the time, and should have known better, but I agreed that we would split up and meet under the giant apple that marked the entrance to the fairground at precisely five that afternoon. Not a minute after, I warned. Susannah blithely promised to be prompt. Of course, she was a no-show. Seven long-distance phone calls and two and a half hours later I learned that Susannah had arrived back at the farm safe and sound, if somewhat the worse for wear. Apparently she had gotten bored well before five, and had accepted a ride home with two teenage boys whom she had just met, but who were "very nice." Unfortunately the boys had even less sense of direction than my sister, and the three of them headed off in the opposite direction from Hernia. They might still be wandering around in the mountains of central Pennsylvania had it not been for their car radio. It was when the Bedford station began to get fuzzy that the three of them figured out it was time to turn around and try another road.

Needless to say, Mama was fit to be tied and the whole fiasco was somehow my fault. Sweet little Susannah had been the victim of my selfishness. I should have taken her to the lamb show and held her sticky hand while she ogled the 4-Hers. Of course, Mama didn't say that exactly, but Mama didn't really know what Susannah was like either. I did. I knew that the Susannah my parents saw was the darling, dimpled daughter of their dotage, while the real Susannah—well, never mind.

I'm sure it didn't even occur to Mama, or Papa either, that I also might have been worried about Susannah. She was my sister, after all, and I loved her. True, I loved her because she was my sister, and not because of any special qualities she possessed—we certainly were not friends—but it was love nonetheless, and they should have given me credit for it. I still love Susannah, although I honestly can't say that I like her any better now than I did then. But she is my closest family, and that counts for something, even though I can't explain why.

"Promise me that this time you'll be here," I pleaded.

Susannah rolled her eyes, but nodded her head. That was as much of a promise as I was going to get. Stupidly, I allowed history to repeat itself.

Eight

There were no closer parking spots past the cemetery entrance, and I had been foolish to look for one. Because of the heavy traffic I had to go at least three miles down the road before I could find a place to turn around. By the time I got back to where Susannah was supposed to be waiting, she wasn't.

Parked where my sister was supposed to be standing was a silver Mercedes-Benz. Somehow it seemed to fit. Not that you'll find a Mercedes at your average Amish funeral. The odds are overwhelmingly against that. What I mean is that if there is trouble, and it involves Susannah, it's bound to be trouble with a flair. My sister has come a long way since riding off in the wrong direction with two teenage boys.

By the time I finally got the car parked, I might as well have stayed home. There was nothing for me to see but a wall of black backs. As for hearing anything directly connected with the funeral, I will confide here that while Bishop Kreider is undoubtedly a godly man, and is in fact almost as old as God, he has the voice of a six-year-old child. Even the deceased, had he not been so, would have had a hard time hearing his eulogy.

I heard other things, of course.

"Move closer this way," a young woman said in Pennsylvania Dutch to a small boy at her side, "and let the English woman pass. She might be an important person."

The boy barely budged, but regarded me somberly. "She looks like Mrs. Troyer."

The woman snorted. "Ach, what a silly thing to say." She cast another glance sideways at me. "Well, maybe just a little. But Lizzie would never wear such worldly clothes."

It was my turn to give myself the once-over. A mid-calf gray coat over a mid-calf gray dress was hardly worldly garb. Even Mama would have approved of my outfit. Of course, Mama would not have approved of my underpants, which had the word "Thursday" embroidered on them in tasteful gray thread. It was only Wednesday, after all.

"Do you mean Lizzie Troyer?" I asked in English. "Married to Samuel? Mother of five darling little boys? Lives on Leesburg Lane?"

They should have both been happy that there were no flies to fill those mouths. "Mennonite?" the woman asked at length.

"Yes. I'm Magdalena Yoder, from Hernia, Pennsylvania. But Lizzie Troyer is my cousin. Well, sort of. I mean, she's related."

The woman nodded knowingly. "Barbara Hooley. This is my little brother, Peter."

There might well have been a dozen Barbara Hooleys in a crowd that large, but I decided to take the chance. "Were you the one engaged to Levi Mast, dear?"

She looked quickly away. "This is my second funeral in just over a week. I'm sure the good Lord has a purpose in all this." Her voice trailed off, and she began to sob quietly into her hands.

If there had been a grave for me to crawl into, I would have. I had not meant to cause the poor woman any distress, but now that I had, what was I to do? I am not demonstrative by nature, and to put my arm around and comfort a stranger was unthinkable. With no one to advise me, I did the best I could. I patted her gently but repeatedly on the arm, and I patted her little brother Peter on the head. They might well have been two farm dogs, fresh home from chasing rabbits.

"Ach, you're hurting me," Peter said, and slipped around to the other side of his sister.

I stopped all patting. "Lizzie told me all about it," I said. "I'm so sorry."

Barbara Hooley wiped her tears on a black gabardine sleeve. "Levi was such a good man," she said. "So good!"

"And a good farmer too, I bet." Too late, I tried to bite off that last word. Amish, and Mennonites more careful than I, do not refer to betting, even as a figure of speech. Gambling is just too big of a sin.

Even with her tear-streaked face, Barbara would have made a pretty bride. "Ach yes, Levi was an excellent farmer, but it was his cheese that was so special. Some say that it was the best in the county. Of course, Yost Yoder made good cheese too," she added generously.

"Ach, yes, Yost made wonderful cheese," someone in front of us said. Clearly the black wall of backs had ears.

"That's why Yost and Levi were asked to form the cooperative," Barbara whispered. "They were the best cheese makers in the county."

"Ah, the cooperative," I said. I would ask the Troyers about that first chance I got.

"It would have been very successful too, Magdalena, if Levi hadn't slipped from the silo, and Yost hadn't drowned."

"I thought Levi jumped from the silo," Peter piped up.

"Levi *slipped*," Barbara hissed.

"But I heard Mama say—" Apparently a gloved hand had found its way over a little boy's mouth.

I should have clamped one of my gloved hands tightly over my own mouth then, but I didn't, and there's no use crying over spilled milk. "Your Levi was too smart to climb up a silo in February," I whispered softly, hoping that Peter wouldn't hear. "It wasn't an accident, was it?"

Barbara not only refused to answer, but she managed to push her way through the sea of black backs before I could stop her.

There was nothing I could do but wait for the funeral to end and the crowd to disperse. Maybe then I would find my sister and whoever it was who drove a silver Mercedes. Of course they were together; I've heard it said that money is a powerful aphrodisiac, and Susannah is—well, herself. On the off chance that the owner was a woman, I would cheerfully eat my hat. After zucchini-and-Kool-Aid butter, what did my taste buds have to lose?

I was right. The "Englisher" was not only a man, but a good-looking man. Not that it mattered to me, mind you. Nobody was better-looking than my Aaron. I was also right about Susannah's reaction to his money. She was wrapped around his cashmere coat like an extra scarf. Neither did it surprise me that this shameless behavior was going on right in front of Bishop Kreider. What surprised and disappointed me was that Bishop Kreider didn't even seem to notice. He certainly didn't look disapproving.

I approached the gravesite as silently as possible. Except for Susannah and her new beau, there remained just the bishop, and a powerfully built Amish man who was carefully filling in the grave, after the family's token shovelfuls.

"Nice service, Rev," I heard the Englisher say.

Bishop Kreider shifted a heavy leather-bound Bible from

one hand to the other. "It was pretty much a standard graveside service," he said in his boyish voice. "You should have come to the funeral itself. That's where you would have heard good preaching."

"Yeah, well, this was nice just the same. Not nice that the fellow's dead, but nice that so many folks came out to see him off."

"Yost Yoder had a lot of friends."

"And family," Susannah said.

The bishop seemed to notice her for the first time. "Yes, the Yoders are a large family." He stared at my sister's outfit. "You aren't a Yoder, are you?"

Susannah laughed with forced gaiety. "Me? No, I'm an Entwhistle."

The man filling in the grave paused for a moment and stared at Susannah. In a far corner of the cemetery a crow cawed.

"Funny," said the bishop, "but you have the Yoder nose."

Susannah's next attempt at laughing reminded me of Mad Elmo's mule. When I was a little girl in Hernia, Elmo and his mule used to go door to door selling rags. Elmo sold the rags; the mule didn't. Mama always used to buy two or three rags (which she later burned), and I was allowed to give the mule a sugar cube. Each time, before I gave the mule his cube, I would tell him to laugh, and he would oblige me by throwing back his head and braying. Susannah hadn't even been born then, but somehow she had perfected the mule's laugh.

"Hyawwwww! No, this is an Entwhistle nose! A Presbyterian nose. Hyawwwww!"

The crow cawed again.

Bishop Kreider stepped back to avoid the spittle. "Wouldn't surprise me if there was Dutch in you somewhere, though. You look very familiar to me."

"Presbyterian back to Adam," Susannah said, as the crow cawed a third time.

It was time for me to step forward. "Susannah! There you are!"

My sister blanched. "Margaret, what a coincidence! Fancy meeting you here."

I refused to play her game. "Not such a coincidence, dear—we came together in my car. You were supposed to save that parking spot, remember?"

Susannah disentangled herself from the Englisher and pulled me rudely off to the side. "How dare you, Mags! Don't you know who that is?"

"Looks like an Amish bishop, an Amish grave filler, and an Englisher to me," I said.

"The Englisher is Danny Hern! *The* Danny Hern."

"Oh, *that* Danny Hern. I think I saw his picture once in the post office."

Susannah paled again. "Did you really?"

"No, but should I have?"

Susannah stamped a long, narrow foot. It might have been impatience, but then again, clog sandals on a freezing day, even a sunny one, are probably not that comfortable. "Of course not! Danny Hern is not a criminal. He's a rock star."

"He is?" What did I know? In another life I had been briefly but madly in love with Mark Dinning, after hearing "Teen Angel" on my friend Cheryl's radio. When I tuned our family radio to the station that played his songs, Mama almost had a heart attack. You would have thought I had invited the devil into our house. Even though I was already in the fifth grade by then, Mama washed *my* mouth out with soap, which struck me as terribly unfair. It was Mark who had crooned the blasphemous words, not me.

"Oh Mags, you are so provincial," Susannah said. She didn't dare roll her eyes outdoors at that temperature, for fear they would freeze in an unflattering position. "Danny Hern and the Vibrators were at the top of the charts for eleven weeks in 1984."

"You don't say."

"Of course, Danny isn't still with the band. For your information, he owns some cheese factory here in Farmersburg. Daisy Duck Dairies, or something like that."

"That's Daisy*bell* Dairies, dear. Now, what I want to know is, how come you didn't save that spot for me?"

Susannah sighed at my stupidity. "Get real, Mags. Would you have saved some dumb spot for me if Aaron Miller had come along in his silver Mercedes?"

"Aaron drives a Pontiac Grand Am, dear."

"That's not the point. Anyway, do we have to talk about this now? Danny is taking me out to lunch at a Chinese restaurant in Zanesville. Moo goo gai pan is his favorite food. Then this afternoon we're driving in to Columbus for a concert. Rock, of course. Danny still has connections and we're getting front-row seats. We won't be back until late, unless it snows there too." She giggled. "So don't wait up, Mags."

"So what do I say to the Troyers?" I asked, but my words encountered only air. By the time I turned around Susannah had redraped herself around the cheese magnate's neck and was hustling him off to his car. She had no intention of introducing me.

Almost as if on cue, the brawny man with the shovel left as well, leaving me alone with just the bishop and the judgmental crow.

I introduced myself correctly to the bishop before the crow cawed even once.

"I knew your papa when he was a boy," said the ancient man with his boyish voice. "That was your sister who just left, wasn't it?"

I nodded shamefully.

"The Yoder nose is not the mark of Cain, you know."

"Certainly not," I agreed. "Cain's nose was much smaller."

Bishop Kreider smiled. "Of course, Yost Yoder was some sort of cousin of yours. You knew him well?"

"Never met him." I looked down at the freshly filled grave. "And I hope it's a long time before we meet."

"Yes, all in God's time. Now it's time we head back to the Yoder farm for the meal. They'll be waiting." I saw him tremble, and I realized suddenly that he must be freezing. If I hadn't seen the lone buggy still parked nearby, I would have offered him a ride in my car.

"Bishop Kreider," I said as we walked, "did you happen to see Annie Stutzman—Mrs. Samuel Stutzman—this morning? She was my father's cousin. She promised to meet me here."

"Ach," the bishop said. "I was supposed to give you a message. Annie has come down with a cold and couldn't make it. She said she hopes you have a pleasant trip back to Hernia."

"I see." Of course, I didn't. Perhaps the bishop had confused my Annie with one of the others. No close kin of mine would let a common virus prevent her from attending one of the biggest social events of the year.

"Well, we'd better be getting back to the house," the bishop said, picking up his pace. "They'll be waiting on me to say grace."

"Yes, of course." I walked faster. "Bishop, do you think Stayrook Gerber will be there?"

"Yah, I think so. Do you have business with him?"

I had to swallow hard before any words could come out. I am not accustomed to lying to bishops. Of course, depending on your interpretation, I wasn't really lying. I did have business to conduct with Stayrook, it just had nothing to do with farming. And even then, you'll have to concede that my motives were pure.

"Yes, it is important that I speak to him," I said.

"In that case, you might have spoken to him a few minutes ago. That was him who just left."

I looked closer at the bishop. Behind the parchment skin of old age, and camouflaged by the boyish voice, there was a shrewd and wary mind. For some reason it pleased me that an Amish man could be so cagey.

Nine

I didn't expect to run into the gal from Goshen at the funeral meal. If she had possessed any class she would have hung out in her motel room and watched whatever it is Susannah watches on daytime TV. I realize that most of those programs would make even the whore of Babylon blush, but Harriet obviously didn't have any morals or she wouldn't have hired herself out as a motorcar-driving mercenary for Mennonite money.

Harriet was certainly glad to see me. "There you are, dear! Honestly, I can't tell you how glad I am to see you. These folks"—she dropped her voice a decibel or two—"might be the salt of the earth, but they are B-O-R-I-N-G."

"This is a funeral, Harriet," I reminded her.

"Not like any of the funerals I've ever been to. Now, an Irish wake, that's what I call a good time. Sometimes they go on for days. Are you Irish, Magdalena?"

"Not by a long shot, dear."

"You sure? Magdalena sounds Irish to me."

"I'm sure."

"Ah, Jewish. Of course, the nose."

Had I not been both a lady and a pacifist, I would have punched Harriet's nose. Many of my regular customers at the PennDutch are Jewish, some even my friends. Their noses come in all shapes and sizes, but the one thing they all have in common is that they don't stick them into other people's business.

"For your information, my last name is Yoder," I said. "I am a Mennonite. These boring people here"—I waved at the crowd—"are my family."

"Well," humphed Harriet, "I should have known as much. After all, you don't have a sense of humor."

I shrugged. "Or else you're simply not funny, dear." I went off to look for Stayrook Gerber.

I found Stayrook in the mudroom talking about the co-agulative property of rennet with several other men. He looked as if he'd been expecting me.

"Stayrook Gerber?"

"Yah."

"I'm Magdalena Yoder, from Hernia, Pennsylvania. Yost was a cousin of mine."

"Yah, I know who you are."

That didn't surprise me. What did surprise, and please, me was that the other men regrouped and turned their backs on us so that we would have some privacy. Of course, they didn't leave us alone on the mud porch; that would have been unseemly, and neither of us would have wanted that. If any of them eavesdropped, that was simply the risk I took. It was my conversation, after all.

"Mr. Gerber—"

"Stayrook, please."

"And please call me Magdalena. Stayrook, I don't know exactly where to begin, or how to say this, except to come right out and state that I don't think my cousin accidentally drowned in that milk tank. Nor do I think that Levi Mast fell from his silo."

Stayrook's big face remained placid, but I saw his eyes widen in the shadow of his hat brim. "Why are you telling me this, Magdalena?"

I'm sure it was only my imagination, but the backs of the other men seemed to stiffen, and there was a brief pause in their conversation. I waited until someone spoke again.

"Someone brought you to my attention," I whispered.

He took a big step backward and nodded almost imperceptibly at me. I obediently closed the gap.

"I am a married man with four children," he said softly. "It is foolish of me to even talk about this."

"Silence won't keep you safe," I said. I know now that it was a pompous thing for me to say. Who did I have to lose? Susannah? She would probably dance for joy at my funeral, because then the PennDutch would be hers. As for Aaron, if that man cared half as much as I hoped he did, he would have long ago bought a diamond ring and popped it on my finger. Rings can be sized up beyond eight, you know.

Stayrook closed his eyes briefly, a habit I've noticed that many people, especially men, engage in just before they lie.

"Whoever told you to talk to me was barking up the wrong tree. I certainly have no reason to share your suspicions."

I stared hard at him. Gave him the evil eye, as Susannah would say. "Two of your friends have just been murdered, and you want to bury your head in the sand? This isn't turning the other cheek, Stayrook. It's cowardice."

The eyes shifted. They didn't roll exactly, but it was

close enough. I would have to check my family tree for Gerbers.

"Stayrook, if you have any idea who was behind these murders, you have a moral obligation to help put them behind bars. You should call the police right now. I'll even call them for you."

The big face began to harden. It was like watching a pond freeze over. His lips moved stiffly. " 'Vengeance is mine, thus saith the Lord.' "

I have seldom been angrier. Two deaths, a widow with children, a bereaved fianceé, and yet Stayrook's principles prevented him from involving himself with the law of men, with English law. God would avenge the two deaths, in his own time, if not in ours.

"Look, you said before that you shouldn't even be talking to me because you have a wife and four children. Well, let me tell you something, Stayrook. You may not have all of them much longer, or they may not have you, if you *don't* talk to me. Obviously its common knowledge that you know what's going on. I mean, someone directed me to you, right? And if the community knows that you know, don't you think the killer knows as well?"

I let that sink in for a moment, while I revamped my strategy. I should have known better than to mention the police, a last-ditch resort for the Amish. Stayrook might still talk, but only if I could convince him that he wouldn't have to be directly involved.

"I run an inn in Hernia," I said calmly. "Last year there was a murder there, and it involved Englishers. The police couldn't solve the murder, but I was able to get the murderer to confess and turn herself in. She hasn't killed anyone since." Okay, so I left out some important details, but I wasn't lying. And in this case, the end certainly justified my means.

Stayrook's eyes were as big as my mama's prize-winning dahlias. "A woman did the killing?"

I waved a hand impatiently. "It happens all the time. We are capable of anything, you know. That wasn't my point. The point is that I have experience in these matters, and might be able to help you. Unless of course, you don't want my help and would prefer the police. At any rate, if you don't do anything about it, then I'm just going to have to call the police anyway. Yost was your friend, but he was my cousin, and I don't have to follow your ways."

Stayrook stared at me. The pond had frozen solid. Under any other circumstances I would have considered it terribly rude. Much to my credit, if I must say so myself, I gazed calmly back at him. His nose was no tiny tater; it was in fact a typical Yoder nose, hidden by the open expanse of a huge face. Perhaps the eye-rolling was a Yoder thing after all, and had nothing to do with Gerber blood.

At last the frozen face thawed enough for the lips to move, but not enough for them to make sounds. Fortunately I had enough experience watching Susannah read to decipher the movements. "I'll talk to you later," they formed.

I nodded. Having run an inn for several years, I was well aware that walls have ears. In the case of a mudroom packed with men, there were more ears per square foot than in an acre of hybrid corn. Stayrook would talk to me later, I was sure of that. In the meantime I needed to find Freni and give her the news from home.

I found Freni in the kitchen slicing pies and cakes. The woman never went beyond the eighth grade, and any fractions she may have learned in school have undoubtedly been forgotten, but nobody east of the Mississippi can match Freni when it comes to dividing a dessert into even portions. Her eye-knife coordination is truly a wonder, and when I found her she was surrounded by a cluster of admiring women. Of course, being Amish, they were careful not to praise her, lest she become proud, but I could see the admiration shining in their eyes.

"Ach, there you are," she said when she saw me. "Why weren't you at the funeral, Magdalena?"

"Well—uh—it wasn't in English, was it? Anyway, Susannah and I went to the burial."

"I didn't see you."

The women dispersed to allow us some privacy. "I was there, Freni. I was standing near the gate."

"Late again, Magdalena?"

I struggled to curb my temper. It is Susannah who is habitually late, not me, and Freni should know that. "No. And I want to talk about something else. I called home this morning."

Freni laid a knife dripping blueberry filling on a cake with white icing. I said cutting was her specialty, not overall neatness. "Did you speak to Mose?"

"No, I spoke to Aaron."

Freni gave me one of her "aha" looks. "And?"

"And we can't go back to Hernia tonight. Western Pennsylvania is snowed in. In fact, it looks like we might be stranded here for a couple of days."

The corners of Freni's mouth began to twitch. "Several days? Why, that's too bad."

"You don't look heartbroken to me, dear."

Freni's mouth had contorted into a rare smile. It was one of the few times I'd seen her teeth when she wasn't yawning. "Of course I miss Mose and all but if you ask me, Ohio is the place to be. Hard work gets appreciated here."

I was stunned. Not only do I pay Freni well, but I am not shy with the compliments. Well, at least I don't intend to be. "Just what is that supposed to mean?"

Freni sliced the white cake, leaving a smear of blueberry on the first several pieces. "Maybe instead of me going back, Mose should come here. We could retire here. Sarah needs someone to help her with the chores, now that Yost is gone."

Freni may have sliced through my heart. "What are you talking about? How can you retire here and expect to fill in for a young man at the same time? Are things so bad in Pennsylvania? Am I that hard to work for?"

Without wiping the knife, Freni began to work on another blueberry pie. "Our son John could come too. He's young and strong."

"And married!" I said. Freni's daughter-in-law Barbara is a sweet girl whose only discernible flaws are that she comes from Iowa and that John loves her.

"Well! At least people here see my side of things. At least here people care. Unlike some, who don't seem to care at all." She pointed the knife at me for emphasis. Globs of blue and white goo clung to it precariously.

I successfully resisted my urge to shake the little woman. The dress I was wearing was still quite new, and I didn't know how easily it would shed icing.

"Freni, you can't pull up stakes and move to another state—especially at your age—just because you don't get along with your daughter-in-law. Have you considered family counseling?"

I might as well have asked her if she had ever considered a career as a belly dancer. Freni began gasping and puffing. She reminded me of Susannah that one time I held her head underwater too long at Miller's Pond. Let me hasten to add that I was a child then, and cannot be held accountable for those intentions now. At any rate, I knew that it was time for me to scoot out of the kitchen. Three hundred years of pacifism have not altered our genes to the point that a full-fledged pie-and-cake fight is out of the question.

Harriet from Goshen was the first to leave after the meal. She left sometime in midafternoon, which just goes to show that she had been exaggerating about those Irish wakes. Even I stayed on until after dark.

Okay, I will confess to being the second to leave. Too much food and the body heat generated by all those mourners had combined to make me sleepy. I know you expect me to say that I was bored, like Harriet, but I truly wasn't. Emma Hertzler saw to that when she accidentally spilled a bowl of cole slaw on the bishop's lap, and if things lagged off a bit after that, they certainly picked up when Jonas Mast choked on a chicken bone and I had to perform the Heimlich maneuver. Unfortunately, Jonas is a widower, quite handsome, and about my age. Even more unfortunate is the fact that no one who witnessed the incident had ever heard of the Heimlich maneuver, and until that bone popped out of Jonas's mouth and bonked Esther Gingerich on the nose, my reputation was at stake.

Even after the procedure, when the more astute were hailing me as a humble hero, tongues wagged mercilessly about the implications of such a thing. No, I assured them, I did not expect Jonas to propose marriage, and yes, it was the first time I had ever put my arms around a grown man other than my father. To fortify myself against the inquisition I had two pieces of pie and three pieces of cake for dessert. So I was both stuffed and sleepy when I staggered out into the starlit night. But I was certainly not bored.

The air temperature must have been about ten, and I remember the crunching sound my shoes made on the frozen grass. I never lock my car doors in weather that cold, lest the locks freeze shut, and so I didn't get my keys out of my purse until after I had slid behind the wheel. I was fumbling around trying to fit the key into the ignition when I felt a tap on my right shoulder.

My scream was almost loud enough to wake the dead. Had it been any louder, the funeral would have all been in vain.

Ten

Sarah Yoder's Amish Sauerkraut Salad

✦

3 cans (approx 16 oz.) sauerkraut, drained and chopped
1 red bell pepper, diced
1 green bell pepper, diced
1 large red onion, diced
3 stalks celery, diced

Combine the sauerkraut and diced vegetables.

Dressing for sauerkraut salad:

1½ cups sugar
½ cup salad oil (extra-light olive oil may be substituted)
⅔ cup white vinegar
⅓ cup water
1 teaspoon caraway seeds

Heat and stir the above five ingredients until the sugar is dissolved and the mixture is well blended. Pour over the vegetable mixture and toss to combine. Refrigerate 24 hours before serving. If kept in glass container, the salad will keep in the refrigerator for up to two weeks.

Eleven

"**S**hhhh!" Stayrook clamped a beefy hand over my mouth. "Somebody might hear you. If I take my hand away, will you promise not to scream?"

I nodded.

Stayrook removed his hand, which, by the way, smelled curiously like licorice.

"Do that again, buster," I hissed, "and somebody will be digging *your* grave."

My vehemence must have taken Stayrook aback some. He didn't say anything until he'd slipped out of the backseat and around to the front.

"Drive," he ordered.

I'm no expert on Ohio, but I doubt that even there it is customary for Amish men to hijack cars. If I laughed, it was because I was feeling such immense relief that it was only Stayrook who had waylaid me. That, and I could appreciate how ridiculous the situation was.

Stayrook could not. "Do you want my help, or do you just want to laugh at me?"

I bit my tongue, and my laugh sputtered to a stop. Even in the dark I could see the hurt look in Stayrook's eyes. "Yes, I want your help."

"Then drive. We can't talk here."

"Where to?"

"That way," he said, pointing north. "When we get to the second crossroads, turn left. Then your first right."

Stayrook's directions brought us to the end of a narrow gravel road that petered out in a streambed. Tall, gaunt trees stood sentinel above dense underbrush. The only lights to be seen were those in the sky, and the place felt wild and forlorn. It was hard to believe I was still in Ohio.

"This is where the young folks come to court," Stayrook said matter-of-factly.

I recoiled in shock. For all their strictness, my Amish relatives were surprisingly relaxed when it came to the latitude they allowed their teenagers. Not that their teenagers would do the same things you're thinking of, but still, it was a lot more than my Mennonite parents would have tolerated. I tried unsuccessfully to conjure up images of black buggies filled with amorous Amish teens, boldly holding hands. It was too much for my blood.

"Here?" I asked weakly.

"Yah." Stayrook grinned. He had straight white teeth, or at least that's what they looked like in the dark. "But don't worry, they won't be here tonight. Because of the funeral."

That relaxed me a little. I certainly wasn't up to a hijacking *and* a passionate display of manual interdigitation. Not on the same night. "So, tell me all you know about my cousin's death," I said. I felt a need to be in charge again.

Stayrook glanced about, as if even there, beyond the pale of civilization, danger might be lurking. "Magdalena, you were right. I do know something more about the deaths of Yost Yoder and Levi Mast."

"Yes?"

"They were not accidents."

"You don't say." Sarcasm is an art form, and Susannah, my tutor, is one of the masters.

Stayrook shifted nervously. "You must give me your word that my name will not be brought up in connection with this matter."

"You have my word," I said solemnly. From one of the gaunt trees an owl hooted.

Stayrook took a deep breath. "Yost, Levi, and I all used to supply milk to Daisybell Dairies. So did our fathers. In fact, most of us in Farmersburg County were connected to this dairy in one way or another. Those of us who didn't supply milk worked in the factory."

"The place that makes the fancy cheese."

"Yah, but that was back when Mr. Craycraft was in charge. Wesley P. Craycraft III, who founded the dairy. He was an Englisher, of course, but like the salt of the earth. He cared about the cheese, and he cared about his workers too."

"Go on."

"Then Mr. Craycraft died, and his nephew from West Virginia came up and took over. Things were never the same."

"How so?"

"Mr. Hern—Danny, he wanted us to call him—started taking shortcuts. Shortcuts that he thought would save him money."

"What kind of shortcuts?"

I could feel Stayrook's gaze boring into me. He must have thought I was stupid. "You ever make cheese, Magdalena?"

"Yes." That wasn't a lie. Once, after Mama died, Susannah and I tried to make cottage cheese by pouring sour milk into a sock and then hanging it up to drip.

"A good Swiss has to age, you know."

"Of course." Our cottage cheese had started out plenty aged, if you ask me.

"Mr. Hern didn't think so. He wanted to cut the aging time from six months to three. Then he cut it back to two. Imagine that!" Stayrook laughed, and the owl hooted along with him. "Two months is not Swiss. Not Farmersburg Swiss!"

"Certainly not," I agreed. Come to think of it, that sour milk might have been in our fridge for two months before we tried to make cheese out of it. After our parents' deaths, before Freni bustled her way into our lives, I sort of lost track of things.

"So, it was false advertising, you see. Mr. Hern was selling this nothing cheese as Farmersburg, and in the beginning he made a lot of money. Without an aging period, he could produce a lot more cheese in the same amount of time."

"Couldn't the public tell the difference?" Once as an economy measure at the PennDutch, I tried serving my guests instant coffee, instead of the real McCoy. That I survived that mistake is due only to the fact that I know a good hiding place or two around the inn.

Stayrook sighed. "Of course the public could tell the difference. Sales started to drop, but not as fast as you would think. A good reputation is a hard thing to overturn."

I certainly hoped so. I planned to be in business a long time. "Well?"

"Well, although sales had begun to taper off, Mr. Hern was still making more money than his uncle ever had. Of course, it wasn't honest money, and that bothered us. Some of us talked about not selling any more milk to Daisybell Dairy. We even took the matter to the bishop."

"And?"

"The bishop said that we should stop selling our milk to Mr. Hern unless he agreed to age the cheese at least four months. Even that would be cutting it close."

"And did he?"

"We never got a chance to see. Before the four months were up, Mr. Hern made improper advances to one of his factory employees. A young woman named Elsie Bontrager."

"Amish?"

"Yah. A good woman. Elsie had just been baptized, but she wasn't married yet. To put it frankly, Magdalena, I have three Holsteins with faces prettier than Elsie Bontrager."

"Tsk, tsk," I chided. "There is no correlation between marriage and looks. Some of us have simply chosen not to tie the knot."

Stayrook coughed politely. "Yah. Anyway, when Mr. Hern bothered Elsie, that was the last straw. All the Amish that worked for Daisybell Dairies quit and we formed our own cooperative."

"Aha. But did Elsie Bontrager press charges against this Mr. Hern?"

I could see Stayrook squirm. "She has gone to live with an aunt in Indiana."

"I see," I said, but I didn't. If Mr. Hern had laid one finger on me, he would now be missing it. In jail, if possible. Perhaps it was just as well my branch of the family was no longer Amish; even as a Mennonite, my attitude was an anomaly. Perhaps I was really destined to be a Presbyterian. I would have to talk to Susannah about it sometime.

"Anyway," Stayrook went on, eager to move the story away from Elsie, "we elected Levi and Yost to head the cooperative, because the actual processing was going to be done on their farms, and because they were younger and had more knowledge of the way things worked."

"With the world, you mean?"

"Yah, with the world. And things worked very well. Since we had eliminated the middleman, we were able to age our cheese the proper length of time, and still sell it for less than what Daisybell was selling theirs for."

I sat up straight. "Daisybell continued to make cheese? How could they do that when you stopped supplying them milk?"

Stayrook shrugged. "Other farmers, English farmers from outside the county, they trucked their milk in to the dairy. But I heard it wasn't the same."

I had to stifle a chuckle. "Amish milk is somehow better?"

Stayrook nodded. "Amish milk in Farmersburg County is." He was quite serious. "Some say it is the richest in the world."

That was quite a claim, coming from an Amishman. Unless it was absolutely true, Stayrook was guilty of pride, the worst of Amish sins.

"Perhaps it is something in the soil," I suggested.

"Yah, perhaps. Anyway, Mr. Hern was not happy with our success. Twice he came to see Levi at the farm when I was there delivering milk, and once I saw him at Yost's place."

"Did you hear what he wanted?"

"Yah, and it was always the same. He wanted to buy out the cooperative and for us to start delivering milk to him again. Of course, we refused. Even after he apologized for what happened to Elsie, we refused.

"Mr. Hern didn't understand that. 'You Amish are making a big mistake,' he said. 'You are in far over your heads.'

We told him that we could all swim and would have to take our chances. 'Then you'll pay for this,' he said. That was the second time I saw him at Levi's farm."

"Sounds like a threat to me."

Stayrook nodded silently.

"You have, of course, told this to the sheriff," I said needlessly.

The sharp sound of Stayrook sucking in his breath startled me. "Ach, no!"

I was incensed, but not surprised. "Stayrook Gerber, the sheriff *has* to be told if there was a threat. And this is not just an Amish thing anymore. Murder is a capital crime, a crime against the state. You can't sit on evidence out of religious conviction."

Stayrook turned and faced the window. Since it had fogged, I knew it wasn't because something outside had suddenly caught his eye. "Magdalena, the Bible says that God will seek his own judgment in his own time. It is arrogant and sinful for a man to interfere with God's plan."

"Ha!" I could no longer restrain myself. "So now what are you going to do? All start working for Mr. Hern again? He could be a murderer, you know, or doesn't that bother you? I suppose you see him as part of God's plan as well."

The Stayrook Gerber who turned from the window and faced me again was a different man. The big brawny gravedigger had somehow shrunk considerably and was now a scarecrow propped up on the seat. "We are going to sell our farms and move."

The owl hooted mournfully.

"What?" I spoke loud enough for the owl to hear me, and he obliged me with an answering hoot. I ignored him. "You are all going to sell and move? To where?"

Stayrook answered in a voice that matched his diminished size. "To Indiana. La Grange County. Most of us have kin there anyway—"

"So what? So do I, but you don't see me living there, and believe me, I've had my life threatened a time or two. What does the bishop think of this?"

Stayrook's voice dropped. "The bishop thinks that Levi and Yost may have been possessed. He thinks that if our people move to Indiana, they can leave behind the forces of evil."

"And you?"

He shrugged. "Have you come across evil before, Magdalena?"

"Have I ever! But I didn't move."

"It is God's will for us."

"Says who?"

"The elders. They are all in agreement with the bishop. That is how we know it is God's will. Part of his plan for us."

I observed a rare moment of silence. I bit my tongue and counted to ten. Twice. The counting, I mean, not the biting. "Well," I said calmly, "maybe I am part of God's plan as well. In fact, you may henceforth refer to me as Phase One."

"Ach du lieber," Stayrook moaned. "As if we don't have enough problems right now. Just who do you think you are, Magdalena Yoder?"

"Whoooo?" the owl echoed.

It was time to turn around and drop Stayrook off at the Yoder farm. If my instincts were right, life was going to be complicated enough without my having to dodge rumors that I was having an affair with Stayrook Gerber. In the words of Susannah, I "peeled out of there and burned rubber" all the way back.

It wasn't yet nine o'clock when I got back to the Troyer farm, but they were already home and in bed. I felt deliciously guilty as I slowly opened and then closed the front door behind me and crept up the creaky wooden stairs. If that had been Mama's house, she would have been out of bed and swinging a rolling pin seconds after the first creak. The pin, by the way, would have been meant for my backside, not a burglar.

Either the Troyers were all asleep or else they were totally uninterested in disciplining me, because no one intercepted me, smelled my breath, or checked my seams. For one intense moment I allowed myself to envy the Troyer boys and the relative freedom they would experience when they hit their teen years. Then I remembered the sardine omelettes. Mama might have been strict, but she was a first-rate cook. Love can come and go, after all, but a stomach is forever.

I was dreaming that Aaron and I were trying to ice-skate on Miller's Pond, in our bare feet, when Susannah crawled into bed and stuck her icy feet against mine. It took me a minute or two to become fully awake.

"Susannah Yoder Entwhistle!" I glanced at the luminescent hands of my watch. "It is four thirty-five in the morning! You should be ashamed of yourself!"

"For what?" she asked sleepily.

Then for the first time I remembered who it was Susannah had been out with. It was the murderer himself, Danny Hern. Even if it wasn't him who pushed Levi from the silo, or held Yost under as he drowned in milk, it was him who had ordered their deaths. I was positive of that. My baby sister, whom I was supposed to protect now that Mama and Papa were gone, and who surely couldn't look out for herself, was dating a cold-blooded murderer. Mama must be spinning in her grave so fast that the people in Tokyo undoubtedly were feeling the vibrations and expecting a tidal wave.

"Susannah, you can't—" I stopped. What my baby sister didn't know couldn't hurt her. At least not yet. But her relationship with Danny Hern could help lead to justice for the Amish community of Farmersburg, whether they wanted that justice or not. Foolishly I kept my big mouth shut.

Twelve

The next morning I passed on the sardine omelettes and left the house while Susannah was still sawing logs. However, that's not saying much. Once, shortly after she graduated from high school, my sister slept for thirty-six hours straight. Aaron tells me that she was probably drunk and none of us knew it at the time, but I don't think that had to be the case. Susannah slept so much when she was a baby that Mama, who was going through the change of life and was easily distracted, forgot to feed her for an entire day. Of course, she hadn't checked Susannah's diaper either, and wouldn't you know, at the end of the day it was still dry. One thing for sure, my sister has a world-class bladder.

Outside it was just beginning to get light and promised to be another cold but clear day. Over in the mountains of Pennsylvania, according to my car radio, eight more inches of snow had fallen overnight, and six more were forecast. It was as if Hernia were in another part of the country altogether, instead of just two hundred miles away. It seemed bizarre to be driving on flat, clear roads when back home everyone was snowed in. I said a quick prayer for Aaron,

Doc, and Mose, who were undoubtedly cooped up with restless guests and numerous complaints.

Farmersburg is easily twice the size of Hernia, but it certainly is no Pittsburgh. Even Somerset and Bedford dwarf it. That was fine with me. I am not a fan of big-city driving, and Farmersburg was just my cup of tea. For a real cup of tea I stopped at Pauline's Pancake House, right where U.S. Route 62 comes into it from the west. Frankly, I didn't expect much from Pauline, but after eating with the Troyers, it couldn't help but be a pleasant surprise. The pancakes were light and fluffy, the butter real, and the syrup warm. That the syrup was only two percent real maple didn't matter to me. Mama gave us only corn syrup when we were growing up; the maple she saved for when we had company, and to this day I can't imagine eating the real thing unless the table is decked out in its finest and I am in my Sunday best.

Pauline, the proprietress, was a plateful herself. I could hear her gum snapping from three tables away. There is something palpable, perhaps a pheromone, that proprietresses emit, and that others of their ilk pick right up on. Whatever it is, Pauline made a beeline for me.

"Hey, hon, where you from?"

Since I could read between the lines, I cut straight to the chase. "The PennDutch Inn, Hernia, Pennsylvania, and I'm only here for a few days."

Pauline's smile of relief was so wide that her gum fell out, but with a practiced hand she caught it and popped it back in her mouth, without missing a beat. "Then welcome to town, honey. It's always good to see a visiting face."

Between the lines that meant she could relax now that she knew I wasn't competition moving in on her territory.

"This is a charming little town, and quite a place you have here, dear. You get a lot of tourists?"

Between the lines I meant that Farmersburg was about

as far off the beaten track as one could get, her restaurant was more than adequate, and did outside troublemakers show up with any regularity?

Pauline slid into the red vinyl seat across from me. "May I, hon? Most of my Joes are home-grown, but we get a few cameras now and then, usually in the summer. The tourist you're talking about is from West Virginia."

"West Virginia?"

Pauline nodded, and her beehive hairdo tilted precariously. Fortunately it was stanchioned with enough bobby pins to secure the Empire State Building in gale-force winds. "Big tipper, but a slow eater, if you know what I mean."

I did. "So he's here for a while," I said. "What's his game?"

Pauline tapped the creamer in front of me. "A little squeeze from the cow, but he's squeezing more than that if you ask me."

Not one to decline an invitation, I asked, "Who's in the juicer, dear?"

"The *Ay*mish."

I gritted my teeth, but held my tongue. Clearly Pauline had once been a tourist herself.

"Do tell, dear."

Pauline glanced furtively around, as if trying to spot eavesdroppers. To be really thorough she might have tried jabbing her hair with a fork. An entire CB unit could have been hidden in that hill.

"The Amish supply me with most of my basics. You have bacon with that?" She pointed at my plate, which had been scraped so clean that even a forensic dietician would have been at a loss to recreate my meal.

"Two orders of bacon," I said proudly. The experts won't agree, but in my opinion fat is where it's at. Better a short, fat-filled life than a long dotage filled with iceberg lettuce. "Let us pray" is all I need of that vegetable.

Pauline snapped her gum extra loud in appreciation. "Good for you, girl. Anyway, what I was saying is I've been buying from those people on a regular basis, so I've gotten to know some of them pretty well. Not that you can ever really get inside their heads, on account of they're so different and all. Sort of like the Japanese, I guess. You know what I mean?"

"What an interesting observation," I said kindly. Professional courtesy prevented me from rolling my eyes even a quarter of a turn.

"Yeah. Anyway, things used to be different before old man Craycraft died. Over at Daisybell Dairies. He was their biggest customer. And not just milk, either. I understand that a lot of them worked at the plant."

"Yes?"

And then she did pick up a fork—fortunately a clean one—and jabbed at the base of the hive. The tines clinked melodically against the metal hairpins. Either that or she was harboring some real bees.

"New dandruff shampoo," she said by way of explanation. "Not as effective as my regular brand. Now, where was I?"

"You were telling me about Daisybell Dairies. How things have changed there."

"Yeah, that's right. You see, when Craycraft died, his nephew came up from West Virginia to run the place. He's the tourist I was telling you about."

"I see."

"Yeah, well, a lot of us wish he had stayed home. The Amish feel that way too. You can tell. Something tells me they weren't given a fair shake over there at the factory, and then there was that business about the girl."

"Oh?" I tried to sound mildly curious.

Pauline gave the hive a final hard jab. If any bees had been in residence, they were certainly dead now. "From what I hear, our tourist, Danny Hern, put the moves on this Amish girl he had working for him."

She paused for dramatic effect, and I obligingly looked shocked. I was shocked, of course, but somehow, when hearing about it for the second time, it didn't quite ring true.

"Go on," I said.

"Well, no sooner did that happen than all the Amish working at the factory quit, and his milk suppliers—all of them Amish—quit their deliveries. Last I heard they was forming their own company. You know, one of them—them—"

"Cooperatives?"

"Yeah, that's it. You gotta admire the Amish. They're real hard workers. It's in their blood."

"You don't say." So it wasn't just wishful thinking, after all. Susannah was adopted!

"Yeah, well." She stood up without checking for clearance. It was a good thing her place lacked ceiling fans. "You stop back in the next *few* days, okay?"

I got up as well. I had room for another order of bacon, maybe even a short stack of it, but Pauline's prices were far from puny. Then I remembered something.

"Pauline, dear—do you mind if I call you that?"

She snapped her consent.

"You said before that you thought the Amish were in the juicer. You think they still are?"

"That's *Ay*mish, hon. Yeah, I know they've got this cooperative and all, but something still ain't right. They look kinda scared. Like they're afraid of their own shadows, if you ask me."

I had asked her, and she had told me more than I'd expected.

★ ★ ★

The county sheriff's office was just across the street, so I left my car at Pauline's and hoofed it. I am a firm believer in exercise, and after jumping to conclusions, walking is my favorite kind. Walking is, after all, a natural form of exercise and was even practiced back in Biblical days. The Apostles, I know, did a lot of it. There is not one verse, however, that mentions them hopping up and down on steps that go nowhere or rowing boats without hulls. That's because they weren't lazy. Susannah, on the other hand, takes an afternoon aerobics class in Bedford that she drives to. Half the time Susannah skips her class because she can't find a parking place close enough to suit her. Go figure.

At any rate, you would think that walking to the sheriff's office would give me plenty of opportunity to read the sign by the front door, but I must have been thinking about home, and Aaron, because I missed it. It was only after I had closed the front door behind me, and set off some sort of signal which alerted the secretary, that I realized the Farmersburg sheriff's office was not where I wanted to be.

"Can I help you?" the secretary asked. She was in fact very pleasant.

"Ah, no thanks. I thought this was the telephone company." Okay, so it was a lie, but a lie told under extreme pressure. If there ever was a mitigating circumstance, it was the sign behind her that read *Marvin Stoltzfus, Sheriff.*

"The telephone company is two stoplights west, then left on Main. Right beside the Baptist church."

"Thank you."

I wheeled and was about to make the fastest exit ever out of a building not on fire, but the front door opened and in stepped the sheriff. There was no mistaking that he was a Stoltzfus.

To be truthful, he didn't look anything like our chief of police back in Hernia, *Melvin* Stoltzfus, who, tradition said, was kicked in the head by a bull when he tried to milk it.

However, every molecule in my body knew they were related. Maybe it was the pheromone things again. After all, if Jack's giant can smell the blood of an Englishman, I see no reason why a Yoder can't smell a Stoltzfus. He probably smelled me too.

"Don't I know you?" asked Sheriff Stoltzfus.

"No." I tried to move around him, but he jockeyed to cut me off.

"Marilyn Memmer, is it?"

"No." I bobbed in the opposite direction but wasn't quick enough.

"Rebecca Kreider?"

"No!" My patience was wearing thin, and I would have to go over him if I couldn't get around him on the next try.

"Agnes Hostetler?"

"Getting warmer," I said, taking a step forward.

"Aha! You're a Yoder, aren't you?"

I stepped back. I'd been caught. My colors were revealed. "But you don't know *which* Yoder now, do you?" I taunted him.

He laughed, something Melvin would never have done, and took two steps forward so that we were nose to chin. His nose, my chin. "Does it make a difference? You Yoders—"

"Yes?" I am five-ten, and I was wearing a winter coat. If I stand straight and extend my arms slightly at the sides I can make most men back off, or at least move aside.

Marvin was unmoved. "You have a record?"

"Just hymns," I said. "But not with me."

"Driver's license?"

"I walked." Perhaps I was being a mite difficult, but the man was blocking my access to the door and I was beginning to feel like a caged animal. Even a docile cow can get belligerent when cornered.

"I asked to see your driver's license," Marvin hissed. He

tapped the badge on his chest authoritatively. "You have to show it to me."

"Why?"

Marvin's right arm moved, and for a split second I thought he was going to reach for the gun in his holster, but instead he took off his sheriff's cap. It was all I could do not to burst out laughing.

Thirteen

Sheriff Marvin Stoltzfus possessed the biggest ears, bar none, that I had ever seen on a human being. They were as big as saucers, and could only have been folded beneath that regulation cap. Suddenly unfettered, the ears trembled and swayed, apparently adjusting themselves to their new environment.

He scratched the top of his head. "I said, give me your license."

Obediently I opened my purse, fished out my wallet, and thrust my license at him. I couldn't help feeling sorry for him after all. Perhaps a look at my DMV mug shot would boost his self-esteem, thereby improving his mood. After all, for years a number of states have been using Pennsylvania driver's license pictures as antidepressants.

My Ohio friends tell me that they have a somewhat humane DMV. They claim it is possible to get their license, complete with photo, at one place, on the same day. Coming from Pennsylvania, I find that hard to believe. The regulations for our DMV were written by the Marquis de Sade and are enforced by refugees from Singapore. These cane-carrying curmudgeons are committed to carrying out arcane and complicated canons.

For instance, in Pennsylvania we must apply for our licenses at a police barracks. This isn't a dormitory for cops, but a vast torture chamber where you wait in line to find out which line to wait in. Then you apply for your license and take a test. If you pass the test you are given a photo application, which you must then send off to Harrisburg, the state capital, and they will mail you (by U.S. Snail) notification of where you must get your photo taken. Invariably the place noted is the police barracks, where you started out to begin with.

It is my understanding that the employees who man the cameras are highly trained psychopaths with degrees from Libyan universities. It is their job to anticipate that exact second when their customers yawn, belch, grimace, blink—you get the picture. Unfortunately.

Marvin Stoltzfus actually smiled when he saw my picture. His ears, which were lined with more veins than my Aunt Clara's legs, and almost as fuzzy as her cheeks, flushed pink with pleasure. He didn't, however, become any nicer.

"It doesn't show your weight here, or your height. How do I know it's you?"

I sighed deeply. Then I obliged him by twisting my face into a grimace that would have put the fear of God into the devil himself. It was really rather easy to do, what with Lizzie Troyer's supper to look forward to that night.

"All right." He handed the license back. "Now what can I do for you?"

"Nothing," I said. "I'm lost. I was looking for the telephone company. I need to pay a bill." Of course, I instantly realized how stupid that was, considering he'd seen my Pennsylvania license.

And Marvin was no Melvin. "Care to try again, Miss Yoder?"

"There's no defense like a good offense," Susannah is found of saying. Of course, she applies that philosophy to eligible men. But it seemed plausible that it could work on a Stoltzfus as well.

"I'm here to see you about the deaths of Yost Yoder and Levi Mast," I said. "I have reason to believe that their deaths were not accidental, but murder. I demand that a thorough investigation be held."

The ears began to flap slowly while he took that in. He motioned me to a hard plastic seat, which I took gratefully. Apparently Pauline's pancakes were not as fluffy as they appeared.

" 'Demand' is a strong word, Miss Yoder." The ears flapped faster. "What are these reasons you have?"

With a Stoltzfus it is always best to start with the obvious. "Amish men don't bathe in their milk tanks. Certainly not in February. In fact, never.

"And they don't climb to the tops of their corn silos in February either. Especially not on their wedding days. Of course, you should know all that, being a Stoltzfus."

The ears went rigid. "I am a Methodist, Miss Yoder, not that it's any of your business."

I swallowed. "Well, back home Stoltzfus is an Amish or Mennonite name. Our chief of police is named Stoltzfus. A real nice guy too." Okay, so that was an out-and-out lie. And yes, I feel guilty.

The ears began to twitch with excitement. "You mean Melvin Stoltzfus?"

"Yes. What a dear sweet man." When it comes to guilt, it might as well be in for a penny, in for pound.

"Melvin is my first cousin!" He actually sounded proud.

"But you said you were a Methodist!"

"Oh, that. Mother's second marriage was to a Methodist. After Daddy died—he ran away from home and became an elephant trainer for the Barnum and Bailey, and that's where he met Mother—she married a Methodist minister. So that's what I was raised." He sounded proud of that too.

"I see. How did your daddy die?" I asked politely.

Marvin slapped his cap back on his head, and in one swift movement scooped both of his ears back and tucked them inside. "He was stepped on by one of his elephants, not that this is any of your business either."

I nodded with new understanding. To my credit, I didn't ask Marvin what it was his mother did in the circus. It was clear though that, given his background, Marvin Stoltzfus knew nothing about the Amish and their methods of farming. And now that I understood the logic of the Pennsylvania DMV, it made perfect sense that he should be sheriff in a county largely populated by Amish.

I decided to switch tactics. "Were you involved in the Elsie Bontrager case?"

He looked at me defiantly. "Yes, of course I was."

"Very interesting," I said. "From what the Amish tell me, they never pressed charges."

The ears must have shifted beneath the cap, because I thought I saw it move. "I didn't say they pressed charges. I said, I was involved in the case. You might say I was a mediator of sorts."

"I see. Who asked you to mediate, the Amish or Daisybell Dairies?"

He stood up angrily. "Just who the hell are you to interrogate me?" He tapped his badge. "*I* am the law around here."

I stood up slowly. "And I'm here visiting family. Amish family. Lots of them."

As I said, he was smarter than his cousin Melvin. "The Amish don't vote."

"But the Mennonites do!" I said, and left.

It was a small victory. Farmersburg County has more

Amish than it does Mennonites, and most of those Mennonites were from the German rather than the Swiss tradition. That is to say, they were Mennonite Mennonites, rather than Amish Mennonites, like me. I don't blame you for being hopelessly confused, because I was hoping Marvin would be confused as well.

Now that I was actually in Farmersburg, I didn't need directions to Daisybell Dairies. The gal from Goshen had neglected to tell me that in addition to being the largest building in Farmersburg, the factory was the only one with a thirty-foot Holstein cow in front of it.

"The statue is exactly twenty-one feet and three inches high, and twenty-eight feet and eleven inches long," said Arnold Ledbetter, as we began our tour.

I gazed up at it appreciatively. "Concrete?"

"Fiberglas."

Much to my surprise, my request for a tour of the factory had been immediately granted. Even more surprising was the fact that my guide was none other than the general manager, Arnold Ledbetter. As for the infamous Danny Hern, he was presumably at home. Apparently the gallivanting cad had taken the entire week off.

I studied the behemoth for a few more seconds. "Ahem, Mr. Ledbetter, I hate to tell you this, but your statue is anatomically incorrect." I was referring to the fact that this cow, unlike normal bovines of the female persuasion, lacked teats. Nipples, for you city folks.

Arnold giggled salaciously. He was a mere snippet of a man, with a shock of black hair that seemed to grow only from the top of his head. I would have to ponder the genetic quirk responsible for that. His glasses were bottle-thick, but only half-moons, and those were top halves. He was every bit as interesting as the cow.

"Yes, well, she was originally fully endowed, but we had to saw them off because of a religious protest."

I found that utterly ridiculous. "Mr. Ledbetter, the Amish see cows in their natural glory every day. I can't believe they were offended by that."

"Oh no, it wasn't the Amish. It was the Baptists."

I breathed a huge sigh of relief. "Oh well, to each their own."

Arnold giggled again. "We filed them off in July. Half expected them to come back on the first cold night."

I cast him my Sunday-school-teacher look. "Shall we continue the tour?"

"Yes, yes, step right this way."

Arnold took me on a much more thorough tour than I had expected. Even Mama, who was a stickler for details, would have been overwhelmed at the amount of information Arnold threw my way. I must say that throughout it all I behaved gallantly, and like a lady. If my inner eyes glazed over after just a few minutes, Arnold never saw me looking bored through his top half-moons.

I will spare you an accounting of what I saw and learned, except for two important things. First, all the employees I saw that day were Englishers, and most probably Baptists. Second, the Swiss cheese produced by Daisybell Dairies—at least that offered to tourists as samples—is incredibly delicious. I had been expecting something that amounted to navel diggings, or even toe jam, but what I tasted that morning was both creamy and firm, and pocked with the requisite myriad of holes. The flavor was sweet and nutty, with just a hint of bite as an aftertaste. And that description holds true for each of the nine samples I tasted.

"Well, it's been a pleasure, Miss Yoder, but I really must be going now," said Arnold, as he snatched the sample plate from my hand.

"Yes, of course. Thank you again for the tour, Mr. Ledbetter. I found it all so interesting. However, I forgot to ask you one thing."

"Yes?" He smiled patiently, but wisely held the sample plate out of my reach.

"What really did happen to Elsie Bontrager, and where is she now?"

"Ha ha!" It was almost a bark. "That was all a misunderstanding, I assure you. Miss Bontrager was a young, naive girl who misconstrued certain things. She was also mentally unbalanced. If I recall correctly, she had a nervous breakdown and has been sent off somewhere to recover."

Arnold Ledbetter didn't seem to realize that my arms were longer than his, and like a crane snatching up minnows, I managed to grab the six remaining samples before he could react.

"Miss Yoder!"

"It really is very good," I said. I hoped that my sincerity showed for a change.

After lunch, which was the cheese, I found a secluded phone and called Aaron. I said secluded, not private. The phone was a public one, inside the vestibule of the public library. As it was a school day, *and,* coincidentally, Bunko day for the Farmersburg Women's Club, the library was all but deserted.

"Hello? PennDutch Inn," Aaron said in his dreamy voice.

"Aaron! It's me."

"Me who?"

"Now cut that out, Aaron. It's Magdalena, and I'm calling from another pay phone. These things eat money."

"What? You don't have a credit card?"

"Don't be silly. I have Susannah for a sister, remember?"

"Yeah, how are you doing, Magdalena?" It was precious of him to ask.

"Fine. And you?" I longed to add the words "Pooky Bear," but wisely restrained myself.

"Oh, me, I'm fine." I heard a female singing in the background, then some high-pitched laughter.

"Who's that? Mose?" Of course I knew it wasn't. Outside of Bishop Kreider, few men can hit clear notes that high.

"Oh, that?" Aaron paused two quarters' worth. "That was—uh, Hooter Faun. She managed to get back here after all. Hitched up with some guy on a snowmobile."

"What is she doing now?"

"Uh—"

"Why, Aaron Miller!" I was about to hang up the phone, but then for the second time that day decided to take my sister's advice. "Now, listen here, buster. You tell that floozy to knock off whatever she's doing and pack her bags. The PennDutch is a respectable place, and no one but Susannah—"

"Magdalena, calm down, will you?" He had the nerve to chuckle. "Hooter was just singing some camp songs for the children. I'm afraid they're bored."

I'd forgotten that in a rare burst of generosity, call it insanity, I'd relaxed my rules and let a young couple with preschool children rent a room. I wouldn't have done it except that the mother is a highly placed government official, and she had just been forced to give up her Bolivian nanny. That, and they were so desperate to get away from reporters that they offered to pay me twice my regular rate. Somehow word has gotten around that I respect my guests' privacy.

"What is Hooter wearing?" I stooped to ask.

Aaron chuckled. "You're going to love this. The power lines are down, so the furnace is out. Hooter is wearing a parka zipped to her neck, and a stocking mask, and she has her hood up. I'm surprised she can still talk, much less sing."

I breathed my sigh of relief with my hand over the phone. "Well, enough of that. I was just calling to see how everyone is doing. You guys getting enough food?"

"We're making do. How did it go yesterday?"

For a split second I considered being the mature and circumspect person I hoped Aaron believed I was. But he has such a sympathetic voice, and I really did need a good listener, so I gave him his money's worth. Actually, it was my money, and I had to interrupt the call three times while I ran to get bills changed at the checkout desk. If the librarian had been helping patrons, or had been a woman less easy to intimidate, I might not have gotten it all said. When I was through, I, for one, certainly felt better.

"Dammit, Magdalena! It sounds like you're in it up to your ears again." The concern in Aaron's voice was music to my ears.

"Well, someone has to look out for these Farmersburg Amish. They're certainly not doing the job."

The music swelled. "But not you! You could get hurt, or worse. Don't you realize that?"

Of course I did. "I have no choice, Aaron. We are our brother's keeper, after all."

The music reached a crescendo. "Well, I'd like to keep you right here in Hernia where I can keep an eye on you. I could kick myself for not having gone with you."

"Maybe you could borrow that snowmobile from Hooter Faun's friend. I'm only over the river and through the woods."

"I'll—"

We'd been cut off. I tried calling three more times and each time I got a busy signal. The fourth time I got a recording saying that all circuits were busy. I left the library resigned, yet strangely hopeful. Fairy tales sometimes do come true, like that time Susannah crashed a Little People of America conference and dated seven men. It was possible that Aaron, my knight, would come skimming to my rescue on a borrowed snowmobile. Then we would ride off toward the sunrise (Hernia is in the east) and live happily ever after. Just thinking that was enough to keep me warm that cold February day.

Fourteen

Even though it was after two in the afternoon when I got back to the Troyers', Susannah was still in bed. She was sound asleep and obviously dreaming by the smile on her face. Although Mama almost always sided with Susannah, I know she would have agreed with me that sleeping past seven in the morning, *and* enjoying it, has got to add up to sin. One can thereby conclude that sleeping into the afternoon, unless you have a night job, is pure, unadulterated wickedness. And in my sister's case, often adulterated as well.

Since I am a God-fearing woman, and my sister's keeper, I did my duty and yanked the pile of quilts off her. To my relief there was no sign of Danny Hern. Susannah was even still wearing the same nightie she'd gone to bed in. Yet all was only temporarily well. Before I could wake Susannah, a snarl escaped the silken shift and Shnookums scrabbled out, snapping. That minuscule mutt is a mangy menace. One of these days I'm going to buy a Roach Motel and send him on his last vacation.

"Tell that rat to stop biting, or I'll feed him to a cat," I said charitably. After all, the Troyers didn't feed their barn cats, but made them work for their lodging.

Susannah yawned and stretched a myriad of times, and finally sat up in bed. Shnookums slid into her lap, where he sat snarling. Four bleary eyes regarded me balefully. It didn't take a genius to tell they were both hung over.

"Is it morning already?" my baby sister asked.

"Where are we talking about, dear? It's already *tomorrow* morning in Japan."

Susannah rubbed her eyes and yawned again. "Oh Mags, you are so mean. What time is it? I mean here?"

"Two-sixteen p.m."

"Is that all?" Susannah flopped back down in bed and Shnookums went flying. Bowsers that small best wear ballast.

"How was your date, dear? You make it into Columbus?"

Susannah forced herself up on her elbows. The cur climbed back to his coveted cove in her concave cleavage. You know what I mean.

"Yeah, Columbus was super. The Vibrators gave a rad performance, and after that we went to the Club Nude downtown. It was awesome."

It amazes me that my sister feels so free to tell me these kinds of things. Even those of you who may have judged me harshly regarding my treatment of Susannah will have to concede that the lines of communication between her and me are definitely open. Often far too open for my liking.

Anyway, I declined to pursue Club Nude. "I take it you had a good time. Did Danny boy behave himself?"

"Of course he did," Susannah said. "That is, until that waitress with the giant—"

I spared us both. "Where is he now?"

Susannah and Shnookums yawned simultaneously. "How should I know? He said he had to go to work today, so we had to come back early. Maybe he's there now."

"Unh-unh."

Susannah sat up abruptly, sending Shnookums flying again. I stepped aside adroitly as two pounds of hair and teeth whizzed by. "What's that supposed to mean?"

"Why nothing, dear. Except that I just came from Daisybell Dairies, and there was no sign of your boyfriend."

"You what?" Susannah was on her knees now, threatening me with a pillow. You'd have thought I'd read her diary again.

"Relax. I didn't stop by to talk to what's-his-name," I said. "I just wanted to take a tour of the plant. You don't expect me to just sit around twiddling my thumbs, do you?"

My beloved sister yawned again, exposing flawless teeth. Rock-hard enamel, our dentist called it, and Susannah, unlike me, had been allowed an unlimited amount of candy as a child.

"You don't even watch TV, Mags, so you're used to doing nothing every day."

Maybe Mama might not have understood, but the good Lord surely would have if I had wrested that pillow from Susannah and smothered her. As proprietress and principal chambermaid, I work twelve-hour days at the PennDutch Inn. Meanwhile, Susannah sleeps, smokes, and slithers through the lobby in search of male guests with strong libidos and weak morals.

"Well, I never!"

"Then don't you think it's about time you did? Use it or lose it, I always say."

I clamped my hands over my ears to protect them from further defilement. "Susannah Yoder Entwhistle! You should be ashamed of yourself. For your information, I am saving myself for the right man, and when he does come along it is going to be very special." Although from what little Mama had told me, and from what I'd picked up from my female friends, *it* was just a little less tedious than rolling up one's hair. And apparently far messier.

"And anyway," I continued, my hands still clamped tightly over my ears, "I wasn't going to tell you this, but now I think I will. Your rich new boyfriend lied to you, because he never even planned to go to work today. In fact, according to the plant manager, he's off for the rest of the week."

I paused to let the information sink in. Even with my ears covered I could hear some of my sister's response, so I had to resort to singing hymns. I can set a mature example, you know. Fortunately Susannah ran out of energy before I ran out of hymns, so I was able to get the last word in.

"*Schteh uff,*" I said in Pennsylvania Dutch. "Get up and get dressed. This afternoon we're going over to cousin Sarah's house to see how she's doing. And don't even think about wiggling out of this. You do want your allowance this month, don't you?" I immediately began singing that old favorite hymn of Mama's, "Work, for the Night Is Coming."

I know that threatening my thirty-five-year-old sister with withholding her allowance might sound punitive, but unfortunately it is my prerogative. If she would get a job like everyone else, or at least help out at the inn on a regular basis, she wouldn't be in that position in the first place. Being on the dole has its consequences, you know. While I don't mind doling out dollars to destitute derelicts who decidedly deserve it, I do mind shelling out shekels to a shiftless sister who shirks work and shies away from responsibility altogether.

Susannah must be a closet Republican, because even though I couldn't hear her reply, I could read her lips loud and clear. However, I stood my ground, and when I drove off to Sarah's house a half hour later I had my shiftless sister and her shaggy Shnookums safely stashed in the backseat.

* * *

Either Sarah had kept her children home from school or the little Amish school down the road had let out for the day. At any rate, the yard was again full of towheaded youngsters, all of whom bore an uncanny resemblance to old photographs of Susannah and me. Seeing Susannah (she was wearing a purple jumpsuit topped by a fake leopard-skin cape made out of the finest polyester), they began to giggle. Dutifully I stomped my foot at them and called them hammerheads in Pennsylvania Dutch, but they laughed harder, so I grabbed a fake leopard-skin glove and whisked my sister into Sarah's house unannounced. We are family, after all.

We found Sarah in the kitchen kneading bread dough. Freni does that whenever she is upset about something as well. There is something very therapeutic about punching and pulling a good elastic dough, and I would recommend it as something to try before one sees a psychiatrist. It is certainly a lot cheaper. Of course, in some cases a therapist is in order from the get-go, while in others bread-making can become somewhat of an obsession. But I won't be mentioning any names here.

"Ach, but you startled me," Sarah said. Our sudden appearance had resulted in floured hands flying to her face.

"The children told us to come right on in," I said. Truly, it was more a rearrangement of the facts than a lie. If I had asked the children for permission, I'm sure they would have given it.

"Freni's not here right now. Jonas and Anna Beiler came by to get her for the day. She's Jonas's second cousin three times and Anna's first cousin twice removed. Does that make any sense to you?"

"Makes perfect sense, dear."

Sarah resumed her kneading. "There is cocoa on the stove. Pour yourselves some and pull up some chairs."

I poured the cocoa and pulled up the chairs, while Susannah watched expertly.

"How are you doing today, dear?"

The fingers moved faster. "It comes and goes. One minute I'm wondering if I should plant two rows or three rows of snap beans this spring, and the next I remember that Yost is dead. Snap beans were a favorite of his, you know. Now he'll never eat them again."

Big tears rolled off her face and splashed onto the dough. Mercifully, bread dough is a forgiving substance.

"Well, at least he won't be hungry where he is now." It was a very Mennonite thing to say, but even as I said it, I regretted it. If something happened to Aaron, I wouldn't want somebody quoting platitudes, even if they were spiritual truths, to me.

Sarah jabbed at the dough with closed fists. "Yah, Yost won't be hungry anymore." She jerked her chin in the direction of the door. "But they will. And children need more from their papa than just food."

"That's for sure," Susannah said. My sister has always maintained that I was Papa's girl, and that the two of us contrived to shut her and Mama out of things. This from a woman who had Mama wrapped around her finger tighter than a tourniquet.

"How are you going to manage the farm by yourself?" I asked.

The heavy wooden table shook from her next blow. "Ach, but I won't be by myself. Yost's youngest brother, Enos, and his wife, Dorothy, will be moving in to help me. They just got married last summer and don't have any babies yet. They'll help me until I can get this place sold."

"What? You're selling?" I remembered what Stayrook had said about the Amish pulling up stakes. Surely that had been an exaggeration.

"Why, I think that's a wonderful idea," my dear sister

said sweetly. "I try to make a fresh start whenever I lose someone I love." Despite her worldly ways, Susannah is as innocent as a newborn babe. I have yet to convince her that naiveté is not the arrival of Baby Jesus on Christmas morning.

"Not that I want to move," Sarah said more to herself than us. "All my babies were born here, and even though Yost died here . . ." Her voice trailed off, and for a moment she stopped punishing the dough.

"Then don't move," I said. "Maybe Enos and Dorothy can stay on permanently here. Or at least until your kids are old enough to make the difference."

"I'd move to Hawaii," Susannah said helpfully. "Or Myrtle Beach. I hear it's cheaper than Hawaii and a lot more fun. The guys are supposed to be cuter there too."

Sarah responded with a sob.

I gave Susannah the kick she was due and patted Sarah on the back. Four hundred years of inbreeding may have made me undemonstrative, but it didn't leave me without feeling. "It isn't time to be thinking of moving, dear. Not now. Give yourself time. And plant three rows of snap beans, because I'll come and help you eat them."

Sarah smiled weakly and wiped her face on her sleeve. Four hundred years of inbreeding had made her strong as nails, the occasional sob notwithstanding. "Yah, now is not the time to think about such things. Would you like to stay for supper, Magdalena? You too, Susannah. We're having frankfurter rafts and sauerkraut salad. The children all love frankfurter rafts."

My mouth watered. I hadn't had frankfurter rafts since the day—I was twelve—Mama discovered TV dinners.

"Thanks, but no thanks," said Susannah, who had never had frankfurter rafts. "Magdalena and I already have plans."

"We do?" That was certainly news to me. I had purposely told Lizzie Troyer *not* to count on us for supper.

While bread and fish might be sound Biblical fare, pies and cakes have their place too.

Susannah gave me what was supposed to be a meaningful look. Anyone else would likely have thought it gas. "Yes, we made plans earlier, remember?"

I didn't. Undoubtedly Susannah had another date lined up with Danny Hern, but that didn't mean I had to be stuck eating sardines in sild oil.

"Actually, dear, I remember no such thing," I said. "However, if you have plans, feel free to run along. But leave me my car, of course."

Even I began to wonder if Susannah had gas. Either that or had gotten something in her eye. I hadn't seen a human face go through so many contortions since back in seventh grade when Ernie Hershberger replaced the lettuce in Lydia Kauffman's BLT with poison ivy. The Pennsylvania DMV would have loved that.

"Are you all right, dear?" I asked kindly.

Susannah's left eye gave a final twitch that would have dislodged her false eyelash had I given her time to apply it that day.

"*We* have plans, Mags. Thank you, Sarah, but we'll have to take a rain check on that dinner."

I could hardly believe my ears. Not only had Susannah displayed exceptional manners in thanking our cousin, but she actually wanted *me* to tag along with her someplace.

"Well, I guess we do have plans after all," I said.

"You can at least stay for another cup of cocoa, can't you?" our cousin coaxed.

We stayed and sipped the delightful brew while Sarah shaped the bread into loaves, put them into well-greased pans, and set them aside to rise.

"It's a funny thing about Yost," she said suddenly, "but he wasn't himself the night before he died."

I was all ears. "He wasn't?"

Sarah didn't seem to hear me at first. She wet some dishtowels, wrung all the water out, and then placed them lightly over the loaf pans before answering. "No, Yost was definitely not himself. I have known him my whole life, but he never acted like that before."

"Acted like what?" Susannah asked. It surprised me that she'd even been listening.

"Ach, I have never seen such behavior. Even in springtime the animals don't act like that."

Susannah ignored my hand signals. "Like what?"

"Like he was crazy." She lowered her voice and glanced at the windows, through which we could hear the distant voices of children. "Maybe possessed."

Fifteen

My Mama's Frankfurter Rafts

✦

8 skinless frankfurters
Bacon grease
1 egg
2 tablespoons milk
1 teaspoon powdered onion
2 cups cold mashed potatoes
1½ cups baked beans
1 cup shredded sharp cheddar cheese
Salt and pepper to taste

Preheat oven to 350 degrees and grease 8-inch-square glass baking dish.

Brown frankfurters in bacon grease. Set aside to cool. Beat egg with milk and onion powder. Thoroughly mix beaten egg mixture with mashed potatoes. Smooth mixture over bottom of baking dish. Cut cooled frankfurters into halves lengthwise. Cut again across the width. Arrange frankfurter slices over potatoes until covered. Spread baked beans over the frank slices. Sprinkle the grated cheese evenly over the surface of the beans.

Bake for 25 minutes or until heated through and the cheese is melted.

Serves four.

Sixteen

I was stunned. Mennonites and Amish don't take possession lightly. We are forbidden Ouija boards and other types of entertainment that claim to make connection with the spirit world. Séance parlors and fortune-tellers are not even discussed, much less patronized. In a society without television, in which "new age" is what you become on your next birthday, the word "channel" is almost never used. Our faith is in God, and we look past the netherworld to the world to come. That is, the Kingdom of God.

Of course, the Bible is full of demons, as well as angels, so we believe that they do exist. We prefer to ignore them, however, as long as we can. If the subject comes up, it is never as a whim, or in jest. Sarah Yoder would not have suggested that her dear departed husband had been possessed unless she had ample reason to believe it. And unless there had been other witnesses.

"Can you describe his behavior for us in a little more detail?" I asked gently. I must admit that my naturally suspicious mind favored a human rather than a supernatural explanation. There is enough evil in the average human heart to make a personal appearance from the devil quite unnecessary.

Sarah nodded, her eyes suddenly brimming with tears. "It was after supper that night. The children were already in bed, but Yost and I were still downstairs. I was reading a book and Yost was writing a letter. Suddenly he looked up at me with the strangest expression on his face.

" 'My eyes must be giving out on me,' he said. 'Suddenly the words seem to be marching right off the page. Look, there they go now. Can you see them?' he asked."

"Wow!" Susannah said.

"At first I thought he was joking. Yost liked to kid around a lot. He was always teasing the children, but he was especially fond of teasing me. I'm what you would call gullible."

"I understand," I said. And I did. Susannah was ten before she stopped believing everything I said. Still, a farm child half that age should have known, without asking Mama, that there is no such thing as a macaroni plant.

The tears began to spill from Sarah's eyes, but she did nothing about them. "We were sitting right here, at this table. Suddenly Yost pushed back from the table and began to cry. The table was breathing, he said. It wasn't a table after all, but one of the cows. The cow had somehow been made into the shape of a table, and it was in pain.

"Then Yost jumped up and grabbed a cleaver and smashed it down on the table. To kill the cow and release it from its pain, he said. Only he was crying."

"Far out," Susannah said.

"Here. Look here!" Sarah scraped some flour out of a deep groove with her fingernail, and we could see that the cut in the exposed wood was fresh.

"Oh God," Susannah said.

I gave her a gentle kick under the table. "Then what?"

"I asked Yost to give me the cleaver, and he gave it to

me. Then he started to moo like a cow. He got down on his hands and knees and mooed like a cow!"

"Jesus!" Susannah said.

I kicked her harder. "Then what, dear?"

"Then Yost started begging me not to kill him with the cleaver. Magdalena, it was like he believed he was the cow!"

I kicked Susannah in time to forestall her next utterance. "What happened next?"

Sarah glanced at the outside kitchen door and shivered. "Then he went out that door, still on his hands and knees, and I never saw him alive again."

"You poor dear!" I thought for a moment. Mercifully Susannah must have been thinking too.

"But Sarah, dear," I said carefully, "I was under the impression you found your husband in the morning when he didn't come in from milking. Is that true?"

She shook her head, and I was glad that the bread was safely covered and in another spot. Bread dough is not that forgiving. "No, that's what I told the sheriff. But what else could I tell him?"

I shrugged. "What else happened?"

"I ran outside after Yost. I didn't even grab a coat first. But I couldn't find him anywhere. Not in the barn, not in the dairy, not even the root cellar. It was like he just disappeared.

"Then I ran upstairs and checked on the children. They were all asleep. That put my mind at some ease, so I went out and hitched up the buggy. I looked everywhere one last time, but still I didn't find him, so I drove to Annie Stutzman's for help."

"Is she your nearest neighbor?"

"Yah. I brought her back here so she could watch the children while I went to get Stayrook Gerber. He is the nearest man.

"Anyway, Stayrook was still up, and he came over right

away. Stayrook and I looked together until Annie made me go back inside and drink some hot milk. She thought it would calm my nerves. Then she sat with me while Stayrook continued looking.

"Stayrook even walked across the north pasture to where we have some hay piled up for winter feed. He thought maybe Yost could be hiding in there."

"But why would he be hiding?" Susannah asked. It was a reasonable question, so I kept my toes to myself.

Sarah looked at Susannah and then me. "I don't know why he would be hiding. But we had to take everything into consideration. We had to think of all the possibilities."

I patted her hand. It was ice-cold. "Of course, dear."

"Of course, Stayrook didn't find him there either. After that he stayed in the kitchen with Annie and me, and we prayed and read the Bible. And waited. It was just after midnight when I heard a noise coming from the dairy. It sounded like someone shouting.

"We all three ran to the dairy, and that's when we found him. He was dead by then. Drowned in the milk tank."

"But naked?" I asked gently.

Sarah froze, her eyes as big as buckeyes. "How did you know?"

"Annie Stutzman told me when she called about the funeral."

Sarah's icy hand grabbed my wrist. "You won't tell the sheriff, will you? You must not say anything to him about that, Magdalena!"

"I won't," I promised. "And Susannah won't either, will you?" I nudged Susannah with the toe of my shoe.

"Of course not. What do you think I am, stupid?"

I sipped my cocoa, which was getting cold.

"But you did call the sheriff," I said after a while. "I mean, you did call him as soon as you realized your husband was dead, didn't you?"

Sarah looked startled. "What? Oh no, we didn't call the sheriff *right* away. I mean, we took him out of the milk first, and then Stayrook drove over and got the bishop."

"The bishop?" Susannah and I chorused.

Sarah gave us each a challenging look. There was indeed mettle there despite the tears. "Yah, the bishop. We wanted his advice before we told the sheriff. You see, Sheriff Stoltzfus is not an easy man to deal with."

Susannah sputtered in her cup. "Stoltzfus?"

"Yes, Stoltzfus," I said. "But Marvin, not Melvin. I'll fill you in later. Go on," I said to Sarah.

She glanced at Susannah, who was still sputtering. "Bishop Kreider is a good and wise man. He said that the sheriff, who is English, might not believe that sometimes the devil or his angels can enter a person and possess them. Like in the Bible. He said the sheriff might order an autopsy, and that there could be a big investigation if he knew Yost had drowned without his clothes."

She looked beseechingly at us, as if our approval was important. We both nodded, and she continued, "The bishop didn't actually suggest it, but he hinted that it might be better if we dipped Yost's clothes in the milk tank and put them on him before we called the sheriff."

"I take it you found the clothes nearby?"

"Yeah, but they were thrown everywhere. It was as if he had ripped them from his body."

"How terrible it must all have been. But I take it the sheriff believed that Yost just happened to fall into his milk tank and drown? I mean, didn't it seem odd to the sheriff, even a Stoltzfus sheriff, for such an *accident* to happen? Didn't he suspect something?"

Sarah shook her head. "What other explanation could there be? Yost was a good man who was well thought of by everyone. You saw how many people were at his funeral."

"Well, to be honest, just at the graveside," I said. "I hope you don't mind, but Susannah and I didn't make it to the funeral itself."

Sarah smiled wanly. "But you saw all the people who came, didn't you? Anyway, Magdalena, strange accidents happen all the time."

"I'll say," Susannah said helpfully. "I dated a guy once whose brother got his finger caught in the coin return of the vending machine. It was on a day even colder than this, and before help could come he had frozen solid. Like a popsicle. Only *he* had his clothes on, of course."

She ignored my kick. "They had to cut his finger off to separate him from the machine, and then wouldn't you know they went off and forgot about it. Well, on the first really warm day that finger came popping out when a little old lady put in too much change to buy herself a Snickers bar. At the sight of the finger she fainted and—"

It wasn't the first time I'd put a hand over Susannah's mouth, but it was the first time she didn't try to bite me. Maybe there is hope for my sister after all.

"So you see," Sarah said stalwartly, "the sheriff wrote it up as an accident and there didn't have to be an investigation. It has all been taken care of."

"I see," I said. But I didn't. My handy little murder theory involving Susannah's nefarious new boyfriend now had a hole in it big enough for a real cow to wander through. Even if Danny Hern, or his goons, had somehow been involved in the drowning, they couldn't be blamed for Yost Yoder's suddenly going bonkers and charging out into the night on all fours. And why would they have bothered to take off his clothes?

It was time to go, because suddenly I had other fish to fry. I am proud to say that both Susannah and I hugged our cousin and told her she would be in our prayers. If Sarah minded being included in Susannah's Presbyterian prayers, she made no indication. We also thanked her for the hot cocoa and complimented her on her bread-making skills. Already the covered loaves had risen above the edges of the pans. I had the feeling that Sarah Yoder was going to be all right.

"Why didn't you tell me Melvin had a cousin here?" Susannah demanded as soon as we got in the car. "Is he cute?"

Wisely I started the car and drove out on the highway before answering. "As cute as Melvin," I said, without adding to the length of my Yoder nose.

"Dreamy," Susannah sighed.

I bit my tongue. My sister believes that anyone who prefers to stand when visiting the outhouse rates an automatic ten on a scale of ten. Uniforms, titles, and fat wallets all add extra points, of course, so Marvin, being a sheriff, probably rated at least a fifteen, which somehow makes sense to her.

"But of course I wouldn't have time to see him anyway, at least not tonight. I mean, we do have our dinner with Danny."

"Say what?" I braked hard enough for Susannah to slam against her shoulder belt, thereby somewhat constricting Shnookums. I assure you that result was quite accidental.

After Susannah had finished comforting the mashed mongrel, and properly chiding me, she remembered my question.

"Ah, tonight," she chortled. "Mags, you will be happy to know that you don't have to sit around with the Troyers looking at four walls. I told Danny all about you, and he wants to meet you. In fact, he wants to take us out to dinner. At the fanciest restaurant in Canton. Cher something."

"That's Cher Bono," I said. I may not listen to popular music, but I do pick up on things now and then. To hear Susannah talk, you'd think I live in a cave.

Susannah howled cruelly. "Sonny and Cher broke up

years ago. Probably before I was born. The restaurant I'm talking about is French."

"I don't care if it's Spanish," I said. "What makes you think I'm going there with you and that criminal? Not after what he did to poor Elsie Bontrager. Or haven't you heard?"

"Oh, that!" Susannah had the nerve to laugh. "All he did was compliment the girl on her eyes. Supposedly they are very blue. Since when did that become a crime?"

I pulled the car over to the side of the road but continued to grip the wheel tightly. "That's certainly not what I heard, Susannah. And Elsie Bontrager aside, this boyfriend of yours has been nothing but trouble for the Amish ever since he inherited his uncle's business."

She whirled in her seat, and if the mutt got mashed then it was her fault. "How so? These are just more vicious rumors."

I reminded myself to tread slowly. Speak now and pay later has not always been a pleasant philosophy.

"I have it from a good source that Danny Hern started taking shortcuts the moment he took over Daisybell Dairies. Eventually the Amish who supplied his milk had no choice but to quit supplying him and start up their own cooperative. Of course, no sooner had they got started on their own than two of the co-op leaders died under suspicious circumstances. Now the Amish are so scared they're thinking of moving away from the area altogether."

"Says who?"

"I can't reveal my source, dear. But I am positive he wouldn't lie."

"So it's a man?"

"Not necessarily. As a matter of fact, it's a woman." I ignored the twitching in my nose, since it was for a good cause. "And she says that your boyfriend, Danny Hern, even issued what could be construed as a threat."

Susannah laughed. "Danny? Threaten somebody?"

I gave her a look that, if harnessed, could have turned milk into aged cheese overnight. "I fail to see the humor here. You could be dating a murderer, you know."

Susannah yowled.

"But come to think of it," I said, thinking aloud, "going out to dinner tonight might be exactly the right thing to do. It'll give me a chance—" I caught myself before I went too far. It had been foolish of me to say that much.

Susannah was laughing far too hard to hear me.

Seventeen

An hour later Susannah was still laughing.

"I am *not* your mother," I said. "If I'd known you were going to pass me off as Mama, I would have stayed home."

The silver Mercedes had just pulled up in front of the Troyers' house, and I suppose I could have balked then and refused to go along with my sister's game. However, there was Lizzie's supper to consider. The zucchini fritters I could handle, but the sardine lasagna was asking too much. Better to play mother to my sister and dine with a criminal than to dine on Lizzie's cooking, which was a crime in itself.

"I only told him that because at first he thought I was too young to date and wanted to ask my mother for permission." Susannah laughed gaily. "When he dropped me off last night he said we would only go out again if I brought my dear, sweet mother along."

"Yeah, right." Susannah is on the shady side of thirty. So shady that even mushrooms can't grow there. Danny Hern was either blind as a bat, in which case he shouldn't be driving, or Susannah was even more gullible than I thought—in which case I have been wrong to tease her all these years.

"So, you're coming, and you're going to pretend to be Mama?" Susannah begged.

I sighed deeply and spun my eyes around a couple of times. It was a small price for Susannah to pay for all the joy I was about to give her.

"All right, I'm coming. And I won't contradict you if you refer to me as your mother, but don't expect me to come right out and say it."

"Love you, Mags!" Susannah gave me a quick squeeze.

I was understandably embarrassed by such sentimentality. "But I'm not going to raise your allowance, you know."

" 'Course not." Susannah reached to hug me again, but I deftly dodged her and hurried to open the door.

It was wise to intercept Danny before he had a chance to knock. The Troyers knew we were spending the evening with him, but there was no point in rubbing their noses in our strange English ways. A silver Mercedes and a grown man in ten pounds of gold chains and a full-length fur coat (some of the skins still claimed their heads) were not the best cross-cultural ambassadors I could imagine. Susannah and I were probably more than enough for them to handle as it was.

"Ah, it's *Chez*," I said, "not Cher. Chez Normandy."

"Same thing," Susannah said. She snuggled deeper into Danny's slain beasts. With Shnookums snuggled in her bosom, she should have felt deep shame.

It had been a quiet ride from Farmersburg to Canton. Every time Danny tried to speak—usually to me—Susannah pelted him with kisses, so any extended conversation would have been perilous to our lives. As a consequence I knew nothing more about Danny after the hour ride than I had before except that he belonged to AAA and had had his oil changed three weeks prior. These things I discovered by discreetly rummaging through the glove compartment. That is a driver's prerogative, you know.

"Park here, darling," Danny directed.

I pulled the sleek silver car into the reserved spot and turned off the engine. One could hardly tell the difference. It had been a joy to drive, really, once I'd gotten over the shock that I was the designated driver.

"He only drinks a little bit," Susannah whispered, just as I'd opened the door to the Troyer house.

What she neglected to say was that he drank a little bit all the time. The menagerie of minks masked a flotilla of flasks. Come to think of it, the poor animals were probably not dead, just stupefied by the fumes engulfing them. That Susannah had managed to make it to and from Canton the night before was a testimony to her guardian angel. That overworked being deserves to retire permanently as soon as Susannah's number is called.

Money does indeed speak, and the amount of cash Danny Hern flashed around that night had a very loud voice. The staff of the Chez Normandy snapped to attention the minute we walked in the door and didn't stop snapping the entire evening. Not at us, of course, but at each other. Money can make people very tense, you know.

As the proprietress of a successful inn I consider myself somewhat of an expert on the restaurant trade, so I feel entitled to comment on what I observed at Chez Normandy. First of all, the tables were far too small. Putting fine white linen cloths bordered in Flemish lace on something the size of a TV table is more than just foolish, it's begging for spills. As for the flocked velvet wallpaper in the gold fleur-de-lis pattern, it made the place look cheap. And whoever heard of a fountain in the middle of a restaurant, much less an obscene one of a boy urinating champagne?

"Why, I certainly don't get fifty dollars just for showing my guests to their table," I felt compelled to say. Okay, so the PennDutch has only one very long table in its dining room, but I do seat the guests, and I have yet to receive a tip.

Of course, I would have seated my guests differently as well. I know that table was small, but there was no reason to seat Danny Hern between Susannah and me. He was a virtual stranger to me, after all. Although I must say, once shed of the pile of pelts he looked rather appealing. Not as a boyfriend, mind you, but as a nephew perhaps. A very young nephew, since he couldn't have been a day over twenty.

"Actually, I'm thirty-six," he said, when asked.

"Months?"

He laughed pleasantly and took a sip of champagne. I do not believe in drinking, but if I ever faltered from the straight and narrow and became a worldly Presbyterian, like Susannah, I might be tempted to try a tonic now and then for cosmetic purposes. Apparently alcohol can preserve more than bug specimens in a jar.

"Plastic surgery," Danny volunteered, as if reading my mind. "Two eyelifts, a chin tuck, a face peel, and collagen injections to fill all the cracks. Hurts like hell when you do it, but does wonders for your self-image."

"Mama looks just fine the way she is, don't you think?" Susannah asked sweetly.

I gave her a swift but sweet little kick under the Flemish lace.

"Your mother doesn't look a day older than you," Danny said. "In fact, you two could be twin sisters."

Susannah choked on the champagne she shouldn't have been drinking. "Well, that's because she isn't my mother after all. Mags is my sister, but she's *old* enough to be my mother. I just said she was my mother as a joke." My own flesh and blood winked wickedly at me.

"Your sister, eh?" Danny's wink was beyond wicked, since it was accompanied by a hand on my knee. That table, as I said, was far too small.

"And what about yourself?" I asked Danny. "Do you have any surviving siblings?"

My hand was now under the table as well. Unlike his, mine gripped a fork.

Danny drooled. "Let's not talk about me, sweetheart. You sisters into a little swinging?"

Unfortunately, since I couldn't see under the table, it took me two tries to dispatch the prick. This called for great stoicism on my part, if I must say so myself. As for Danny, he was an even greater stoic, or else the booze blocked the brunt of his pain. He barely grunted, but the hand was immediately removed from my knee. Susannah, I'm sure, didn't suspect a thing.

"Miss, could I please have a clean fork?" I remembered to ask when the waitress came to take our orders.

The waitress cheerfully brought me a clean fork, so I knew right off she wasn't French. She was, in fact, a young American gal named Tina, with one brown eye and one blue eye, and very friendly. It was her first day there, she said, would we cut her some slack? We all agreed, most of all Danny Hern, who was becoming slacker by the moment.

Because the menu was all in French, which no one but me could read, there was a great deal of confusion, and by the time we'd placed our orders I had all but forgiven the horrible insult. There are other ways to extract vengeance besides toes and tines.

"She'll have the *escargots* and the *ris de veau*," I told the waitress. "He'll have the *anguilles frites*, and I'll have a *filet mignon*, rare, with *pommes de terre à l'anglaise*." Mama was right about one thing. The French I took in high school did come in handy one day.

No sooner had the waitress disappeared into the kitchen than a waiter came bustling over. This fellow, a genuine Frenchman, was preceded to the table by his nose. Apparently he had overheard me order.

"Is madame quite sure that's what she wants to order?"

"Quite."

He pointed to Susannah with his nose. "But is the mademoiselle sure?"

"Of course."

The nose aimed at Danny Hern. "And the monsieur?"

"Yes," I said tiredly, "and we are all hungry and want to eat as soon as possible."

"Will that be all then?" he sniffed.

"Come to think of it, I'd like some steak sauce with my filet," I said pleasantly.

The nose bobbed a haughty retreat.

Everyone within a block of Chez Normandy knew when Susannah's escargots arrived. "Ugh, slugs!"

"No. Snails, dear." I winked mischievously. "They are absolutely delicious dipped in that garlic butter there."

"But they're still in their shells!" Susannah cried. "They might even be alive!"

"Nonsense, dear." I grabbed one of the slippery snails with the special holder and pried it loose from its house. "See? Dead as a doornail."

Susannah's shade of green did nothing for her. "Gross! It's totally disgusting. Even that holder-majiggit is disgusting. My gynecologist—"

"Now this," I went on, pointing at the sweetbreads, "is a positive treat for the taste buds."

"Looks interesting," Susannah said. "What is it?"

"Brain food." I winked again.

My brave little sister tried the sweetbreads. "Not bad," she said, "but Freni's scrambled eggs are better. These are a little too salty." Nonetheless, she wolfed them down.

I dug into my filet before it could get up and walk off the plate. As for Danny Hern, he seemed to be enjoying his eels. Between I interrogated him. Skillfully, of course, so that he didn't know what was going on.

"So, I hear you're originally from West Virginia, Mr. Hern. Just where, exactly?"

"Huntington."

"Go to school there?"

He nodded. When his mouth wasn't full of eel, it was full of champagne. The little boy with the bladder problem was working hard to keep up with Danny Hern's thirst.

"West Virginia University?"

"Yep."

I tried to hold him in a gripping stare, but bleary eyes are hard to connect with. "Marshall University is in Huntington," I said. "West Virginia University is in Morgantown."

He smiled amiably. "Went there too."

I tried a different tack. "How do you like living in Farmersburg?"

"I don't."

Now I was getting somewhere. "After Huntington, those Farmersburg folk must all seem like yokels to you, right?"

He swayed but managed to keep his glass still. "Nah. I meant I don't live in Farmersburg. I live right here in Canton."

"What?"

"Get real, Mags," Susannah said, chasing the last bite of sweetbreads around on her plate. "What would a man of Danny's experience be doing in Farmersburg?"

"But you work there, don't you?"

This time the glass swayed and Danny kept still. "Well,

I own Daisybell Dairies, but I don't exactly work there. Although I guess that depends on what you mean."

I ignored the sordid chuckles from my two dinner companions. "What I mean is, are you involved in the running of Daisybell Dairies?"

"Well . . ." He looked to Susannah for help, which just shows you how much he'd been drinking.

"Danny believes in delegating his responsibility," Susannah said blithely. "Like I do."

"You're kidding!" I waved my fork to get Danny's attention again. "But you spend time at the dairy, don't you?"

"Yeth."

"So you must have been aware of the shortcuts that took place, which, along with a certain incident, caused all your Amish employees to quit?"

"My Amish quit? Why they go and do that?"

The man was fading fast, so I had to cut to the chase. "Did you molest a young Amish woman by the name of Elsie Bontrager?"

He stopped in midsway. "Blue eyes, Elsie. Nice blue eyes."

"Well?"

"Nah. I din touch her. Just admired her eyes."

"I see. Mr. Hern, why did you drive out to the farms of Levi Mast and Yost Yoder when they were running their cooperative?"

"I did?"

"You certainly did. I have it on good authority you visited the Mast place at least twice, and the Yoder place once. Was that to threaten them and get them to disband their cooperative?"

"Magdalena!" Susannah's voice was so sharp that Shnookums took up the call to arms and began yapping. Fortunately my sister was able to quiet him by dropping a snail—sans shell—down her blouse. No doubt the Chez Normandy frowned on four-legged furballs at the table, unless they wore mink.

I ignored my sister. "Well?"

Hern squirmed and the champagne sloshed, but his speech was surprisingly lucid. "I was interested in how they were going to make their cheese without the resources of Daisybell Dairies. Call it professional curiosity."

"Yes, of course. And this from a man who cares so little about cheese-making that he delegates his responsibilities at his own factory?"

The bleary eyes bulged. "I don't have to sit here and take this, you know."

I dug into my purse and pulled out the keys to his Mercedes, which dangled just outside his reach. "No, you don't. But you probably won't get very far, unless you take a cab."

Danny boy lunged for the keys, but the chains of champagne restrained him and he passed out on the table, facedown in Susannah's snails. It happened so quickly that it wouldn't have caused a scene had Susannah been more circumspect.

"Magdalena Yoder! Now look what you've done!"

I looked. "I'm afraid he did it to himself, dear."

"Garçon, garçon, garçon!"

Susannah began to scream for the waiter, who, being an actual Frenchman, took his own sweet time getting there. Unfortunately this allowed Shnookums time to work himself up into a furry froth, so eviction was inevitable. It was also inevitable that I had to pay the tab, since I was the only one with money who was conscious enough to write a check (I eschew credit cards, unless they are offered to me).

Having paid that enormous sum, I felt entitled to speak

my mind. "That fountain statue is obscene, your tables are far too small, and my sister says the calf thymus glands are too salty."

I was not responsible for what Susannah did next.

Eighteen

I let Susannah sleep in the next morning while I went to visit Annie Stutzman. I know, I should have paid a courtesy call on our cousin much earlier, but Annie is a lot like a watermelon rind pickle: tough on the outside, pithy on the inside, and all-around tart. Perhaps I shouldn't be casting aspersions, but it has got to be the Stutzman in her. We Yoders are nothing if not sweet.

Annie's mother was a Yoder, but her father was a Stutzman. She married Samuel Stutzman, who, incidentally, was less closely related to her than her parents had been to each other. Both of them were descended from the patriarch Jacob Hochstetler three times, whereas Samuel was descended from the patriarch only once. Susannah and I, incidentally, are descended from this man through two of his children, but in five different ways. If this sounds confusing to you, then think of my people as a map of New Jersey. It is crisscrossed by hundreds of roads, but they all lead to Hoboken. Or so says Susannah.

Anyway, after putting Danny in one cab and ourselves in another, we managed to get back to the Troyers' in time for me to catch my requisite eight hours of sleep before lunch, but of course not for Susannah's sixteen. Actually I made it downstairs just after the last zucchini waffle disappeared at breakfast, but discreetly retired to our room until I could hear Lizzie doing the dishes and was sure that the coast was clear. No doubt it was ungracious of me to sneak out without saying good morning, but when faced with Annie Stutzman, one needs a full reserve of charitable feelings.

I had met Annie only once before that I can recall, and that was at a family reunion near Hernia. My impression was of a monstrous woman with piercing dark eyes and a light mustache. Unfortunately I made the mistake of pointing cousin Annie's attributes out to her, and Mama saw to it that I ate a bar of Camay soap.

Of course, I was only four at the time and I could have had things turned around. Annie Stutzman could well have been a light woman, with monstrous eyes and a dark, piercing mustache. Not knowing what to expect, I approached the woman I saw sweeping Annie's porch with caution.

"*Gut Marriye.* Could you please tell me where I can find Mrs. Samuel Stutzman?"

The woman, who had not looked up when I drove into her yard, continued to be fixated on her porch. "I know a lot of Mrs. Samuel Stutzmans," she said. "How do I know which one you want?"

"Are you Annie Stutzman, first cousin to the late Amos Yoder, of Hernia, Pennsylvania?"

"Could be," she said, turning her back further, presumably to sweep out a corner, "but Amos Yoder is a common name. Even in Hernia, Pennsylvania. I might not be that Annie Stutzman you're after."

Even without a glimpse of her nose, I knew this was the right woman. "The Annie Stutzman I'm after is fat and has beady eyes and a mustache," I said, proving that two could play that game as well as one.

"*Ach du Heimer!*" Annie whirled around, accidentally striking me on the shins with her broom. At least I think it was an accident. "Why, Magdalena Yoder! You haven't changed a bit. I can see you have that same mean streak in you that you had last time I saw you."

"I was four then, Annie. I'm meaner now."

"So you are," she agreed. "Well, now that you're here, you may as well come on in. I have a cold, you know. No point staying out here and catching my death of pneumonia."

"No point at all," I said. I followed her into a spotlessly clean house. At least the broom hadn't been a sham; not only were those floors clean enough to eat off, but open-heart surgery on them was not altogether out of the question.

Annie motioned me to sit in a straight-back chair, while she settled into a much more comfortable rocker. "Of course you're a day late, dear."

"I beg your pardon?"

"The funeral was the day before yesterday. When I didn't meet you at the cemetery, I fully expected you to come by and see how I was. If not that day, then surely the next. Any daughter of dear, departed Amos would have done that."

"Well, this one didn't." I thought of Susannah, undoubtedly still asleep under a pile of comforters, a cantankerous canine her only concern. Why am I the only one of my parents' offspring expected to toe the line?

Annie's sniff was unrelated to her cold. "The Pennsylvania branch of the family has always been—"

"Annie dear, I'm here now. So, how are you doing?"

I had been partially right. Although my father's cousin was of average weight for her age and height, she did have beady eyes and a mustache that would make most men proud. I suppose she was near my father's age, had he been alive, which would put her close to eighty. Perhaps it was the bead in her eye, or the way she'd handled that broom, but in person Annie Stutzman came across much younger than I'd expected.

"I have a cold, of course," she snapped. "At my age that could be dangerous, you know."

"Then what were you doing outside on the porch, dear? It's fifteen degrees."

"Cleanliness is next to godliness," Annie sniffed. This time it was the cold.

I pulled a tissue out of my bra and graciously handed it to her. "And you'll be next to God sooner than you expect if you don't start taking care of yourself. Would you like me to make you some tea?"

"Ach, just like your father," she said, but the protest ended there.

I meandered to the kitchen through a series of spotless rooms. It wasn't until I had the water heated and was pouring it into the teapot that it struck me that something was missing from all those rooms. There was no sign of a man. Even in the mudroom, which should have been full of boots and coats, there was only one set of lady's galoshes and a woman's coat.

"There's some brown sugar pie in the saver," Annie called from the front room. "Made it just this morning. Help yourself if you want, and bring me a piece."

I cut two large slices and scooped them onto chipped dinner plates. Brown sugar pie is my favorite food in the whole world. It would make a dandy late breakfast, and if Annie didn't want a piece as large as that, lunch as well.

"My, a bit generous with the pie, aren't we?" Annie asked when I returned.

I put the tea tray on a table between us. "How is cousin Samuel?"

Annie blanched, which made her mustache all the more

visible. "Why, you're even meaner than I thought. As if you didn't know."

"Know what?"

I must have sounded as innocent as I was, because Annie believed me. More often than not I am tried, convicted, and hanged simply because my tone of voice may be slightly off. As a consequence I have been accused of breaking every one of the Ten Commandments *except* the one involving adultery, whereas in reality there is at least one other commandment I have yet to break.

"Well, tongues must not wag in Hernia as much as they do here. I thought everyone in the world knew about Samuel by now. After all, it happened almost thirty years ago."

I took a big bite of my pie, which tasted as good as it looked. "Not me, and I kept my ear to the ground."

Her beady eyes scrutinized my ears. "A good soap can take care of that, dear. You sure you didn't hear anything?"

"Positive. Anyway, back then Mama covered my other ear with her hand."

Annie sighed. "You may as well hear it now, I guess. Things like that are pretty tame by today's standards. Besides, those were troubled times. You remember how it was."

I shook my head. "Mama kept her other hand over my eyes."

"Ha! Ha! That sounds like your mother, all right. Ha! Ha!"

I'd forgotten that dear Annie could bark like a dog. "Do go on, dear," I coaxed.

Annie took a dainty sip of her tea and then carefully wiped both her mouth and the cup rim. "It was like this. Some New York hippies—on their way west, they said— asked if they could camp in our pasture. Just for a night or two, mind you."

"Of course."

"Well, they ended up staying almost six months, and during that time we were very kind to them."

"I'm sure."

"Too kind, even. We gave them milk from our cows, and let them eat all the fresh vegetables they wanted from our garden. They were very excited about that; called them organic."

I rolled my eyes just to be polite.

"Anyway, they were full of questions about our ways, so we spent a lot of time with them. After all, they were pacifists, and so were we. It was surprising how much we had in common."

"Free love?" I asked.

"Ach, no! You should be ashamed of yourself, Magdalena Yoder! Still"—the beady eyes brightened—"that's not to say one can't learn a thing or two from the English."

"Tsk, tsk," I said. Mama had been right to cover my ears.

"Anyway, to make a long story short, Samuel spent too much time with the hippies. Eventually he got sucked into their ways." Anna began to whisper. "In the end he ran off with them. Just up and left. And me with three children."

"You don't say!" And to think I almost left Farmersburg without paying a visit to our dear cousin.

"Yah. My Samuel, always a good Christian man, ran off with those hippies, and I never saw him again." She paused, and her voice picked up strength. "But I did get a letter once, telling me how happy he was in his new home, and with his new *religion*."

"I beg your pardon?"

She nodded. "India. That's where my Samuel went. A place called Ashram."

"That's a thing," I said, "not a place."

"What?"

"An ashram is a religious retreat for Hindus. Paul McCartney stayed at my inn once. He told me all about it."

"Whatever. The point is, my Samuel's gone."

"And your children? Did he take them with him?" Come to think of it, I couldn't remember ever hearing about my Stutzman second cousins.

"Ha! Ha! The children were too little then. Maybe Samuel was ready to be hippy, but he wasn't ready to change diapers. I got to keep the children. Ha!

"But they're gone now, of course. All of them. Off to Indiana. How could they be expected to stay in a place where their father had done such a thing? 'Your father ran off with the hippies,' the other children used to tease them. 'Englisher! Englisher!' Ha! It's a wonder they turned out normal."

"A wonder, indeed. But you stayed."

"Yah, I stayed. And here I am, all alone. Still, I should count my blessings. I have my health, after all, except for this cold."

"And the farm too," I added helpfully.

"Ha! Not the farm. Just this house. I sold the farm off years ago. A woman can't run a farm by herself, you know."

I decided not to argue and poured myself some tea, taking care to add tons of sugar and gobs of thick cream, like the good Lord intended. "Who did you sell it to?"

"I sold it to my neighbors. I split it in thirds. That third"—she pointed east—"I sold to Christian Yoder. He was Yost Yoder's father, and the land was a wedding present for his son.

"And that piece there"—she pointed straight ahead—"I sold to Lazarus Gerber, who farmed across the road. Lazarus gave his piece to his son Stayrook.

"Which leaves that piece to the right, which went to Jacob Mast. I expect his son Levi would have inherited it, but he died recently. Now I suppose it will go to Enos, Levi's younger brother."

She threw back her head and barked briefly. "Of course, none of that matters now."

I took a sip of nectar. "You mean because the Amish plan to sell off their farms and leave Farmersburg?"

She nodded, the beady eyes suddenly brimming.

I handed her another tissue. "Wouldn't you go with them?"

"Ach, I'll be eighty-one this May. How could I move? I was born less than three miles down the road on my parents' farm, and I've lived in Farmersburg County my entire life. No, I think I'll die right here."

Perhaps I nodded absently.

"Magdalena, have you fallen asleep?"

"Did you say before that the Levi Mast who fell from the silo lived there, and the Stayrook Gerber who dug Yost's grave lives there?" I pointed in the appropriate directions.

"Ach, you Pennsylvania Dutch are a slow lot," Annie said, not unkindly.

I swallowed a sip of ambrosia and took another bite of pure heaven. "Good neighbors over the years must have been a comfort."

"Ha! The Masts have always been good enough neighbors, but the Gerbers . . ." She leaned closer and whispered again. "I don't have any Gerber blood in me, you know. You either, for that matter. Between you and me, they're a funny lot."

"Yes?" I took another long, luscious sip.

"There were eight of those boys—Stayrook was the oldest—and they were wild. Stayrook was a teenager when those hippies were here, and for a while it looked like it was going to be him, not Samuel, who ran off and became a Hindu."

"You don't say." Amish traditionally allow their teenagers a great deal more freedom than the public imagines. This freedom is predicated on the belief that once their wild oats were sowed, the young adults will return humbly to the fold and thereafter toe the line. Usually this plan works. But as teenagers, my Mennonite friends and I would look with envy on the Amish youth, whose parents always seemed to look the other way. Not my parents, of course. Consequently I was deprived of sowing a single wild oat. Corn is the only crop I ever got to harvest.

"Yah, Stayrook Gerber was a wild one, all right. Hanging out with those hippies almost as much as my Samuel did. Ha! But now it's Samuel who's a Hindu, and Stayrook the Christian. A very strict and pious man, too."

"The salt of the earth," I said.

"Yah, and a deacon."

"Really? Well, maybe your Samuel is a guru by now."

"*Ach, gut Himmel!* You talk like a sausage."

I took that as a compliment and made the mistake of offering to wash the tea things. In any other house that would have meant what the words imply, but not so with dear cousin Annie. By the time I got done ironing the used dishtowels and scouring out the tea kettle, I was exhausted, but still hadn't gotten Annie to divulge anything important. In a stroke of genius, I reached for my purse.

"You know, I saw the devil himself," Annie said suddenly, sensing I was about to leave.

"Oh?"

She waved me to a kitchen chair. "Of course, he wasn't wearing a red suit with horns, and he wasn't carrying a pitchfork either."

"Of course not. What did he look like?" I asked politely.

"Like Levi Mast."

"Come again?"

"I saw Levi Mast possessed by the devil." She said it matter-of-factly, and it gave me chills.

"What do you mean, exactly?"

"I mean I saw Levi Mast climb up on a silo the morning of his wedding and crow like a rooster. Doesn't that sound possessed to you?"

"Well, I don't know." If Aaron and I were to get married, and he crowed on our wedding day, I would take it as a compliment.

"What if he flapped his arms as well?"

"Levi Mast crowed and flapped his arms?"

"Like this," Annie said. She gave me a mercifully brief reenactment of Levi Mast's final moments. Whether it was intentional or not, she came across more like a lunatic than a rooster.

I felt the hair on the back of my neck stand up. "You saw this?"

The beady eyes brightened. "I was taking a walk when I saw it all happen. Just like I showed you. *Now* what do you think?"

"Well, I'm no expert on possession, but—"

"Ha! That's what I told Jacob and Catherine. Of course, they didn't want to hear it. They claim Levi was just fine until the minute he died. But they didn't see it. I did!"

"And of course you were at the Yoders' the night Yost drowned, and know exactly what really went on there, right?"

The mustache twitched. "Who told you that?"

"Sarah. She said she came and got you to stay with the children while she and Stayrook searched for Yost. Is that true?"

"Yah. And talk about possession! An Amish man, naked, in a milk vat. Can you imagine that?"

I shook my head. First Levi Mast acting like a rooster, and then Yost Yoder acting like a cow. Now both of them dead. Something was very wrong in Farmersburg, and it looked like it was up to me to get to the bottom of it. As soon as I found a phone to call Aaron, I would swing back over to the Mast place. Jacob and Catherine were undoubtedly in denial, but they were having company, whether they liked it or not.

Nineteen

aron picked up the phone on the first ring. "Magdalena?"

"Why, Aaron Miller," I chided him pleasantly, "you should be ashamed of yourself. You're supposed to answer 'PennDutch Inn.' "

"I was worried," Aaron said. "Are you all right?"

"Is the Pope Jewish?"

"What?"

"Nothing. I mean, I'm fine." Of course, I couldn't explain to Aaron that not only did he light my fire, he mixed my metaphors as well.

"Are you about ready to pack your bags and come home, Magdalena?"

"Any day, Aaron. I just have one or two loose ends to tie up here."

I could hear Aaron suck in his breath. "What loose ends? Magdalena, shouldn't you be letting the sheriff handle that?"

"The sheriff is Marvin Stoltzfus, first cousin to our very own Melvin, remember? Besides, I'm not so sure that he isn't one of the loose ends that need to be tied up."

"Dammit, Magdalena, you *are* getting yourself in over your head. As soon as this damn snow lets up, I'm coming out to get you. Even if I have to walk."

I bade my heart to still. When a Mennonite, even a lapsed one like Aaron, swears—not once, but twice in the same breath—you can be sure some strong emotion has been tapped. It was as clear to me as the drool on Susannah's pillow that Aaron Miller, my would-be Pooky Bear, felt every bit the way I did. It was official, we were in love.

I'll confess, I was singing as I drove up the lane to the Mast place. Aaron Daniel Miller loved *me*, Magdalena Portulaca Yoder, which just went to show you how wrong Mama could be. My being five foot ten and a carpenter's dream may have delayed the process a little, but it hadn't placed it out of my reach. And Mama should have known better, because Susannah, who is only an inch shorter than I, and concave rather than flat, had been in love many times while Mama was still alive. Of course, none of Susannah's experiences could hold a candle to mine. There was only one Aaron Daniel Miller in the world, and he was mine. It would have been a sin not to sing with joy.

I suppose it's also a sin to carelessly run over men unloading buggies, and that's what I almost did. Not that it would have been entirely my fault. Jacob Mast barely cleared the hood ornament on my car. How was I supposed to see him doubled over with the weight of a bag of flour? As for his son Enos, it takes a smart and loving son to jump out of the way of a moving motor vehicle. Had I hit his father, he could have gone for help.

"Ach," Jacob said when he could catch his breath, "for a minute I thought I was going to see my Levi today."

I picked up the flour for him, and could possibly have picked him up too, had I been faster. The man couldn't have weighed more than seventy pounds. Enos, on the other hand, was almost tall enough to see his brother Levi up in heaven without having to die. Four hundred years of inter-breeding have produced a lot of homogeneous characteristics among my people, but height is not one of them. To the contrary, the stature genes seem to have polarized, even within families, making the passing on of hand-me-downs impractical.

"I'm so sorry, Mr. Mast," I guessed. "It was all my fault. I mean, I should have seen you. Are you okay?"

Jacob brushed the dirt from his coat with hands the size of my thumbs. "Ach, I'll be fine. I'm just startled." He peered up at me through bifocals. "You're a Yoder, yah?"

"Yah. Magdalena Yoder. From Hernia, Pennsylvania. I came here for Yost's funeral."

A shadow flicked across his tiny face. "Yah, I saw you at the funeral. It was our second in two weeks. First my Levi, and then Yost. Two terrible accidents, one after the other. Still, God's name be praised."

Enos stood mutely by.

"I'm all for praising God, Mr. Mast, but I'm not sure these were accidents. In fact, that's why I'm here. I'd like to talk to you about your son's death."

Lilliputian fingers combed through a graying beard. "There is nothing else to say, Miss Yoder."

I handed him the bag of flour. "Of course. I'm sorry to have bothered you. Well, maybe I'll see you later. Like at the next funeral, after the next terrible accident."

Jacob glanced furtively around, as if there was even a chance some scurrilous scoundrel might be skulking about. "Mother has made an exceptionally good dinner today," he said loudly. "Would you like to join us?"

I'm only half as dumb as I look. "Yes, that would be very nice."

"Good. Mother will be happy to have company."

I followed the little man and the mute giant into the house. Even before I stepped into the mudroom I received confirmation that Mother was indeed a good cook. The huge slice of brown sugar pie and the copious amounts of cream and sugar consumed at Cousin Annie's were all going to be reassigned retroactively to breakfast. Dinner, the main meal among most Amish, was about to begin with a clean slate.

It didn't surprise me one whit when Jacob's wife, Catherine, turned out to be six foot two and their daughter, Sophia, two foot six. Okay, maybe I fudged a foot or two on the latter, but you get the picture. My point is that the family was decidedly lopsided.

A psychiatrist—a *guest* of mine, mind you—once told me that he thought Amish men were remarkably free of sexual insecurity. I tried explaining to him that Amish men didn't have sex, but he wasn't quite convinced. Anyway, this psychiatrist seemed impressed by the fact that among contemporary societies, the Amish are unique in that their men don't have to prove their masculinity by driving fast cars, going off to war, hunting, yelling obscenities at sporting events, or flicking remote controls. But what amazed this man the most was the number of short Amish men who felt totally comfortable marrying tall Amish women.

"That shows they are comfortable in themselves," he said. "They don't need to act macho or dominate in order to prove that they're real men. In fact, I would hazard a guess that they make superb lovers."

"Amish men don't have sex!" I practically screamed at him.

"Then how do you explain their large families?" he asked smugly. "Are those all virgin births?"

The double dose of heresy was too much for me to bear, and I cracked. "Well, maybe the women have sex," I said, "but the men don't." The fact that I had just condemned all

Amish mothers as adulteresses was lost on me until much later.

Considering that they were still grieving, the Mast family were remarkably cordial to me. Catherine seemed neither surprised nor upset to see an extra face at her table. She seated me beside the diminutive daughter, who I judged to be about fifteen, and across from the gargantuan Enos, who might have been eighteen. Three older daughters, I'd already been told, had married and left the nest.

"Will your mother be joining us?" I asked politely of Jacob.

He seemed startled. "Ach, Mama passed on to glory ten years ago."

I kicked myself under the table for having been so stupid. Clearly the mother he'd referred to earlier was Catherine, the mother of his brood.

Fortunately, soon after that the food was passed and I refrained from opening my mouth except to fill it. Unless, of course, I was spoken to.

"We might be moving, you know," Sophia announced, as she crammed a forkful of egg casserole into her mouth.

"To where?" I tried to sound surprised.

"We don't know yet. Maybe Indiana. Where are you from?"

"Pennsylvania. I live in a little town called Hernia."

"Are you English?"

I coughed uncomfortably. "Well, I suppose that depends on your definition. I'm a Mennonite."

"Do you have a television?" Sophia asked, her mouth full of food.

"No." The fact that I allow Susannah to own a little black-and-white set was irrelevant, wasn't it?

"Do you listen to rock and roll?"

"No."

"Do you go to the movies?"

"No."

"Do you hang out in the malls?"

"Not when I can help it."

"Do you have a boyfriend?"

"Yes."

She breathed a sigh of relief. "Do you kiss him?"

"If you want to enjoy the rest of your meal, I'd stick to the less personal questions," I said sweetly.

She nodded. "Have you ever met Michael Jackson?"

"No." That time I had to fudge as well. The pair of white women who reserved a room under the names Jones and Smith might well have been who they said they were. It was only Susannah who claimed to recognize them as Michael Jackson and Lisa Marie Presley. As for the fat man in a rhinestone-spangled jumpsuit who booked the adjoining room—that could well be a coincidence. And just for the record, I did not clean the pair of blue suede shoes I found outside his door that evening.

"Do you drink wine and other things?"

"Other things," I said, "but not with alcohol."

"Ach," Sophia said, the disappointment evident in her voice, "and I thought you were a Mennonite!"

"I am a Mennonite, dear. Perhaps you thought I was a Baptist."

"Speaking of baptism," Catherine said gracefully, "our Enos is of age now and is going to be baptized next Baptism Sunday."

"Is that so?" I asked pleasantly.

"Yah." A typical boy in his late teens, Enos apparently preferred eating to talking, and had already consumed as much food as your average salad bar patron, or a medium-sized Third World country. His parents perhaps should have been considering limiting his calorie intake unless they wanted to raise the ceilings.

"Well, you certainly have grown into a fine young man," I said.

"Levi was taller," Sophia said.

There was a shocked silence, and Enos even stopped chewing.

"Well, he was!"

Catherine recovered first. "Yah, Sophia, you're right. Levi was a few inches taller. And very strong too, like an ox." She smiled at her second son. "Of course, Enos is very strong too."

"But Levi was stronger," Sophia said. "He could lift the front end of our buggy off the ground with one hand." The admiration in her voice was unmistakable.

"So?" Enos asked. His face was suddenly red.

"So, I don't think it was an accident when Levi fell from the silo. Even if he slipped, he could have grabbed one of the ladder rungs and held on with one finger."

The second shocked silence lasted longer. Fortunately I had the sense to see it as opportunity knocking.

"I think Sophia may have a point," I said. "Levi doesn't sound like someone who would accidentally fall from a silo."

"It's winter," Jacob said. "The ladder could have been icy."

"Then why would he climb it?" I asked.

Enos's jaw had begun to twitch, even though he was no longer chewing. He glanced at his parents and then at me. "We don't need any English outsiders sticking their big noses into our business."

"Enos!" Catherine turned to me. "He didn't mean it, I'm sure."

"That's all right," I said. "I know I'm sticking my big nose in where it doesn't belong. But I hate the idea of you moving when you don't have to. There has got to be another reason Levi fell, besides slipping and possession."

Sophia's eyes widened. "Possession?"

"I told you she would find out sooner or later," Catherine cried. She was staring at her husband.

"Mama, is it true?"

"I suppose God only knows for sure, but there were signs," Catherine said. Her eyes beseeched her husband. "You tell her, Jacob."

Enos stood up. "I'm sorry, Mama, but I don't want to listen to this again."

"Enos! Sit down," Jacob said softly. "It's time we all talked about this. Sophia as well."

They may have been small pants, but it was clear who wore them in the Mast family. Enos sat down obediently, although he looked like an animal about to bolt.

"Levi was my brother, and we didn't always get along," he said, "but I know he wasn't possessed. And I don't think what he did that morning proves anything."

"You mean when he crowed and flapped his arms like a rooster?" I asked gently.

Four pairs of eyes stared at me, one more intensely than the others.

"Papa, is that true?" Sophia asked.

Jacob nodded. "You've always been a heavy sleeper, Sophia. I thank the good Lord that you slept right through it."

"How did you know this, Magdalena?" Catherine asked. I could see that she was trembling.

Mama used to tell Papa that our walls had ears. Of course, she meant Susannah and me.

"Let's just say that your cornfield has eyes," I said. "Catherine, please understand that I really want to help you. And I agree with Enos. Your son Levi was not possessed. Something else happened to him that morning, and that's what I'd like to find out."

"But what?" Hope and anguish mixed in her voice.

"Maybe he was drunk," Sophia said.

"Ach du Heimer!" her father said. "Levi didn't drink. He was already baptized, a member of the church. Those days were behind him."

"But Papa, he did drink sometimes. Just ask Enos."

We all looked at Enos. I prayed that he wouldn't bolt.

"Is this true, Enos? Did your brother drink? Even after joining the church?"

I once saw a deer in my headlights with the same expression on its face. "Ach, Papa, how can you ask me that?"

"Enos?" Catherine's eyes were brimming with tears, surely the most effective weapon a mother has.

"Ach, Mama, Levi was my brother! And it wasn't often, Mama. Just once or twice when he rode along with us on Saturday nights."

I knew what Enos meant. Teenage Amish boys, prior to baptism and membership in the church, have been known to drive their buggies into town and tipple a bit. Their parents don't approve, but they sometimes turn a blind eye. That blind eye, however, sees very well when it is turned to young men who have been baptized, and thereby formally joined the church. Then, strict obedience is paramount, and excommunication and even shunning can be the reward for deviance.

I felt it was time to butt in. "I'm not an expert on drinking, Catherine, but I'd have to say alcohol, even a lot of it, wasn't responsible for what happened to Levi. As I understand it, alcohol slows you down, and your silo is pretty high. If Levi had drunk enough to jump from the silo, he probably wouldn't have made it up to the top anyway."

"Yah, you're right." The tears were now streaming down Catherine's face.

"Then it was the possession," Jacob said quietly.

"No!" I hadn't meant to be so sharp, so I took a deep breath and counted to three before continuing. "It doesn't have to be that either. It could be something totally different. Like . . . like . . . well, maybe a medical condition of some sort."

"Jacob?" Catherine asked softly.

Jacob shrugged. "Yah, it's possible, I suppose."

"Like Great-Aunt Veronica?" Sophia asked. "She thought she was Mary Magdalene, and nobody said she was possessed."

The other three nodded, but they didn't look as if they were convinced that Levi and Great-Aunt Veronica belonged in the same padded cell.

"What did the medical examiner say?" I asked. "What was the autopsy report?"

"There was no autopsy," Jacob said. "The sheriff agreed that it was an accident."

Catherine and Jacob exchanged looks.

"All of us did," Jacob said. "Catherine, me, Stayrook. Even Annie Stutzman."

"Stayrook Gerber?"

"Yah, his farm is just over there. I sent Enos to get him."

"Annie showed up on her own," Catherine said. "That woman knows everything about everyone's business."

"Mother," Jacob chided gently.

"Yah, but—"

There was a knock on the door to the mudroom, and before anyone could get up and answer it, Stayrook Gerber strode into the room. He seemed tremendously relieved to see me.

"Ach, there you are! I've been looking all over Farmersburg for you."

"Is something wrong?" I demanded. Experience has taught me that there is seldom time to panic after a disaster has happened, especially if immediate action is required. Those of us who revel in distress had best do it when we can.

"It's your sister, Susannah. Apparently something terrible has happened."

"Dead?" I asked. And no, I didn't sound hopeful.

Stayrook shook his head. "No, according to her, it's worse than that."

Twenty

Annie Stutzman's Brown Sugar Pie
(Milche Flichte)

✦

1 unbaked 8-inch pie crust
1 cup brown sugar
3 tablespoons all-purpose flour
Dash of salt
1 12-ounce can evaporated milk
2½ tablespoons butter
Ground cinnamon

Preheat oven to 350 degrees. With your fingers, mix the brown sugar, flour, and salt directly in the pie shell. Spread evenly. Slowly pour the evaporated milk over the mixture, but do *not* stir in. Dot with lumps of butter and sprinkle cinnamon liberally over the surface. Bake for 50 minutes.

The filling is supposed to be gooey. The pie is best eaten at room temperature.

Serves eight, although Susannah has been known to down an entire pie at one sitting.

Twenty-one

I found Susannah slumped in a heap at the foot of our bed. She wasn't alone, of course. Four of the Troyer boys (the oldest was in school) ringed her like curious island savages finding a stranger washed up on their beach. At least they weren't crying. As for Lizzie, she was downstairs in a tizzy. The crazy English houseguests had clearly been too much.

"Is she dead?" Benjamin, the oldest son present, asked. He poked her with a bare toe.

Shnookums, who was perched precariously on a hunched shoulder, snarled.

"I think the rat bit her," Solomon said.

"Rat bite?" asked Elias the baby, taking a cautious step backward.

"The rat's a dog," Peter said. At three, he was the most intuitive of the Troyer boys. No normal boy looking at Shnookums would come to the same conclusion.

I shooed the boys out of the room and knelt down by my sister. "What's wrong, sis?"

Shnookums snarled again but went silent as soon as I

raised a practiced hand. Of course I would never smack a dog, or even a rat for that matter, but Shnookums, totally lacking in intuition, doesn't know that. Apparently some of Susannah's boyfriends have cuffed the cur upon occasion. And no, I don't feel guilty for having played upon that mutt's neurosis—not when my sister needed me.

Susannah slowly lifted her head, like Lazarus must have as he prepared to climb out of the grave. Her eyes were red and swollen and her mascara had streaked, forming miniature batwing patterns across her cheekbones.

"It's all your fault!" she sobbed. The ducts opened and a fresh flood of tears cascaded down her cheeks, moving the batwings before them.

"What's my fault, dear?" I racked my brain for something I might have done in recent memory to cause her such anguish. Blacking out her name and phone number on the men's-room wall at the rest area on our way to Farmersburg couldn't have been that big of a deal. Undoubtedly there were still plenty of rest areas within a three-state radius that carried her message.

"It's your fault my life's over!" she wailed. Shnookums wailed sympathetically along with her, only three octaves up the scale.

I was concerned. Truly. "How is your life over? Susannah, are you ill?"

"It's your fault Danny Hern dumped me," she shrieked. "If you hadn't given him the third degree and forced him to eat eels, I might have had a chance with him. I could have been rich! Rich, Magdalena! Now it's all gone because of you."

I held my tongue well beyond the count of ten. When Susannah gets hysterical, it's best to let her get it out of her system. When the shrieks turn back into sobs, one can approach the water again, but cautiously. Susannah's emotional life is strewn with dangerous shoals and hidden riptides. Only an exceptionally strong swimmer or an utter fool would voluntarily plunge into that sea.

"There, there," I said gently, when the water had abated some. "There are other fish out there."

She stared at me through swollen slits. The batwings had migrated down to the corners of her mouth. "I don't want *other* fish, I want *Danny.*"

"But dear, you've only known the man for a couple of days."

"Oh, you wouldn't understand!" The ducts began to leak again, pushing the batwings farther south.

"What do you mean, I wouldn't understand?" I bristled. "I have Aaron. And I've known him a lot longer than you've known Danny."

She was strangely silent.

"And anyway," I said, pushing my luck, "how do you know Danny has dumped you? Have you spoken to him this morning?"

She shook her head.

"See? No news is good news, right?"

She shook her head again. "I told you that you didn't understand. Danny and I were going to be married. This morning. We were going to elope!"

I slumped down on the floor beside her. Sometimes Susannah is more than I can bear. Maybe if Mama and Papa hadn't gotten themselves killed, things might have turned out differently. Maybe Susannah would have gone to college, maybe even become a doctor. Maybe Susannah would have married a Mennonite instead of a Presbyterian, and *still* be married, with four or five little boys of her own.

"But no, you had to go and spoil it all," Susannah said mercilessly. "You just had to go and ruin my life again."

"How?"

"By making a fool out of everyone at the restaurant," she snapped. "That's why Danny dumped me. I just know it."

Shnookums, taking a cue from his mistress, snapped at me.

I snapped back.

I did what any loving big sister would do. I drove Susannah and the mangy mutt around both Farmersburg and Canton looking for the reluctant groom. Of course it galled me to do so, but what choice did I have? With Lizzie in her tizzy I couldn't very well leave Susannah there. The murders of Yost and Levi were just going to have to wait while I attended to my sister's needs.

With Susannah in the backseat, propped up on pillows, we drove first into Canton. Of course, we called first, but the phone number Danny had given Susannah was bogus. That is to say, both times we dialed we reached the residence of one of Canton's rabbis.

"Rabbi Kalmanson here," a cheery voice answered.

"Oh, sorry, I must have made a mistake. I'll make my call over."

"Yes, steak can be kosher. Provided it comes from a kosher animal, of course."

"Pardon me? I was trying to reach the residence of Daniel Hern, in Canton."

"Yes, the cantor's job is still open. Do you wish to audition?"

"How much does it pay?" I asked. I am a firm believer in exploring all opportunities.

"No, I don't have time to audition you today. How about tomorrow? Say around five?"

"That'll be fine," I said, and then hung up before he could accuse me of asking for wine.

We found Danny's condominium easily enough, thanks to my sister's slack morals. No one answered the door, however, and the silver Mercedes was nowhere to be seen. At Susannah's insistence I practically tackled an elderly resident as she came out of the adjoining condo, but she had seen neither Danny Hern nor his car since the day before.

Jacques, the chef at Chez Normandy, was only a little more helpful. Two men were driving the car away just as he arrived at work. No, neither of them was Danny. Both men appeared to be wearing dark clothes, and possibly dark hats. That was all he could recall. Even a five-dollar bill couldn't jump-start his memory.

I thanked Jacques nonetheless, adding that the filet mignon the night before had been just a little tough.

"Ah, the woman who ordered escargots!"

"For my sister," I said, pointing at Susannah.

He lunged for Susannah, beaming. She accepted his first hug stoically. His second hug she greeted with wanton enthusiasm, so I tactfully separated them.

"That's all, Jacques. We're in a bit of a hurry now."

Tears welled up in his Gallic eyes. "She is my first customer ever to order escargots!"

"It was me, dear, remember? Anyway, if no one ever orders them, how did you happen to have some on hand?"

He threw up his hands impatiently, an appropriate response to my stupidity. "*Mon Dieu!* They were my pets, of course! I kept them in a terrarium in the kitchen window. The generations before them had all died of old age, but these—"

"I think I'm going to be sick again," Susannah said, as I sportingly spirited her away.

Arnold Ledbetter was not surprised that Danny couldn't be found. "I told you before, Miss Yoder, that Mr. Hern has taken the entire week off. For all I know, he could be in Timbuktu."

"Is that in Pennsylvania?" Susannah asked.

"Hardly, dear," I said kindly.

Susannah was undeterred. "Well, wherever it is, maybe

Danny got snowed in there and left a message for me on his office machine."

To his credit, Arnold Ledbetter snickered softly. "Well, there aren't any messages to that effect on his machine now. I just checked it. Miss Entwhistle, I have absolutely no idea where he is—no, wait. One day last week, when I was passing by his office, I thought I heard him ordering two plane tickets for Aruba."

"Aruba!" I said.

Susannah giggled giddily. "Isn't that romantic?"

"But I wouldn't even have been there to see the wedding! That is really unfair of you, Susannah!"

Okay, so I probably would have refused to go, no matter the location, but a gal has a right to be invited to her sister's wedding. Especially if it's in the Caribbean.

"I didn't think you cared," Susannah had the nerve to say. "Anyway, when I told you earlier that we had planned to elope, you didn't get all in a huff. Why the sudden change of heart?"

"Because eloping to Canton and eloping to Aruba are not the same thing."

Susannah smiled sweetly. "I would have sent you a postcard. You know, one of some muscular guy sitting alone on a beach. Wish you were here. That kind of thing."

I confess that the sticky-sweet sentiment just expressed swept me away and I forgave her on the spot. After all, Susannah has never once given me as much as a birthday card. Too moved for words, I patted her arm affectionately.

Arnold Ledbetter peered up at us through his half-moon glasses. "Ladies, I'd like to stand here and chat, but I don't have all afternoon."

I shook myself loose from my reverie. "We understand," I said.

"Well, I don't," Susannah said. "Danny said we were

eloping this morning, and he would have been there unless—"

"Unless what, dear?"

"Unless he meant *tomorrow* morning?" Arnold suggested.

Susannah frowned. "Well, maybe. I do tend to get my days mixed up."

"She's not really used to days," I explained.

"Then I'm sure that's the reason for the mix-up," Arnold said, and without further ado he dismissed us by strolling off down the hall.

Just to be on the safe side, I persuaded Susannah to stop in at the sheriff's office and file a missing-person report. Much to my horror, the secretary had already gone home for the day, leaving only Marvin to deal with. A root canal would have been more fun.

"No can do," Marvin said before I even finished telling him what I wanted.

"Why not?"

"The guy has to be missing forty-eight hours, that's why. Anyway, what does his missing have to do with you? You the next of kin?"

"Certainly not!"

"I am," Susannah said. "I mean, I would have been if he wasn't missing. Isn't that the same?"

Marvin stared at Susannah. It was the car headlights staring at the deer. "You love this guy?"

The deer stared back. "Would that make a difference?"

The man with the deer-sized ears smiled. "Maybe, maybe not."

"Then let's say I don't love him." A crude but observant person might have noticed that Susannah's bottom twitched then, and her posture improved considerably.

Marvin's ears twitched in response to Susannah's bottom. "Then let's say it does make a difference."

"How big of a difference?" Susannah tottered suggestively forward on her clogs.

"Well, maybe I'll just have to let you wait and see." He winked with his left eye, which for some strange reason caused his right ear to wiggle.

"This is disgusting," I said to both of them. "Even animals are more discreet."

Neither of them heard me.

I tugged at a swirl that was Susannah's sleeve. "What about Danny Hern? I thought you were engaged to him."

"Who?"

"Danny Hern," I almost shouted. "Mr. Big Bucks. Drives around in a silver Mercedes, not some dilapidated county vehicle. He was going to make you a rich woman this morning, or have you forgotten?"

"What?"

"Rich," I said. "Lots of money—dough, moola, greenbacks, dinero."

Susannah merely grunted and continued to totter closer to Marvin, who was twitching eagerly closer to her. It was like watching a pair of puppets propelled by internal magnets.

I couldn't believe my eyes and ears. "We have a missing person here," I reminded them. "There are more important things in life than hormones, you know."

"Name one," they said in unison.

"God," I said. "Good health. Friends."

But it was too late. The pathetic puppets had begun to paw each other.

I thought I would puke.

Twenty-two

Take it from me, nothing settles the stomach like a good hot meal. Fortunately Pauline's Pancake House lives up to its name, and the same menu is used all day long.

"Jumbo tall stack, real butter, double order of bacon, and three smoked sausages," I said pleasantly.

There was a staccato burst of gum popping and then a moment of silence. "I see you're hanging around town. You're fixing to move in on my territory, aren't you, hon?"

I smiled politely at Pauline. The poor dear had undoubtedly been on her feet all day. Even the beehive atop her head had wilted and was slouched over to one side. If given the chance I would clue her in on industrial-strength bobby pins.

"Western Pennsylvania's been snowed in, dear. I'll make tracks as soon as the roads clear. I promise."

I have yet to hear a diesel truck backfire louder than Pauline's gum. "Shoot it to me straight, hon. You've got your eye on the old Pork and Cork on Taylorsville Road, don'tcha?"

I shook my head.

"No use lying to me, hon. I've seen that hungry look before." She plopped herself down on the red vinyl seat across from me. "But it ain't gonna work out for you, and I'll tell you why. It ain't gonna work out for the same reason it didn't work out for Buzzy Reaves—he used to own the Pork and Cork. And here's why." She leaned halfway across my table, as if to divulge a secret. "Folks don't want to go out that far from town to eat. Just as soon eat in Canton if they gotta go that far. Only the Aymish live out that far, and they don't eat our food, you know."

"Is that a fact?"

"God's honest truth. And if it's Aymish food you want to serve to the tourists, you're too late. Place called the Dutch Kettle, just over the county line and across the interstate, packs them in by the busload."

"Competition is the backbone of a thriving economy," I said, just to tease her.

Pauline was not easily amused. "You're liable to get your butt stomped if you try that here. A woman by the name of Jenny Wilson owns the Dutch Kettle, and I hear tell she's one mean woman."

"You don't say."

She nodded, the gum popping in rhythm. "So give it up, hon. Go back to Pennsylvania where you came from. And don't even think about opening up a restaurant within city limits. This here's a one-restaurant town."

I tried to flash her my friendliest smile. Unfortunately this attempt has at times frightened infants and on several occasions motivated people to offer me aspirin.

"Pauline, dear, I own a very successful bed-and-breakfast back in Hernia, Pennsylvania. It takes up all my time, *and* it supplies me with all the money I care to spend. As soon as the roads clear back home, I'm out of here. In the meantime, I'd like my supper."

The popping paused. "You ain't just pulling my strings, hon?"

"Negative, dear. So relax, before you get them tied in a knot."

"Seen you coming out of Marv's office a minute ago," she said, sounding calmer. "What's up?"

I grimaced involuntarily. "Bad choice of words, dear. I went in there with my sister to report a missing person."

"Anyone I know?"

"Yes. Danny Hern."

There was a gasp and the gum came flying at me. However, in a remarkable display of hand-and-eye coordination Pauline caught the errant wad and popped it back in.

"You mean Danny Hern of Daisybell Dairies?"

"That's the one. Apparently he and my sister, Susannah, were going to elope this morning, but he never kept the date. We checked, and he's not at home. He'd taken the entire week off from work, but we checked there anyway to see if there were any messages. There weren't. Oh, and his car is missing too."

"Aruba?"

"What?"

"Did he say he was taking your sister to Aruba?"

"Yes. How did you know?"

I waited patiently for Pauline to stop laughing. "Well?"

"That slime bucket never changes. When he first blew into town—after his uncle died and left him the business—he sweet-talked me into eloping too. And guess where we were going to honeymoon?"

"Not Timbuktu?"

"Aruba, imagine that! I'd say at least five Farmersburg gals, and who knows how many in Canton, have been promised Aruba, and not gotten as much as a rutabaga." She found her own joke immensely funny and had to catch the gum several times before she calmed down enough for it to stay put.

"So Susannah was just used?"

"Like this gum." Pauline plucked the offending wad from her mouth and stuck it firmly to the underside of my table. "Now, was that two orders of bacon and one of sausage, or the other way around?"

"Two bacon, one sausage. Leave a little play in the bacon. I don't like it so crisp that it cracks. And be sure the sausages are evenly browned."

I would like to say that Pauline was a professional and my order arrived as dictated. Unfortunately the bacon shattered on impact, and as for the sausages, the limp pink links that lolled across my plate reminded me of something I once read about in Susannah's diary.

If I was a young Amish woman, I'd be nervous too if an Englisher drove up, unannounced, after dark.

"Yah? Who is it?" Barbara asked through a closed door.

"It's me, Magdalena Yoder. We met at the cemetery, remember?"

"Yah?"

"I came to talk with you, if that's all right. Your family too."

"My family has gone to visit a neighbor. Could you come back tomorrow?"

"Why yes, I suppose I could. But I'd be happy to talk with just you. It involves the death of your fiancé, Levi, and it's rather personal."

The door opened a crack. "Miss Yoder, I have nothing more to say about Levi's death. I thought I made that clear at the cemetery."

Pointed shoes have several uses, and I managed to keep the crack open as I spoke. "Yes, I realize the subject must be very painful for you, but I know that you knew Levi's death wasn't an accident. I also think that you know it wasn't possession either."

The door opened wide enough for me to slip in.

Perhaps it was the absence of the black outdoor bonnet, but Barbara Hooley looked different from the way I remembered her in the cemetery. Although the white everyday prayer cap covered most of her hair, which had been pulled back tight in the traditional knot, the hair in front of the cap was a pale golden blond. She was tall and thin, like Susannah, but far from flat-chested. What Yoder blood she had did not show up in her nose. In the eyes of the outside world, Barbara Hooley was a knockout.

"This way," she said and led me through the kitchen to the front sitting room.

As in all Amish sitting rooms, the furnishings were functional rather than decorative. No framed photographs or paintings hung on the walls in the conventional sense. There was, however, a plethora of calendars, each with a brightly colored picture attached. Calendars are first and foremost functional, the bishops have ruled. I selected a sturdy wooden rocker beneath a calendar depicting the Grand Canyon in a February snowstorm.

Large baby-blue eyes, the color unaltered by contacts, gazed steadily at me. "Miss Yoder, my family will be coming back soon. What is it you wanted to say?"

"I've been investigating the deaths of your fiancé and Yost Yoder, dear, and I am positive that neither of them was an accident. I am just as positive they weren't possession."

"Nor suicide," Barbara said firmly. "So that only leaves murder."

"I quite agree, dear. And although I can't prove anything yet, I have a pretty good idea why both men were murdered, and who was behind it."

"Please, go on."

"You know as well as I do that the answer to both questions somehow involves Daisybell Dairies. Someone there didn't want the cheese cooperative to succeed, and went to extreme measures to see that it wouldn't. Just who is actually pulling the strings I'm not sure."

"Mr. Hern, the new owner?"

I rocked silently for a moment. "Maybe, maybe not. He doesn't seem all that competent to me."

"Do you think it could be Mr. Ledbetter, then?"

"It could be. Anything's possible. Do you know him well?"

She nodded. "Before the boycott, I worked at Daisybell Dairies. I graduated eighth grade when I was fourteen, and as soon as I turned sixteen Papa let me go to work. I worked there almost four years. Anyway, I was there when Mr. Craycraft died and his nephew took over.

"When Mr. Craycraft was alive he was always in charge. Even though Mr. Ledbetter was the general manager, everyone knew who was the boss. If there were any problems Mr. Ledbetter couldn't handle, we knew where to turn. Mr. Craycraft liked it that way. He said he liked staying in touch.

"But when Mr. Craycraft died, things changed. Suddenly Mr. Ledbetter was acting like the boss, even though the nephew, Mr. Hern, moved right up here from West Virginia. If you ask me, that's what started the bad feelings at the dairy, not what happened to Elsie Bontrager."

"Ah. That's very interesting. Did you know Elsie well?"

Barbara smiled, revealing perfect white teeth. Harrison Ford wouldn't stand a chance with her. "Elsie was exactly my age and in my special group of friends. I've known her as long as I can remember."

"What was she like?"

"She was beautiful," Barbara said, and I could hear the wistfulness in her voice. Undoubtedly the woman had never looked in a mirror.

I smiled. "I mean, her personality. Would you say she was reliable?"

"Ach, Elsie was the salt of the earth. Some people think she made up the whole terrible story, but I know she didn't. Elsie only spoke the truth."

"Yes, dear, I'm sure. How would you describe her after the incident?"

The perfect face frowned. "That was the worst part for me. Seeing her changed so. She wasn't the same Elsie at all anymore. It was almost as if—"

"She'd been possessed? Is that what you mean to say?"

Barbara stared at me. "Yes, that's what I mean. That's exactly what I mean. People began saying that she was 'off,' that the experience itself was so horrible that she was coping the only way she could. She was making herself crazy. But I don't agree. It was something more than that, Miss Yoder. It had to be. Elsie was such a strong girl that even if what they say happened did, I don't think it would be enough to make her act that way."

I felt a shiver run up my spine. "You just said '*if* what they say happened.' Do you think it might have been otherwise?"

Barbara shrugged. "I just mean that I never heard it from Elsie's lips directly. One day Elsie wasn't at work, and then I heard from someone who heard from someone who heard from someone. You know how that is."

"Yes, of course." It was that way the day Mama and Papa died. For some reason the sheriff who had been there at the scene never did talk to Susannah and me directly. News of our parents' death spread like wildfire, and by the time Reverend Detweiler, our minister, drove out to break the news, we were among the last to know.

"Barbara, forgive me for being personal here, but did Mr. Hern ever—you know, try—with you—"

"Miss Yoder! Of course not!"

"I'm sorry, dear, it was just something I needed to know. So, if he didn't bother you, then I suspect he may not have bothered Elsie, either."

"But Elsie was beautiful!"

"And what are you, dear, chopped liver?"

She stared at me.

I decided to rephrase it in lingo she might understand. After all, not everyone gets exposed to the same cultured folks that I do at the PennDutch.

"Barbara, dear, in case no one has ever told you, you are very beautiful. There are movie actresses who spend thousands of dollars trying to look like you, but never get anywhere close. Believe me, I know. I've met a few."

She colored. "Ach, Miss Yoder, please don't. That is *Hochmut*. Pride."

"Why? Is it a sin to be naturally beautiful? I don't think so. After all, beauty is a gift from God."

"But not to be shown off in public," she said quickly.

It was time to change the subject. "Were you there when Sheriff Stoltzfus came out to investigate Levi's death?"

"No. By the time I got there, Mr. Stoltzfus was gone."

"But you have met him, right?"

"Yah. On other occasions."

"What do you think of him?"

She sat quietly for a few minutes, composing her thoughts. I knew it was against her principles to speak unkindly of anyone. Finally she cleared her throat.

"I had a kitten for a pet once. Not a regular kitten, but a wildcat Papa found in the woods. I named him Samson. When he was little, Samson acted just like a regular kitten. But when he grew up, I learned that Samson couldn't be trusted. After he killed three of Mama's chickens, Papa made me give him away to the zoo in Columbus."

"I see. Theoretically speaking, Sheriff Marvin Stoltzfus could be killing a few chickens on the side, eh?"

She gave me the blank stare I deserved.

"So, do you suppose your family will be moving away, or do you plan to stick it out?"

She shrugged. "We are praying about it, Miss Yoder. It is a very difficult decision for my parents to make. Still, if so many of us move to Indiana . . ."

"Do you know of any families that plan to stay regardless?"

"Yah. The John Augsburgers. They're in their nineties and feel they're too old to move. Their sons John and Joseph would stay too. Along with their families. Then there is Daniel 'the Red' Yoder and his family. They have fourteen children. Let's see, I think Tobias and Rachel Lehman plan to stay. They only have nine children. Of course, Stayrook and Elizabeth Gerber and their children. Oh yes, Elias and Amanda Schlabach—but their children are grown. Maybe a few more."

"Did you say Stayrook Gerber and his family? Isn't he convinced that Levi was possessed?"

"Yah, but he is an ordained minister. Stayrook would be—"

"Stayrook Gerber is an ordained minister? Annie Stutzman told me he was a deacon."

"Sometimes Annie gets confused," Barbara said kindly. "Anyway, Stayrook would be staying on account of the others."

"That's mighty big of him."

My sarcasm was lost on her. "Stayrook is a man of great faith."

"Well, I'm praying that you stay. I firmly believe that's the right decision."

She looked surprised.

"We Mennonites pray too, dear."

She laughed. "Yes, I know. It's just that your feelings are so strong. You have so much confidence in what you think."

"Well, some people have called me bullheaded." Something occurred to me. "What will happen to the cheese cooperative if most of the people leave?"

Barbara suddenly sat bolt upright, one ear turned to the sitting-room window. "I hear my family coming back. They haven't turned yet off Hertzler Road. Do you mind leaving now, Miss Yoder?"

I knew better than to ask how on earth she could hear horse hooves a quarter of a mile away. When an Amish girl says she hears horse hooves, the odds are she does. I thanked her for her cooperation and skedaddled into the dark cold night. Just after I turned out of the Hooley driveway I saw the buggy turning the corner. My visit to Barbara was our little secret. As far as I knew.

Twenty-three

I owed Lizzie Troyer breakfast. After having put up with two crazy Englishers all week, the woman deserved some form of recompense. Eating her sardine omelettes and zucchini muffins was a small enough price to pay.

"What an interesting idea. I never thought of combining sardines in mustard sauce with eggs," I said charitably.

Lizzie beamed. "You can also get sardines in tomato sauce, with jalapeños, or just plain sild oil. Even," she whispered, "in wine sauce. For those days you might be feeling a little naughty."

"Do tell!"

"Ach, there is so much in this world to see and do. New things to try. Tell me, Magdalena, what's it like to be of this world?"

I exercised tremendous self-control and barely bristled. "I am not of this world! 'As it is, you do not belong to the world, but I have chosen you out of the world,' " I said, quoting Jesus himself.

Lizzie was not convinced. "Oh, but you are. Just look at

you. You're wearing red today!" There was no mistaking the admiration in her voice.

"Lizzie, dear, wearing red does not make me of this world."

"But red is the traditional color of harlots," she said knowingly.

"I beg your pardon! I am not a harlot!" I prayed that the boys were too busy with their eggs to hear. Fortunately Samuel had eaten earlier and was already out working.

"No, of course not. But you do drive a car, and can go anywhere you want. Say, isn't that lipstick you're wearing?"

"Just a trace, dear. And frankly, you could use a trace yourself." I dug into my pocketbook, which was propped against my chair, and brought out a tube of Cranberry Kiss.

The last time I saw wistfulness of that intensity was the Christmas when Susannah was eight, and Papa told her Santa would spank her if she wasn't good. From then on Susannah has broken every rule she can.

"No, I couldn't," Lizzie said, as she snatched the tube out of my hand.

"Sort of pucker like this, and try to outline them first. Then smack your lips together to spread it all around."

Five pairs of eyes—Isaac, the oldest boy, had yet to leave for school—were trained on their mother as she made her maiden voyage into the world.

"Mama, are you a harlot now?" Isaac asked seriously.

Lizzie turned as red as my Cranberry Kiss and fled from the room. When she returned, not only was her mouth scrubbed clean, it was set in a firm, narrow line.

"Don't tell Papa," she warned.

"Why?" Benjamin asked.

"Papa doesn't need to know everything, that's why."

Isaac nodded sagely. "Papa doesn't need to know that I broke his saw after school yesterday, does he, Mama?"

Lizzie looked at me accusingly. "Speaking of school,

you're going to be late, Isaac. And don't forget to take your lunch today. It's in the cooler."

"Shall I tell Papa I ripped my Sunday pants?" Solomon asked.

"Papa no, Papa no," Peter and Elias chorused.

After the door banged behind Isaac, Lizzie sat down and let out a long sigh. "Well, you could have warned me, Magdalena. I had no idea that the world could get me into so much trouble so fast."

"You should really get to know Susannah better," I suggested. "By your standards she's probably out of this world. Maybe out in space even."

Lizzie frowned. "Ach, Magdalena, I am not as sheltered as you think. Maybe I'm not in the world, but I do know what's going on." She put a shielding hand next to her mouth to protect her boys from what she said next. "Sometimes in the store I even glance through those magazines."

"No way!" Imagine that, Lizzie Troyer reading about three-headed babies with alien fathers.

Lizzie nodded vigorously. "How else do you think I learned to cook English?"

"I beg your pardon?"

She pointed to my breakfast, most of which was still on my plate. "Authentic English food," she said with English pride.

I bit my tongue. Perhaps those were alien recipes she'd been following.

Lizzie sighed and glanced sideways at the boys. "But I suppose English food is as far as I'll ever get. Samuel doesn't mind that on account of he has no taste buds. But wearing lipstick and red dresses—I just don't think I have it in me. It must be so much easier going the other way around. Like the Gerbers did."

"Come again?"

"Like Lazarus and Mary Ann Gerber. Stayrook's folks. They were Catholics, I think. From Germany."

"Go on."

Lizzie excused her boys from the table and turned her full attention to me. "I don't know much about it, really. Just that they settled here from Germany. Farmersburg didn't have a Catholic church—still doesn't, I don't think. Anyway, the old Gerbers—Stayrook's parents—took to our ways because it was easier for them than learning English. Their German was different, but they could still get along okay, if they spoke slowly."

"I see. And they stopped being Catholic and were baptized Amish?"

"Yah. Of course, that was before I was born. But Stayrook is about my age, and I remember when he was baptized. The year before I was, as a matter of fact."

"How interesting. I can't imagine giving up things like a telephone, once you have them. Did they make good Amish?"

"Ach, very. Look at their son, Stayrook. He's been ordained a minister. Someday he may even be a bishop. No, Magdalena, the difficult thing would be to go the other way. To leave the straight and narrow behind and go out into the wide, wicked world where there are no rules. You must be very frightened."

"Terrified."

My sarcasm was lost on her. "I will speak to Bishop Kreider if you like. He can recommend somebody better than me to teach you the *Ordnung*, our rules of behavior. Do you think your sister will be joining us as well?"

"Ha! Not likely. Not if chastity is required."

She smiled patiently. "Yah, we do stress showing chastity to the poor."

"That's charity, dear."

"What?"

"Never mind, dear. Would you like some help with the dishes?"

"Yah, that would be nice. But what about Susannah? Will she be eating breakfast?"

"Not here, dear."

A gleam appeared in her eyes. I'm sorry to say I've seen similar gleams many times out in the wide, wicked world. "Yah? With a man?"

I bit my tongue, which incidentally was tastier than the omelette. "I'm afraid so. Oh well, I may as well tell you, because you'll probably find out anyway. The man is Sheriff Marvin Stoltzfus."

"Ach du lieber!"

"You can say that again. As you can tell, I'm not exactly thrilled."

Lizzie may not have been thrilled either, but she was certainly interested. "How long has she known this man? I mean, Sheriff Stoltzfus?"

I looked at my watch. "Let's see, by now it's been about fourteen hours."

"And—and—?"

I nodded. "Now Lizzie, let me ask you a question. How long have you known the sheriff?"

I thought I would have to use CPR to get her breathing again. When I was sure she could hear me I rephrased my question.

"Well, I've known the sheriff ever since he was elected. That's about three years, I guess. He's not from around here, you know. He's from down Sarasota way I think. That's where they have the circus museum."

It didn't surprise me that Lizzie knew about Sarasota. Many Amish, especially the elderly, spend their winters down there.

"Lizzie, you weren't satisfied with Marvin Stoltzfus's investigation, were you?"

I could see and hear her squirming. Lizzie and I may resemble each other in the face, but she has a good twenty pounds on me. "I know that only God can deliver true justice," she said, "but Sheriff Stoltzfus didn't even give justice a chance. It was like he'd made his mind up beforehand."

"Like he was in somebody's pocket?"

She stared at me.

"I mean, like somebody had paid him not to see certain things."

"Yah, maybe. I mean, the milk tank was only three feet deep."

"I get your point. But why didn't anybody call him on it?"

She shrugged. "Yost was dead, wasn't he? Causing a fuss wouldn't bring him back."

"No, but it might put a murderer behind bars. Unless, of course, Levi and Yost weren't murdered, but somehow died as a result of possession," I said, testing the waters.

The waters ran cold. "They weren't possessed, Magdalena. Both men were baptized members of the church. Good men. They didn't live on the edge."

"I'm sure they were veritable saints, dear. However, it has come to my attention that young Levi was sometimes a little loose in following the *Ordnung*. I hear he tipped the bottle from time to time."

"Ach, how you talk of the dead! I don't know who told you that, but it doesn't make any difference. Both Samuel and I believe they were murdered."

"Whoever killed Levi and Yost could kill again. Have you considered that?"

She glanced at the boys, who were wrestling in a heap in the doorway to the kitchen. "Yah, I've thought of that. Samuel thinks it would be a good idea if we moved to Indiana, and I agree. Samuel has two brothers there, and I have a sister. Things will be different there, I'm sure."

"I'm sure. And if that's what you really want, I hope you'll be happy there."

She smiled. "Thank you, Magdalena. I want you to know that I've enjoyed your being here. Your sister too. If you ever come out to Indiana, will you visit us?"

"In a heartbeat," I said, then remembered her cooking.

"PennDutch Inn." It was the silky, sultry voice of a harlot, and I recognized it at once as belonging to Hooter Faun.

"Ach du mio!" International clientele can play havoc with one's vocabulary.

"Is that you, Miss Yoder?"

"You bet your bippy, dear. What on earth are you doing answering *my* phone?"

"Well, I'm the only one here at the moment, Miss Yoder. Did you wish to leave a message for someone?"

"Maybe, maybe not. Where is everyone?"

"Well, let's see. Mose and Doc Shafor have hitched up Sadie, and they're giving all the guests sleigh rides through the woods. That is, everyone except Mrs. Ingram, who's upstairs nursing a bad chest cold. But don't you worry about a thing. I made her a nice bowl of chicken soup, and put the humidifier by her bed. Oh, and I hope you don't mind, but I gave her an extra blanket from that cedar closet downstairs."

"Aaron! Where is Aaron?"

If I shouted it was only because pay phones often contain static and I wanted to make myself heard.

"Aaron? Oh, you must mean Aaron Miller."

"Yes!"

"Tall, right? With thick dark hair, and blue eyes?"

"And very much spoken for, dear, so you can keep your grubby mitts off him. Now put him on the phone."

She had a charming laugh that was utterly disgusting.

"I'll say he's spoken for! Unfortunately, Miss Yoder, Aaron Miller isn't here."

Four hundred years of pacifism would not have prevented me from wrapping that phone cord around her neck.

"Don't you play games with me, you trysting trollop. You march straight up to your lovenest and kick my Pooky Bear out!"

That cultured laugh was twice as annoying the second time around.

"Why, Aaron Miller isn't even in Hernia, Miss Yoder. I'm afraid he's already on his way to see the woman who's spoken for him."

"Who? I demand to know this instant. Does she live in Bedford?"

"Why, it's you, Miss Yoder."

"Me? I mean, he can't be on his way here. What about all that snow?"

"Well, he bought the snowmobile from that kind gentleman who brought me back from Somerset. He—"

"Yeah, yeah. What time did he leave?"

"That's what I was trying to tell you. He just left about fifteen minutes ago. He plans to take the snowmobile as far as he can and then rent a car. He said if you called to tell you to expect him by tonight for sure."

"Thanks. I mean, I'm sorry if I jumped to conclusions."

"That's all right. I understand completely."

"You do?"

"Yes. Oh, and one more thing."

"Yes?"

"He said to tell you he loves you."

Twenty-four

Of course I was in a tizzy the rest of the day. You would be too if Aaron Daniel Miller of Hernia, Pennsylvania, had just declared his love for you, albeit via a helpful harlot named Hooter Faun. Not that Aaron's declaration came as a surprise, mind you. I knew from the day we met, in his father's cow pasture, that we were intended for each other and would eventually live happily ever after. I just didn't know when the after would start. Men, I'm told, are often the last to see what's in their hearts.

I'm sure you'll agree that it is hard to concentrate when one is in a tizzy, so I hope you'll understand when I tell you that chasing down a murderer was no longer my number one priority. Right then what mattered the most was finding someone to share my joy with. Someone to validate the most important phone call of my life.

I found Freni in Sarah Yoder's kitchen rolling out a pie crust. Freni, incidentally, makes the flakiest pie crusts in the world. As a child I firmly believed that Freni was Betty Crocker in worldly clothes. Freni's skill at pie making and the constant compliments she receives have got to be a monumental burden for a woman who is militantly humble.

"Freni, dear, you'll never guess what just happened!"

"Susannah got married?" Freni didn't even glance up from the spreading dough.

"What?"

"Annie Stutzman was just here. She says Susannah got married last night to someone named Mark. A Stutzman, I believe."

"That's *Marvin Stoltzfus,* dear, and as far as I know, they're not married. You know how Susannah is."

Freni, blood kin that she is, rolled her eyes in sympathy. "That child is as loose as a square lid on a round jar. Anyway—"

"Anyway, as *I* was saying, I was just on the horn to Hooter in Hernia and—"

"Eat!" Freni commanded, and she shoved a plate of still warm shoofly pie under my face. "I cut this for Sarah, but she decided she wasn't hungry after all. Ach, I worry about that woman. If she keeps on grieving like this she's going to be nothing but skin and bones."

I, who am skin and bones, gratefully accepted Sarah's slice. If what Susannah read in a magazine is right, it is possible for me to work my way up to a B cup simply by putting on pounds. Unfortunately that's hard for me to do. All that jumping to conclusions and eye-rolling burns off enough calories to give me a figure like a fence post. Some of my women guests have openly declared their hostility toward someone so "thin," but they forget that plumpness has its positive points. And I mean that literally. As for me, my Wonderbra is still wondering.

"Freni, please, you have to listen to me this time. Aaron Miller just said he loves me!"

Freni put down the rolling pin so she could devote her full attention to staring.

"It's true, Freni. I called home and spoke to Hooter Faun. She said that Aaron said to tell me he loves me. Can you imagine that?"

Freni put a floured hand to my forehead. "Ach, you poor child. You must be starving to death. Has that Lizzie Troyer been feeding you sardines and zucchini again?"

"Freni! Listen to me!"

"But I am listening. If what that woman said is true, then why didn't Aaron get on the phone himself? And who ever heard of a man saying such a thing to a woman anyway?" Leave it to Freni to knock the wind out of my sails during a hurricane.

"Aaron didn't say it himself, Freni, because he wasn't there. He's on his way here. Right now!"

She pulled up a chair and practically threw me in it.

"Stay off your feet, Magdalena, until you've had some real food in you. As soon as I'm done here I'll fix you an early lunch. I'm sure Sarah wouldn't mind."

"Freni Hostetler!"

"It's Poor Man's Goulash."

"With lots of onions?"

"Three onions. As big as your fist."

I ignored the reference to my hand size. "Okay."

Freni beamed. "Now hush, Magdalena, and eat your pie. I'll be done here in a minute."

I ate, but I didn't hush.

"Aaron is so on his way here. He bought a snowmobile and is taking it as far as he can. When the snow peters out he's going to rent a car. He'll be here before tonight, I just know it. So what do you have to say to that, Freni?"

I don't think she heard the question. Her eyes had glazed over and she was weaving. I popped out of my chair and shoved it at her, but she pushed it away.

"Ach, don't be so silly. I'm perfectly all right. I was

just thinking about Mose. About how much I miss being with him."

I smiled. "Now who's being silly, dear? Put down that rolling pin and hop in the car. We'll go find a phone and you can talk to him."

Freni frowned. "I don't want to talk to him. I miss *being* with him! But of course you wouldn't understand, not being married and all."

I smiled patiently. "But I do understand. And I still say we need to find you a phone. If you can't be there, the phone is the next-best thing."

Freni looked at me as if I'd lost my mind completely. "Ach, how you talk! Not even married, Magdalena, and you talk like that. Your mama would be ashamed."

I shook my head vigorously, hoping to loosen a few of the cobwebs. "I beg your pardon?"

Freni was weaving again. "I'll admit, I didn't like it that much when we first got married. There didn't seem to be much point to it, unless you wanted children, and we—"

"Freni, are you talking about what I think you are?"

I might as well not have been there.

"Of course, after a while I got used to it. It still seemed kind of silly, considering all the bother, but if it made Mose happy, then it was fine with me. After all, I could always use the time to plan my menus. Then one day Mose—"

"Freni Hostetler! Stop it right now. I don't want to hear another word."

"But I miss being with my Mose," Freni practically wailed.

I was scandalized, and did not stick around to hear more. How I ever managed it out to my car on such wobbly legs, I'll never know. Honestly, I had never been so shocked since the day I found Reverend Detweiler's dentures in the bottom of the communion cup. Imagine, a woman in her seventies, and Amish yet, pining after the way of the flesh!

I started to drive back to the Troyers', but then I remembered what Freni had said. Not about missing Mose, but about Susannah getting married. I was ninety-nine point nine percent sure that wasn't the case, but then again Annie Stutzman seemed to know everything that went on in Farmersburg, sometimes almost before it happened. If Susannah was married to Sheriff Marvin Stoltzfus, I was entitled to know. I turned around.

Marvin's secretary was, as usual, very polite.

"Oh, I'm so sorry," she said. "I thought you knew."

"Knew what, dear?"

"Sheriff Stoltzfus and that woman—I mean your sister—left town last night." She laughed nervously. "A little impromptu vacation, I guess. I suppose by now they're halfway to—"

"Aruba?"

She nodded.

"Are you sure about this, miss?"

"Oh, quite. Sheriff Stoltzfus had me make the plane reservations. It left this morning just after seven. Apparently they spent the night in Columbus so they could be at the airport in time."

I willed myself to remain calm. When it involves Susannah, nothing is over until the fat lady sings, and Susannah is anything but fat. As for her singing, her attempts have been known to attract stray dogs from miles around. Until I saw that marriage certificate signed by an Aruban official, there was no real need to panic.

"Of course, you made the reservations at a travel agency and saw the tickets yourself," I said. "Right?" I was still looking for chinks in her story, some clue that my baby sister hadn't lost all her marbles and gotten married again just for a free trip to Aruba. And this time to a Methodist!

"No, ma'am. All I did was book him the flight from my

phone here in the office. He was going to pay for the tickets in person when he got there."

I swallowed. "But at least you went down to Columbus and saw them off. You know, waved bye-bye at that unmentionable hour this morning."

"I haven't seen the sheriff since he and your sister left the office yesterday evening."

"What time was that?"

"Six. The time we normally close up, unless there are emergencies."

My line of questioning was coming up as dry as our two cows, Bessie and Matilda, two summers before. Of course, their problem had to do with Dorothy Ediger sneaking in from town and milking them because she'd read in a health magazine about the benefits of bathing in raw, organic milk. My problem, on the other hand, had to do with too many riddles to solve, on top of being distracted by my Pooky Bear's imminent arrival.

"If either of them calls, please tell them that I'm frantic," I said.

"I certainly will. And I'm sorry again, Miss Yoder. I thought you knew about your sister's plans."

"It's not your fault, dear. But you can do me a favor."

"Yes, ma'am. Anything."

"Tell Susannah that this marriage has violated the terms of her trust fund. Tell her that at the moment she said 'I do' in Aruba, she said goodbye to whatever it is she had coming to her from our parents' estate."

The secretary winked cheerfully. "Will do."

Then, since Freni hadn't made me that lunch, I went across the street to Pauline's.

"You again?" Pauline looked as pleased to see me as my bank clerk does when I bring her bags of pennies.

"Can it, dear," I said calmly. "I told you last time I had no intention of competing with you. I just came in here for some food. Believe me, as soon as it's possible, I'm heading back home with my Pooky Bear."

"Pooky Bear?"

Of course, I was mortified. I wouldn't have dreamed of using those precious words aloud in a conversation. But as I said, I was distracted and anxious. Not to mention scandalized.

"My boyfriend. Pet name." I tried to make it sound casual, as if I were Susannah. Unfortunately I must have sounded too much like Susannah.

"My boyfriend called his Wee Willy. That was before he ran off and married someone else."

"I'll take two tall stacks, one buttermilk, one buckwheat, a double order of bacon, with play, not crisp, and a large glass of orange juice. Preferably the kind with pulp."

When one is distracted, anxious, scandalized, *and* mortified, it is best to head straight to the bosom of Aunt Jemima. She and Uncle Ben are my only relatives who never criticize me and who always manage to make me feel good inside.

Pauline didn't bother to write down my order. A good waitress, one worth her tips, could memorize the *Congressional Record* if she wanted. But Pauline was owner as well as waitress and didn't have to answer to anybody except her customers. I had a feeling most of her customers preferred to defer. I, however, chose not to.

"I ordered pancakes and bacon," I said kindly, when she finally got around to bringing food to my table.

"So?" Pauline's hostility seemed to transcend professional rivalry.

"So, you brought me a ham-and-cheese omelette and a side of French toast."

"So?"

"So, that's not what I ordered."

The gum popped loud enough to make one middle-aged

man, probably a Vietnam vet, flinch. "Does it really matter? Food is food, after all."

I thought for a moment. "Nah, I guess you're right. It doesn't matter. Food is food."

Pauline's victory smile betrayed a crumb of bacon. "I suppose you're happy about your sister getting married."

"My, how tongues wag. But for the record, dear, I'm less than thrilled."

"Why? A normal woman would be thrilled to have Marvin Stoltzfus for a brother-in-law."

"Then I'm definitely not normal. My sister just broke with another man. This has got to be the world's fastest rebound. Something is wrong with this picture."

"Marvin takes a beautiful picture. He's a photographer's dream."

I got to what was really bothering me. "I wasn't even invited to the wedding! How do you think that makes me feel?"

"You? How do you think I feel?"

I shrugged. My mouth was full of the ham-and-cheese omelette, which was surprisingly good, considering it had been foisted on me.

"I feel lousy, that's how! Well, I would feel lousy, if I believed the stupid story. Which I don't. Marvin Stoltzfus would never marry a sleaze like your sister."

I have long ago decided to ignore insults directed at Susannah. I have enough trouble countering the ones aimed at me.

"How come? Was he already married?"

"No! Marvin is *my* man."

"I beg your pardon? Marvin is Wee Willy?"

"Don't play dumb with me, toots. You've known all along about your sister making a play for my man, haven't you?"

I tried explaining that Susannah and Marvin had only

just met the night before, and that if Pauline really wanted to keep track of what was going on she needed to keep an ear to the ground. Preferably one of Marvin's ears.

The woman was still in a snit when I paid my bill.

"Wait a minute!" she called after me, as I walked away. "This isn't the right amount."

I stopped and turned obligingly. "So?"

"So? So your bill comes to five twenty-five, and you only gave me a dollar and a quarter."

"So?"

"So you owe me four dollars."

I smiled sweetly. "Does it really matter, dear? After all, money is money, right?"

I knew when I walked out that it had better be my last visit.

Twenty-five

Catherine Mast's Egg Casserole

✦

10 hard-boiled eggs
1 can cream of mushroom soup
½ 12-ounce can evaporated milk
½ teaspoon Worcestershire sauce
1 can French-fried onions
1 tablespoon butter

Hot cooked rice

Preheat oven to 350 degrees. Slice hard-boiled eggs in egg slicer and layer half the slices in bottom of buttered 8-inch glass baking dish. Blend soup, milk, and Worcestershire sauce until smooth. Spoon half the mixture over egg slices. Layer the remaining slices on top of sauce and spoon remainder of sauce over them.

Bake for 25 minutes. Sprinkle French-fried onions on top of casserole and return to oven for another 5 minutes. Serve over hot cooked rice.

Serves four.

Note: To get boiled eggs to peel easily, always start with eggs as fresh as possible. Slip eggs into boiling, salted water. Turn down heat and simmer ten minutes. Pour off hot water and rinse with cold. Rinse again in hot water. The expansion and contraction will loosen the membrane inside the shell that often makes peeling eggs so difficult. Rinse in cold water one more time. Allow eggs to reach room temperature before peeling.

Twenty-six

Amish bishops are chosen by lot from among the ordained ministers, who in turn are chosen by lot from among the baptized men. Amish bishops, like Amish ministers, receive no special training. Neither do they receive any pay.

It did not surprise me to find Bishop Kreider out in his barn shoveling away at his *Haufa Mischt,* pile of manure.

"Best to do this kind of thing on a cold day," the bishop said, smiling.

I smiled back. "Same thing goes for cleaning chicken houses. Do you have a minute?"

The bishop put down his shovel without protest and directed me to sit on a bale of hay that was visible from the open barn door. Propriety, like courtesy, must be observed at all times.

"Yah? Is something wrong, Miss Yoder?" the good bishop prompted in his twelve-year-old's voice.

I scratched my head and discovered a piece of hay that had managed to imbed itself in my hair in record time. I love barns, but whenever I'm in one, I soon start looking like a scarecrow.

"Bishop Kreider, I may be leaving soon. I mean Farmersburg. But I wanted to talk to you about something first."

"Yah?"

"You don't really think that Yost Yoder and Levi Mast were possessed, do you? Or that young girl from the factory, either?"

"Possessed?"

"Yes, you know, like possessed by the devil. Or whatever. The reason you're packing up your flock and taking them with you to Indiana."

Bishop Kreider stared at me.

I stared back. "Well? Do you or do you not believe they were possessed?"

"Where did you hear that? Annie Stutzman?"

"My sources are irrelevant, sir. And you still haven't answered my question."

The bishop was still staring. I dug another piece of hay out of my scalp and brushed a handful off my lap.

"I know, I must look a fright. Hay and I just don't seem to get along. Maybe it's some kind of static thing I have going. You should see—"

"Miss Yoder, who have you been listening to?"

"What do you mean?" She may be only a cousin once removed, but I wasn't about to tell on Annie.

"Please don't play games with me, Miss Yoder. There is much for me to do."

"I'm busy too," I snapped. "My boyfriend is coming in from Pennsylvania on a snowmobile, and I hope to be going back with him at my earliest opportunity. In the meantime it has become absolutely clear to me, as it should have to you, that the recent deaths in your community were neither accidents nor the result of possession. They were murders. So far I appear to be the only person in the entire county who wants to see justice prevail, but I can't deliver it by myself."

I strode to the barn door, then wheeled. It may have been a dramatic gesture, but I've seen it work for Susannah.

"Oh, and one more thing. My sister just ran off to Aruba to marry a Methodist. If you don't think my plate is full, then think again."

Before I could wheel again and complete my exit, the bishop put up a hand.

"Please, Miss Yoder. I can see that we have a lot to talk about. May we start again?"

I shrugged. "It depends. Will you give it to me straight?"

"I try only to speak the truth," he said softly. He looked genuinely offended.

I stepped away from the door and the freezing wind. "Then why the hell are you so damn hard to pin down on this possession thing?"

Believe me, I was more shocked than he at what had just come out of my mouth. My first swear word ever, and it had to be addressed to a bishop. On the bright side, Mama would undoubtedly start spinning in her grave so fast that she'd spin all the way through to the other side of the earth and out into orbit. Maybe then her grip on me would be loosened.

The bishop, however, seemed unfazed. "Yes, I do believe those two men were possessed."

"You do?"

"I do."

"And the girl?"

"Yah, her too."

"Then why didn't you just say so?"

"I didn't expect you to understand."

"Because I'm only a Mennonite?"

"Yah."

It was as simple as that. Despite our common bloodlines

and shared values—such as pacifism, humility, and an emphasis on spiritual rather than material wealth—Bishop Kreider saw me as an outsider. Someone who couldn't be trusted with the truth. Perhaps he expected me to run to the press with this revelation. Maybe he feared that by confiding in me, he would be opening the door to network television shows broadcasting remotes from cow pastures and cornfields all over the Farmersburg area.

"I am offended," I said. There was no need to elaborate.

He looked away. "I'm sorry. What else was I to think? In a world where so few truly believe in God, how many do you suppose believe in the power of the devil?"

"Not many, but I do. Mennonites do."

"Yah." The bishop gestured to the bale of hay, but I shook my head.

"May I?" he asked, sitting down. "It's been a long day, and my arthritis has been acting up. I expect we'll have snow here before morning."

"By all means, make yourself comfortable. Now can we talk? I mean, *really* talk?"

"Yah, now we can talk."

"Remember, you promised the truth," I reminded him.

It was important that I believed the bishop. The world is a much tidier place when clergymen tell the truth. Unfortunately, that isn't always the case. I will admit to having my faith shaken once before by a minister. In fact, everyone in Hernia was stunned when Reverend Detweiler, whose teeth I found in the cup, skipped town with the church's building fund and a lover named Pat. After that, however, they barely blinked when Pat's wife became an atheist and moved to Texas to be near Madeline Murray O'Hare.

Bishop Kreider is no Reverend Detweiler. I am convinced that the man is without guile. He most certainly is without lust. Not so much as a lustful thought was directed my way, at least not that I could tell. Jimmy Carter would have been proud of both of us.

We talked calmly and seriously for a long time.

"Do you really think you can escape the devil by running off to Indiana?" I asked finally. It may not have been a tactful question, but he got the point.

"No, of course not. The devil is everywhere. However, I do think that by moving to Indiana we can escape a lot of the temptations we have here. Temptations that the devil feeds on."

Temptations? Here?" I didn't mean to snort. But even I, who is as innocent as a day-old chick—or so says Susannah—could not see Farmersburg as a hotbed of temptation.

"Pride," Bishop Kreider said.

"Pride?"

"Pride in our cheese. In Indiana the cheese won't be so good. It was our pride that led to the possessions."

I nodded. I understood perfectly now. An Amish person—indeed, even most Mennonites—would rather walk naked through Times Square than be proud. Even if that pride is somehow justified. Utter humility is our ultimate goal. We are, as Susannah puts it, proud of our humility.

I glanced at my watch. Almost six hours had passed since Hooter Faun had said the magic words that were destined to change my life. Of course, the words weren't hers, but Aaron's, but you know what I mean. The point was, even if he jogged all the way from Hernia, Aaron was going to arrive sooner rather than later. In the meantime, I had a lot left to do.

"Thanks for everything," I said.

I was being sincere. Bishop Kreider had at least convinced me that he was an honorable and God-fearing man. If, however, he ran off to Indiana with a parishioner named Pat, I would have to reconsider my opinion.

"Godspeed," the Bishop said. "It's too bad you aren't

Amish, Miss Yoder. I have a brother-in-law, now a widower—"

I left the bishop to his *Haufa Mischt.* I have nothing against Amish men, but Aaron Daniel Miller was closing in by the minute. I know it sounds ridiculous, but I could feel his body heat. Waves of it were wafting in from the direction of Hernia, undoubtedly melting the snow and hastening my Pooky Bear's arrival. The last thing I wanted to do was stand by a manure pile while an Amish yenta fixed me up with a widower in black suspenders.

Blissfully I made a beeline for my car and boogied on in to Farmersburg.

Although I could feel Aaron's approaching body heat, nobody else in Farmersburg could. Certainly not the thermometers. The one on the aluminum hinge attached to the knee of the Daisybell Dairies cow read six degrees. Wisely I refrained from sticking out my tongue and licking the monstrosity.

When Shirley Stutzman licked the flagpole during recess in third grade it took two thermos bottles of hot water to thaw her loose. Even then, part of Shirley's tongue decorated the pole until the next warm spell. After that, every time we lined up to say the pledge of allegiance Miss Kuntz put Shirley in the place of honor, directly in front of the pole. After all, it was because of the pole that Shirley Stutzman could no longer say her *s*'s.

Much to my surprise, Arnold Ledbetter seemed glad to see me.

"Come in, Miss Yoder. Here." He pushed some papers off a leather armchair and pulled it in front of his desk. "Sit down. I've been hoping you'd drop by."

"You have?"

"Yes. I have some news for you about Mr. Hern."

"Is Danny Boy all right?"

"Fine as frog hair," Arnold said. He had the nerve to laugh at his own little joke. "You see, frogs have such fine hair that it can't be seen!"

I gave him my best Sunday-school-teacher look. "Actually, Mr. Ledbetter, the speckled Congo cavern croaker has an epidermis covered with very coarse hair. Only the reticulated blue-and-green Bulgarian bullfrog is more hirsute. In fact, up until 1927 it was believed to be a species of small porcupine."

"You don't say!" His look of respect should have made me feel guilty, but as long as public libraries exist in this country, the truly gullible deserve their fate.

"But I do say. And not only that, if you ever get the opportunity, take a good look at the woolly Siberian catfish. It will knock your socks off. Of course, I'm not here to discuss zoology, am I? Somehow we got steered off the subject at hand."

He rubbed a stubby hand across his own hair, which formed a black island on the very top of an otherwise bald head.

"Yeah, well, we were talking about Mr. Hern. I was about to tell you that he's been located."

"In Aruba?"

The dark eyes which peered out from under the inverted half-moon glasses contained not a glint of humor.

"No, in Charleston, West Virginia. He has a sister there he's very close to. Someone he can turn to in times of need."

"Danny Hern is in need?" I asked. "Did the backseat bar in his Mercedes run out of peanuts?"

"Very funny, Miss Yoder. I'm not talking about a man's material needs here. As it so happens, Mr. Hern is in a state of emotional pain."

"So he isn't fine after all. What gives?"

He wagged a short fat finger at me. "You. You're what

gives. It's you who are responsible for Mr. Hern's condition."

"I?"

"Yes, you. You were the one who introduced him to your sister."

"I most certainly did not! I simply went to park my car, and when I saw Susannah again, the two were entwined like vines on an unpruned trellis. I take no responsibility whatsoever for their liaison. And what does this have to do with emotional turmoil, anyway?"

"Ha! Denial seems to be the disease of the nineties, doesn't it? Well, just to refresh your memory, your sister set a trap for Mr. Hern, and once she'd caught him, she heartlessly let him go. Broke their engagement just like that." He tried in vain to snap his pudgy fingers.

Thank goodness I didn't have any brothers and Papa, despite Mama's protests, had taught me how to snap my fingers, as well as whistle and launch a mean spit wad. In all modesty, the snap I produced then sounded like a chicken bone cracking.

"Have you got it wrong, buster! It was Danny Boy who dumped Susannah. Not the other way around. And it is I who should be consoled. Because of your boss, my baby sister is off in Aruba consummating her marriage to an inept sheriff."

Arnold smiled, proving he had lips. "You mean, *our* sheriff? Marvin Stoltzfus?"

"Yes, good old Marvin Stoltzfus, who missed his calling. Somewhere there is a circus cannon waiting to lob him across center ring. So you see, I'm the one who's supposed to be upset here, not Danny boy.

"And speaking of whom, what's his sister's number down in Charleston?"

"It's an unlisted number."

"What's her address then?"

"Sorry, but I'm not privileged to divulge that kind of information."

"I see. Well then, do you have anything to prove that Danny Hern is even alive, much less staying at his sister's place in West Virginia? I mean, for all I know he could be inside one of your cheese presses getting the headache of the century."

Arnold jumped up and practically yanked that leather armchair out from under me.

"I don't have to take this kind of abuse, Miss Yoder. You want to make your snide little accusations, you take them outside. Mr. Hern is fine, like I told you. Now get the hell out."

I am all for liberated women, but the fact remains, the average man is stronger than the average woman. Still, the shoe marks on his office linoleum attest to the fact that, by becoming dead weight, women can retard the process of eviction. As for the teeth marks on his hands, I plead the Fifth Amendment.

Twenty-seven

It was getting dark by the time I knocked on Annie Stutzman's door. I don't blame her for being cautious, but there is a limit, you know. She made me stand outside in the bitter cold while she grilled me like she was the Gestapo. Understandably, I was slow to reveal a few identifying facts about myself.

"Okay, my middle name is Portulaca, and I'm forty-six. But I won't tell you my weight."

"Then you're not coming in!"

"All right. I weigh one hundred and ten in my clothes and ninety-nine dripping wet."

"You do not! You might be flat on top, Magdalena, but you've definitely got a Yoder bottom."

"Aha! So you do know it's me. Now open up, Annie, before I freeze to death out here. It's almost zero degrees."

The door cracked just wide enough to tease me with a ribbon of warm air and the smells of supper.

"You by yourself, Magdalena?"

"Yes. Please, Annie, let me in. I need to talk to you."

The door opened wide enough for one of my shoes, and

it was all over but the pushing. Once I was inside, Annie seemed glad to see me.

"I was expecting company, but it looks like they won't be coming after all. You want to stay for supper?"

"That depends. What's cooking?"

"Skillet pot roast. It was my Samuel's favorite."

"What's for dessert?"

"Chocolate crazy cake. I just baked it this afternoon."

"Well—"

"Please. I'll even whip up some cream for the cake."

I relented and sat down to a sumptuous feast that couldn't possibly have been intended for one woman alone. The crazy cake, when it was served, seemed to confirm this observation. Although it had been freshly iced, I detected several dozen little holes, about the size made by birthday-candle holders.

"Annie, dear," I said over my third helping of cake, "you wouldn't by any chance consider yourself a nosy, interfering gossip would you?"

"Why I never, Magdalena!"

"Of course, I meant that as a compliment, dear. Some people are just more observant than others. There are those who say it's a gift."

"Oh well, that's true," she said, "but I would hardly call myself nosy. And I'm certainly not a gossip!"

"Of course not, dear," I agreed. "But it would be a shame if those astute observations of yours were kept all to yourself. Nobody would benefit from them, right?"

"Right." Annie folded her napkin into precise thirds before carefully tucking it into a wooden ring.

"On the other hand, if some of those observations were inaccurate, and they involved your friends and neighbors, and you passed them along anyway, then you could be accused of spreading rumors."

Annie's fork froze just outside her mouth. "Now what's this about me spreading rumors?"

"Oh, did I accuse you of spreading rumors?"

"Don't you be coy with me, Magdalena. I've known you since you were in diapers."

I licked both sides of my fork. That frozen stuff in tubs can't hold a candle to freshly whipped cream.

"It's just that a number of people have quoted you as a source of misinformation on a very sensitive subject."

"They have?"

"Yes, dear, they have." I pointed politely to my upper lip.

Annie, sharp as a tack, wiped the whipped cream off her mustache. "What have these people been saying?"

"That you've been telling everyone Levi Mast was possessed."

"But he was! I saw him myself. Flapping his arms and crowing like a rooster. That's something only a possessed man would do, isn't it?"

I caught her gaze and did my best to hold it. "Is it? Do you honestly believe that Levi Mast was possessed, dear?"

"Well, uh—"

"Or was he acting like those hippies sometimes acted? You know, the ones who led your Samuel astray."

"Levi Mast was not a hippie!"

"That's beside the point. The point is, you've been telling everyone that Levi was possessed. Yost too. Do you realize what that has done to this community?"

"But the bishop thinks it's possession, Magdalena. And so does Stayrook, who is an ordained minister."

"But you don't, do you?"

She wouldn't answer.

"You didn't want to tell anyone that you suspected drugs because that would remind them of your Samuel, and how he ran off with the hippies, right?"

She nodded.

"Then why didn't you just keep your mouth shut altogether?"

Annie's face looked just like the one on my rubber doll after Papa backed over it with his pickup truck. Of course, Molly didn't have a mustache.

"So I may have embellished things a little from time to time, Magdalena. And maybe left a few things out. But I don't see any harm in that. When you get to be my age, and are living by yourself, you need to do—" She paused to wipe tears from her eyes with the corner of her apron.

"Do what, dear?"

"Well, certain things so that people will pay attention."

I patted her sleeve. "Negative attention isn't what we really want, is it, dear?"

She jerked her sleeve away and began gathering up my dishes.

"Just you wait and see, Magdalena. You might not understand now, but you will. Forty-six and still not married. You'll see what it's like to be lonely.

"Now when Samuel was here—" The apron made another pass. "When my Samuel was here, things were different. But an old woman alone is just that. You'll see soon enough."

But I won't, I thought. I'll have my Pooky Bear and we'll rock away our old age on the porch of the PennDutch, provided it isn't winter. I glanced at my watch. How had I let so much time get away from me? Even if he crawled, Aaron could be at the Troyers' by now.

"Thanks for a delicious supper," I said, jumping up. I did my duty by grabbing what dishes were left and carting them over to the sink.

"Ach, you're not going yet, are you, Magdalena?"

"Why yes, dear. *Tempus fugit.*"

"Please, no slang."

"I'm expecting company myself, Annie. I have to get back to the Troyers'."

"But you can't leave me alone tonight. Not now that you're here." She must have seen the resistance in my eyes. "Can't you stay at least a little bit longer?"

I reached for my purse. "Maybe next time. I've really got to go now, dear."

Annie's touch on my sleeve was softer than a cool spring breeze. "Please stay, Magdalena. Please stay at least until I'm asleep."

"What? What's going on here, Annie?"

"Tonight is my Samuel's birthday." She swallowed hard. "It's also the anniversary of when he left to go with those hippies off to India. The supper you just ate was for Samuel. I make it every year, just in case he might decide to come back.

"I used to think that time would take care of everything. Maybe dim my memory. At least heal the pain. But it doesn't, you know. Not very much, at least. I can still see Samuel riding off with those hippies in their car painted like a rainbow. Riding off and laughing."

She shuddered. "Today it was thirty years. I thought he'd come back today. Of course, he didn't. But you did, Magdalena. You came and ate Samuel's supper with me. You made tonight bearable. Please, Magdalena. Please stay a little longer. Just until I'm asleep. Please?"

"Well, I—uh—"

"Please, Magdalena. You're my cousin's child. You're all I have. You're my only friend. You can't abandon me now."

It would have been impossible for me to leave just then. There was something in both Annie's voice and her words that dredged up all the guilt that Mama had tried but failed to produce in me. Even Mama's favorite standby, the thirty-six-hour-labor story, was impotent compared to this.

I suppose a lot of it had to do with the fact that Annie

Stutzman was alone, a veritable hermit, in a community where aloneness is unheard of. Whether it was shame or defensiveness that motivated her I don't know, but Annie Stutzman had succeeded in all but alienating herself from her friends and neighbors. To put it bluntly, she had become a pest. And even though it was clear to me that the distance that existed between Annie and her community was one that she was primarily responsible for creating, I couldn't help feeling sorry for her. At a time in her life when Annie should have felt particularly loved and cherished—gathered up to the bosom of her church, so to speak—she was alone and lonely.

What made it all so tragic was that it needn't have been so. True, Annie's children had left the community, possibly even the faith, to get away from their father's legacy, but had they remained behind in Farmersburg, the community would have continued to offer their loving support. Of that I am sure. After all, there probably isn't one Amish family in Farmersburg, or anywhere for that matter, that hasn't, in its history, had at least one troubled soul defect from the fold.

Although it broke my heart to hear the woman claim me as her only friend, it was, as I said, the guilt that gave me no choice but to stay. How could I abandon Annie, as Susannah says I abandoned her?

Please understand that I never intended to abandon my sister. In fact, for years I honestly believed that I hadn't. After all, I was also in shock when our parents died, and felt just as cut loose as Susannah did. True, I was ten years older than my sister, but I had the burden of the farm placed suddenly on my shoulders. I tried to look out for Susannah, I really did, but I obviously failed.

If I had given more of myself to my sister in those early days, I'm sure she wouldn't have run off and married that Presbyterian. She surely wouldn't have felt a need to throw herself at anything in pants, and wouldn't, at that very moment, be trying to validate her worth by consummating a marriage to a man she didn't even know, and whose ears were large enough to span two time zones.

"Of course I'll stay with you, dear," I heard myself say. If my Pooky Bear was in town, and had meant what he'd said, then he would wait.

"Ach, Magdalena, you are so sweet," Annie cooed.

My guilt barometer plummeted further. I am *not* sweet. I only agreed to stay to assuage my guilt for having abandoned Susannah. I certainly was not doing it out of kindness. Nor did I intend to do it cheerfully.

After I washed the dishes and helped Annie finish one of the quilts she was working on, I literally tucked her into bed. The fact that I made her a cup of cocoa and read her some comforting passages from the Bible is incidental. I'm sure Annie knew I was eager to leave. Consequently, I will accept no credit for charity.

As soon as her eyes closed I was out that door like a stallion who smells a brood mare. Only the other way around, of course. If Annie Stutzman woke up in the middle of the night I would be only a pleasant memory, making, I hoped, pleasant memories of my own.

It was snowing. Not flakes, just that fine powdery stuff that is the result of intense cold. Even my headlight beams revealed only a vague general whiteness, as if the clouds were being fed through flour sifters. But the snow was coming down at a good rate and had obviously been doing so for some time. In the time it had taken me to assuage my guilt, several inches had piled up, and I had to clear off the windshield before going anywhere. In retrospect I could have saved myself a lot of trouble if I had taken the time to clear the rear windows as well. But I was in hurry to see my

Pooky Bear and couldn't be bothered with such minor issues as personal safety.

Mine is an old car, and it took a few miles for the heat to kick in. Until then my teeth chattered so hard I was afraid I'd lose a filling. When it finally came, the first blast of warm air on my ankles made me groan with joy. Only heaven can possibly offer a sensation more delicious than warm air swirling around your feet on a zero-degree night.

If it hadn't been for the distraction of such bitter cold, I might have noticed the faint smell of cheese before I even got in the car. If the air in the car had been warmer—at least moister—I'm sure I would have smelled it long before I did. As it was, I didn't notice the telltale odor until I was smack dab in the loneliest stretch of road between Annie's place and the Troyers'.

Then I noticed the smell. And then, before I could react, a hand clamped around my mouth again.

Twenty-eight

had the presence of mind to take my foot off the gas before I bit the hand that gagged me.

The man screamed.

"Serves you right."

I braked expertly, despite the slick conditions, and pulled to the side of the road.

"Out, buster! And I mean now."

"Keep driving, Magdalena. Do exactly what he says and you won't get hurt."

"Stayrook?" I couldn't help but laugh. "You're Amish, Stayrook. You don't believe in violence any more than I do. What are you doing here? What do you mean, I won't get hurt?"

Something cold and metallic nuzzled my neck.

"He might not believe in violence, Yoder, but I do. And I say drive."

I recognized the voice of Arnold Ledbetter. He was a little man and I could probably pin him down in a wrestling match, but I was not going to argue with a gun. Little men wielding guns have been responsible for some of the largest trophies, and I didn't fancy having my head mounted on the wall of Daisybell Dairies. Not now that I knew Aaron loved me, and happy-ever-after beckoned.

I willed my foot back on the accelerator and pulled slowly back onto the road. It was snowing so hard now it was impossible to see the line that divided the highway. The fine white silt sifting down from the sky was as opaque as heavy fog, and I wouldn't have seen the lights of an approaching car until they were on top of me. I prayed that I was still within my lane.

There was nothing I could do but creep along. Arnold must have realized my helplessness, because he allowed me to drive at my own rate. Even just a few miles per hour faster and we might have decorated a fence post once the blizzard stopped.

"Where's that damn turnoff?" Arnold demanded.

I took a deep breath. "What turnoff?"

The barrel prodded me again. "I'm not talking to you, Yoder. This is between me and him. You shut up and do what you're told."

Mama would have been proud of me. For once I kept my mouth shut. My lips were clamped tighter than if I'd been offered a piece of her rhubarb pie.

"Turn left just up ahead," Stayrook said suddenly.

"What?"

The point of the gun barrel pressed against that soft spot behind my ear. "Do what he says."

In a split second I chose to obey. Please don't think I'm a coward, but as I saw it, a bullet to the brain was certain death. Decorating a fence post, on the other hand, was still iffy. However, there might well be a deep snowbank between us and the fence, which would bury the car, and we might not be discovered for days. But even in that case I stood a better chance of surviving than did they. Two large helpings of pot roast, four large homemade rolls, and three pieces of chocolate crazy cake smothered in whipped cream certainly gave me a head start in staving off starvation. As for the fourth piece of cake, resting securely within my purse, I would keep it a secret until the two of them were too weak to do anything about it. Ditto for the rolls in each of my pockets.

Unfortunately, Stayrook was intimately acquainted with the local roads, and outside of some light skidding, which I deftly managed, we made the transition to the intersecting road without event.

"Not bad, Yoder," Arnold said. The admiration in his voice disgusted me.

"Now turn right," Stayrook directed.

I did what I was told. This time we didn't even skid.

"Way to go, girl," Arnold shouted.

I stuck my tongue out, but since the rearview mirror was fogged over, Arnold's half-moon glasses probably were as well. Undoubtedly it was a wasted movement.

"Just keep going straight until I tell you," Stayrook said softly.

I knew he was trying to be reassuring, but frankly, I was insulted. Obviously, straight was all I could manage without direction. I couldn't see more than five feet in front of me, even with the high beams on. Did I look like the kind of idiot who would turn willy-nilly into a blank wall of white?

"We'd better not be headed to that Amish parking spot," I said meanly. "You can shoot me for all I care, but I'm not about to make out with either of you two buzzards."

Arnold laughed rudely. "Fat chance either of us would want to, Yoder. You're not exactly prime rib."

"You mean like Elsie Bontrager?"

"Ach," Strayrook said, the distress in his voice quite clear.

"Elsie was a fine piece of work," Arnold said. "Too bad she wouldn't play the game. Still, she came in useful."

"I'll bet she did," I growled.

"What did you say?"

"Nothing."

"Then say nothing quieter. It's hard enough to think with all that snow. Why the hell did you stay so long in that old biddy's house?"

I tapped the brakes just hard enough to launch us into a short skid, and Arnold into the back of the front seat. Annie might be a busybody troublemaker, but she was my kin. Nobody, especially a gun-toting criminal with upside-down glasses and a bad toupee, was going to bad-mouth my blood and get away with it.

"You goddamn bitch!" Arnold bellowed.

That did it. Nobody swears in my car without paying the fiddler. The last time Susannah tried it, she ended up walking almost the entire length of Stucky Hollow Road. Not that I didn't end up paying dearly for my stand. Susannah has yet to let me forget that Stucky Hollow Road is eight miles of gravel lane. But was it my fault my sister chose not to wear shoes that day?

I wear a seat belt, but my car was too old to have come with an air bag. Still, since I was the one with the plan, I was able to brace myself when my foot stomped on the brakes with the same force it stomps on roaches (not that we have any at the PennDutch, mind you). What happened next was positively exhilarating, although frankly, I was disappointed with the acoustics. The teenage boys in Hernia who stand on their brakes are rewarded with loud squeals from their tires, as well as from their girls. Because of the snow cover, my car slid silently, and the grunts and curses from the backseat were no match for the shrieks emitted by Hernia High cheerleaders.

I can't remember for sure, but we must have spun around three or four times, bouncing off snow-covered road banks, small trees, and other unseen obstacles. Eventually we came to a stop in the middle of the road. Except for a hissing from the front of the car and loss of one headlight, the car seemed to be in one piece. Even the windshield wipers were still clacking away rhythmically.

Quickly I checked myself for broken bones and gushing blood. My arms were a little sore from having braced myself against the wheel, but otherwise everything was intact. It is a horrible thing to have to admit, but I didn't even check the backseat. On the other hand, did David check on Goliath after he slew him? As for poor Stayrook, Mama used to say that each Amish person has an extra guardian angel assigned, to protect him or her from motorized traffic. Since Arnold undoubtedly had none, I figured the fight was fair.

The driver door was jammed, and the front passenger door was not immediately cooperative, but I managed to kick it open. Fortunately I was able to locate my pocket book, with its precious cargo of crazy cake, under the dashboard. All told, within seconds of coming to a stop, I and my worldly possessions were slipping around in the snow. Where we were headed, I hadn't the foggiest idea.

Not that it mattered. The blizzard may have muffled the gunshot somewhat, but it was still loud enough to make me scream. The fact that the bullet actually grazed my left ear I hold responsible for my dampened bloomers. I am proud to say, however, that I didn't drop my pocket book.

I will spare you the profanity that issued forth from Arnold Ledbetter's mouth. Suffice it to say, it was clear his mama had never washed his mouth out with soap. At any rate, the gist of his expletives was that I should stand stock still and not even as much as breathe if I valued my life.

I did what I was told. With Pooky Bear officially in my life, I wasn't about to bite the dust anytime soon. That went for snow as well. In retrospect, I might have been better off continuing my mad dash.

"Where the hell is she?" I heard Arnold say.

It was a good question. Although I was only feet from the car, I could barely make out its dark hulk through the swirling powder. I couldn't see Arnold at all. The shot that trimmed my ear hair had been a fluke.

I stood absolutely still, debating whether or not I should call out my position. If Arnold really wanted to kill me, why make it easier? On the other hand, why be the recipient of a bullet that was meant as a warning shot? While I debated I heard mumbling, and then some more angry curses from Arnold. The gun went off again. This time I bolted blindly, much as Susannah does when she sees me carrying dirty dishes.

"Magdalena, stay right where you are," Stayrook called. "I got the gun away from Arnold. Stay right where you are, and I'll find you."

Stayrook was as good as his word, although the fact that he ran into me a few seconds later was purely coincidental.

"Ow," I moaned, rubbing my nose.

"Shhh!" Stayrook warned. "He can't see us. If we zigzag a little we can lose him entirely."

"Where's the gun?" I demanded.

"I threw it away," Stayrook said.

He grabbed me by an arm and began pulling me up the road. Or was it down? With zero visibility it was impossible to tell which direction we were headed.

We zigged and we zagged. In the receding distance we could hear Arnold yelling obscenities, body names for parts God has yet to invent. After about fifty yards Stayrook steered me toward a sharp left.

"We'll get off the road here. Even if he gets the car started he'll never find us."

"Of course he won't get the car started, I—" I gulped. "I left the keys in the ignition!"

Stayrook was gallant enough not to blame me. "These

things happen," he said. "Now careful, there should be a barbed-wire fence right about here."

I couldn't see Stayrook, much less strands of wire, so I did the ladylike thing and let him go ahead. Much to his credit he didn't curse when he located the invisible wire. A sharp intake of breath and a faint moan barely expressed his discomfort.

"Watch your hair," he said.

He held open two strands of barbed wire for me to step through. I ducked, but not low enough. Or else there was a third strand. At any rate, the next thing I knew I was Rapunzel. Mama was right, I am too vain to wear a hat in cold weather. But I learned my lesson, Mama. The fistfuls of hair I had to leave behind will make some bird a nice soft nest come spring.

We plodded across a frozen field, avoiding the bigger drifts by trial and error. This time Mama was wrong. The snow up my dress would not have been an issue if Mama hadn't made such an issue out of women wearing pants. "Only harlots and hussies wear pants," Mama was fond of saying. "God wants you to dress like a lady, and that means skirts." She said this so many times that I was utterly brainwashed, and even after Mama herself started wearing pants, I was stuck with skirts. Why God would prefer a cold crotch over snuggy jeans is beyond my ken, but I am powerless to change my ways.

It was by the grace of God that we stumbled across the barn. It was a small barn, and even though it had once been painted red, we didn't see it until it loomed close enough to scare us. Had we been walking just twenty feet to the left, we never would have seen it. Stayrook's extra angel had definitely been pressed into service.

Excitedly we fumbled our way along the side of the barn until we found the great sliding door. Stayrook, ahead of me, struggled with the door for a few minutes before I volunteered my help. Snow had frozen in its track, and it took both of us, one pushing, the other pulling, to break it loose. Then we cracked the door just wide enough for us to slip through. Once we were inside, Stayrook lit a succession of matches.

"Yikes!" I think I said. Whatever the word, it was certainly no worse than that.

I had been in many barns before, but none quite like this. It was immediately obvious that the barn hadn't been used for years. The floor was covered with dust and bird droppings. Spiderwebs hung from the rafters like garlands. In one corner a slat from the roof was missing, and snow was sifting in, forming a long, narrow drift. In the opposite corner a pile of hay moldered. Leaning up against it was an old pitchfork with one tine broken off.

"Doesn't look too bad," Stayrook said. *"Graddle nie."*

"What?"

Stayrook pointed with a lit match to the miserable hay pile that was little more than refuse. "Crawl in there. If you can sort of dig your way into that haystack, it will help you stay warm until I get back."

I grabbed the hand he was pointing with. "Forget the haystack. What's this about you getting back? Where are you going in the first place?"

The match burned out, and I dropped his hand.

"To get help, of course."

"Where?"

"The Hooley place. They live less than two miles away."

"How do you know that?"

He stamped the snow off his shoes, and I could smell the dust rise.

"I recognize the pitchfork," he said. "Sam Hooley broke the tine trying to move a boulder."

"Well, Sam must have broken his back as well, Stayrook,

because this place hasn't been used in years. Not by humans, at least."

He chuckled. "This is Sam's old barn. He switched from grain to dairying about ten years ago and needed a bigger barn. He was going to add on to this, but then his house burned down.

"Sam's wife, Leah, always wanted to live on the other side of Neuhauser Road so she could have a view of the woods. When their house burned down, that's where they decided to build the new one. Built a new barn there too. This one isn't used until the haying season, and then only as temporary storage."

I breathed a huge sigh of relief. "Well, in that case, if the Hooleys live less than two miles away, I'm coming with you."

"Ach, no! Even though I know where we are, I could easily get lost in this storm. You must stay here where it's safe, Magdalena."

I was touched by the concern in his voice, but somewhat irritated by his stupidity.

"Safe? Arnold Ledbetter is out there. He could stumble on this barn any minute, just like we did. You call that safe? No sirree, buster. I'd rather take my chance out there with Mother Nature than with the mad manager of Daisybell Dairies."

Stayrook lit another match and held it dangerously close to my face. "Mr. Ledbetter isn't likely to find this place. Not in a storm like this. And if he does, you'll be hidden. I'll help bury you in the hay before I go."

It seemed like a stupid plan to me, and I made another attempt to dissuade Stayrook from his foolhardy mission.

"But I must go," he said stubbornly.

The years I'd spent arguing with Susannah came in handy. "You aren't making a lick of sense, dear," I said calmly. "Think of it, Stayrook. If it's snowing so hard Arnold can't find us in the barn this far from the car, then it's for sure you're not going to find the Hooleys' two miles away."

"*Ach du lieber!* You nag worse than my wife," he said. "It is my duty to go to the Hooleys' for help."

For a moment I felt like his wife.

"Your duty? You didn't take me hostage at gunpoint and force me to drive off the main road in the middle of a blizzard. Come on, Stayrook, you were a hostage yourself, weren't you?"

My only answer was the heavy barn door sliding shut behind him.

I am not ashamed to admit that I am terrified of the dark. It's Mama's fault, you know. I was eight when Grandam Yoder died, far too young in my opinion to view a dead body. But Mama thought otherwise, and to keep her quiet I agreed to peek into the upstairs bedroom where Grandma was laid out, in her Sunday best, on her bed.

Mama said she never meant for me to go up there alone, and that if I'd but waited a minute or two, she would have held my hand. Well, she should have said something at the time. I took a good long look at Grandma, who, incidentally, somehow managed to wear a bigger scowl in death than she had in life. And that's saying plenty.

At any rate, I was standing at the foot of Grandma's bed, alone, when the lights went out. The house was plunged into utter blackness, and me just inches from Grandma on her bed. I'm not saying it was a supernatural event or anything, but when I checked with Aaron Miller, who lived across the lane, and with Sadie Schrock, who lived on the next farm down, both of them denied having power outages at their houses.

For one horrible minute that lasted half my lifetime, I thought I would die of fright. When the lights came back on, Mama would find me with hair turned white, eyes glazed over, and turned into a statue, just like Lot's wife.

Of course, that's not what happened. What happened was even worse. When the lights came on I saw immediately that the scowl on Grandma's face had turned into a smile. Sadie said she heard my screams all the way to her house, and with the windows closed.

Now almost forty years later, I was surrounded by darkness in the barn, and my heart began to pound. I'm not talking about the kind of pounding required to pound a nail into a wall in order to hang a picture. I'm talking about pounding so hard it could tear the walls down. If I didn't do something constructive, and quick, I was going to have a heart attack.

Almost instinctively, I dove for that pile of rancid hay and burrowed into it with the speed of a rabbit chased by a fox. Forget about heat loss. It was my need for something to be around me, other than blackness, that was my motivation. It was the same need that drove me under my covers every time a floorboard squeaked for over a year after Grandma's death. And while it may not have been a pile of blankets, the mound of moldy hay was certainly an improvement over standing out in the open. I was just starting to breathe normally when an icy hand grabbed my foot.

Twenty-nine

I screamed loud enough to wake the dead in China. I yanked my captured foot, but whoever or whatever was holding it yanked back. I kicked at the restraining hand with my free foot, but to no avail. I screamed again. I writhed, kicked, and screamed, like a hog being trussed for market. Then I played dead.

"A little late to play possum, don't you think?" a muffled voice said, as the hand released me.

My intent was to scramble out of the hay pile, but I barely had time to flex a leg muscle when the cold fingers closed around my ankle again.

"Not so fast, Miss Yoder. You're much safer in here than you are out there."

"Danny? Danny Hern?" Of course it was him. The odor of rancid hay is hard to describe, but it is nothing like bourbon.

"Yeah, it's me all right. Come on in."

"In where?"

"In here." Danny tugged again, and this time I cooperated by shooting backward on my belly.

"Well, I'll be," I said, sitting up.

I couldn't see where I was, but I'll describe it as a little room. A very little room. More like a big wooden box on its side. It was as dark as the inside of a dog's stomach in there, and just as warm. Frankly, it must have smelled just as bad, what with the bourbon and an obviously unwashed Danny.

"It isn't the Hilton, but I made it myself," Danny said proudly.

"You?"

"Yeah. Originally the hay was over in the corner, and this—"

"This is an old wagon bed," I said triumphantly.

"Yeah, well, this was turned upside down, so I tipped it on its side. Then I moved the hay over here, and *voilà!*"

"You're a master architect, Danny, but what on earth are you doing here in the first place? Slumming it a bit, aren't we? No offense, but this isn't exactly your lifestyle."

I could hear Danny swallow a sip of something. "Yeah, that's just it. I don't know what the hell I'm doing here. Went to bed one night—yeah, that same night we ate French—and woke up here."

"Did you drive?" I didn't remember seeing a car outside, but then again, there could have been a fleet out front and we would have missed them.

"Don't know."

"Well, let's see, dear, by my reckoning you've been here at least two days. Have you even bothered to step outside?"

"Can't."

"Never say can't, dear," I said, quoting Mama. "Just keep putting one foot in front of the other."

"Yeah, well, I tried that. Door's locked."

I smiled patiently in the dark. Sometimes exercising the proper facial muscles can influence our speech. "The door isn't locked, dear. Maybe it was just stuck. Stayrook and I had a hard time opening it just now because snow had frozen in the track."

He passed a loud, flammable belch. "Wasn't snowing when I tried that, Miss Yoder. I could see that much through the hole in the roof."

I'd had enough of his quitter attitude. Susannah is like that. At the least little obstacle she flops down in a heap and declares the going impossible. Once, during the middle of a ten-mile Girl Scout hike, my sister literally threw herself on the ground, refusing to budge another step, and all because of some dinky blisters on one foot. After she was carried out, I told Susannah that the incident was her own fault for having worn high heels. The Girl Scouts simply told her they were going to get a new leader.

"Danny, dear, persistence is obviously not your forte. I'm going to prove to you now that door isn't locked."

So saying, I crawled out of our snug, but redolent, nest and braved the dark to the door. But try as I might, I couldn't get the door to budge either. Even thinking about the time Rita Lantz won the spelling bee in fourth grade just because Miss Speicher couldn't hear right—which still makes me so mad I can lift or move anything—didn't work. That door was definitely stuck. Maybe even frozen shut by now.

"So?" Danny asked, in an explosion of putrid fumes.

"I bet we could open it if we worked together. Stayrook and I did."

He took a deep swig. "No use bothering now, is there? Makes more sense to wait until the storm blows over. Here, have some of this. It'll help you relax."

He shoved a bottle at me, and I politely shoved it away. Alcohol is the devil's drink, and I'm proud to say that not a single drop has passed these lips, except for that time I accidentally discovered Papa's snakebite remedy in the cellar back home. Of course, that was really medicine, and so it doesn't even count.

"Suit yourself," Danny said amiably. "There's plenty here. Don't know where it came from, but it's here. Bourbon, scotch, vodka, you name it. Can't read the labels, 'cause it's dark, so you're gonna have to taste around until you hit something you like." He laughed wickedly. "But I'm not on the menu. Not unless you ask first." He laughed again.

"Why I never!"

I scooted as far away from him and his lewd ideas as I could get. The wagon bed was about eight feet long, so I didn't have to touch him. His bottles, however, were another story. They seemed to be rolling around everywhere.

"Well, if I recall correctly, you never told me how you got here," he slurred. "How the hell did you get here?"

I thought of not answering, but I needed to do something to pass the time. Twiddling one's thumbs, in the dark, while wearing mittens, is not entertaining.

"You ought to know," I snapped. "It was one of your employees who kidnapped me."

"Brenda? Brenda Jenkins?"

"What?'

"Was she wearing a black teddy? Last time Brenda kidnapped me—"

"Can it, buster," I said. "It was Arnold Ledbetter, your plant manager. And I didn't see his underwear."

"Arnie? Little Arnie with the toupee? He kidnapped you?"

"He had a gun, dear."

"He did? What kind?"

"One that shoots bullets. How should I know? Anyway, he shot me."

I'd quite forgotten about that. The intense cold and the excitement had made me forget all about my grazed ear. I removed my right mitten and reached gingerly up to touch my ear. It hurt like the dickens. But then again, so did my left ear. Bare ears on a zero-degree night can lead to frostbite in no time.

I tried to feel for blood, but all I could feel was cold. I smelled my fingertips, but they smelled like mittens, and, strangely, like whiskey. If my ears really were frostbitten, they might have to be surgically removed. Then my Pooky Bear wouldn't be able to nibble on them, as I'd seen Susannah's boyfriends nibble on hers. My potential loss suddenly seemed enormous. I began to cry.

"Geez, Miss Yoder, just asking. You don't have to tell me what kind of gun if you don't want."

"And I'm still a virgin," I wailed.

"Yeah? Well, why didn't you say so? A good-looking babe like you—imagine that! Not to worry, though—Danny boy's here."

"And he'll stay right where he is if he doesn't want a job in the Vienna Boys' Choir," I said, exercising formidable restraint.

"Ooh, tough talk. I've always liked that in a babe. Not like your sister at all."

"Not even close."

"Couldn't even get to first base with her, man. All talk, but no action."

"Really?"

"A total wipeout. Flirted something crazy, but screamed bloody murder the minute I laid a hand on her buttons. Stupid dog screamed too. Wanted to throw that stupid bitch across the room just to shut her up."

"You just watch your mouth! Susannah might not be perfect, but she's the only sister I've got."

"Naw, I didn't mean I wanted to throw your sister. I meant the dog. Snookie, or whatever."

"Shnookums is a male dog, not a bitch," I said. "And

watch how you talk about him as well. I've always been very fond of the little rascal."

Believe me, it is possible to choke on words. When I got done my throat was raw and dry and I was in desperate need of something liquid. I briefly considered scooping up some of the snow that had sifted in through the roof, but who knew where the bird droppings started and stopped. Without a proper light I was liable to ingest something that was hazardous to my health.

"Hey, Danny," I said casually, "does any of those bottles contain anything that could properly be considered medicinal?"

He was too much of a gentleman to laugh, I'll give him that. "Yeah, babe, think I've got something here. Yeah, here it is. Strawberry liqueur."

That sounded medicinal to me. Grandma Yoder, who was always tight with the sugar, made the tartest rhubarb pies imaginable. Even though I complained bitterly about eating them, Mama insisted that I did, on the grounds that rhubarb was good for me. Full of vitamins, she said. Of course, it wasn't rhubarb pies I was being offered, but it was close. Every now and then Grandma, who was in her own way more flexible than Mama, would sneak a few strawberries into the pies to make them palatable. Ever since then I associate the two fruits with medicine.

I took a mouthful of the proffered medicine and promptly spit it out. It is no wonder the Indians called it firewater.

"This is horrible," I choked. "My grandma's rhubarb pies were better than this."

Danny laughed. "I prefer straight whiskey myself. Liqueur is for sipping, not gulping. And if you think that's strong, try this."

I don't know what made me try the next bottle. Intense stress, extreme cold, high anxiety? They were all valid reasons. Maybe underneath it all it really was the devil making me do it. At any rate, I did it. I joined Danny Hern in his bottle ballet. And no, I'm not proud of it, I'm simply stating the facts. Being totally honest. But you must also understand that since that night, I have never taken a sip of anything stronger than vanilla extract. And that was only to check for freshness.

"You still maintain you have no recollection of getting here?" I asked amiably. I'd finally latched on to a bottle that wasn't half bad. Something Danny called Baileys.

"Not a clue. Maybe Arnie brought me as well."

"Probably. How well do you know the guy?"

"Not well. He worked for my uncle, so he was here when I got here. Only he's a hard guy to get to know."

"You can say that again. Why'd you keep him on, if you don't mind my asking?"

"Well, I, uh—I don't know a whole lot about the business, Miss Yoder—"

"Magdalena."

"What?"

"You can call me Magdalena."

"Yeah, well, thanks. Anyway, I'm not too good at business details, and Arnie is, so I just let him run things like as usual."

"Says who?"

"Whaddaya mean?"

"You look at old records? Check the books?"

He took a long swig. "That's important, isn't it?"

"Only if you want to stay in business. What involvement, if any, did you have with the business end?"

"I signed checks."

"What kind of checks?"

"My paychecks."

I took a ladylike sip. "That's it?"

"I signed other checks, too. And documents. Things Arnie brought me."

That was worth two sips. "Did you at least read the things Arnold brought you?"

He didn't answer until I gave him a businesslike kick. "Naw. Not really."

"Why not?"

"Hey, what is this, the Spanish Inquisition? Come on, Magdalena, I trusted the guy. He was there on the scene before I arrived, remember? If my uncle trusted him, that was good enough for me."

"Don't count on it."

"But he was there. That much I do know."

It took three sips in a row then to keep a civil tongue in my head. "What I mean is, don't count on the fact that your uncle trusted Arnold. He may have been keeping a close eye on him."

"Yeah, I guess you're right. Maybe I have been a little lax since I took over."

"Understatement of the year," I said generously.

"But I didn't sign the last document Arnold brought me," he said proudly. "That one I read."

"Oh? What was it?"

"The deed. The deed to Daisybell Dairies."

"Good boy! You realize, of course, that *not* signing that deed is the only thing that has kept you alive."

"Huh?"

"Danny, dear, as soon as Arnie gets your signature on that deed, it's curtains for you. Now I, on the other hand, don't even have a piece of paper to keep me alive."

It was a sobering thought. We sat in silence while he swigged his whiskey and I nursed my medicine. To repay his generosity, I shared the crazy cake in my purse and the rolls in my pockets. After a while it began to get very warm in our hideaway. So warm that I took off my coat and rolled it up for a pillow. The day's exertions had finally caught up with me, and I was having a hard time staying awake.

"Keep an ear open for Stayrook," I said. "I'm feeling a bit drowsy and might nod off now, if that's all right with you."

Arnold answered me with a loud snore.

Thirty

Freni Hostetler's
Poor Man's Goulash

◆

1 pound lean ground beef
1 large onion, diced
Olive oil
2 celery stalks, cut into slivers
1 can condensed tomato soup
½ can water
¼ cup tomato ketchup
1 teaspoon paprika
½ teaspoon Worcestershire sauce
1 bay leaf
Salt and pepper to taste

1 pound noodles or elbow macaroni

Brown meat and onion together in a little olive oil. Stir in remaining ingredients and simmer over low heat approximately 25 minutes. Stir occasionally, adding water if necessary.

Cook noodles or macaroni in salted water until almost tender. Drain. Fold into goulash mixture and simmer an additional five minutes.

Serves four.

Thirty-one

I was rudely awakened by Susannah screaming. I knew at once that I wasn't dreaming. I also knew conclusively that the screamer was Susannah. Her screams, at their zenith, have been known to curdle milk and put the hens off laying. There is even one documented case in Hernia in which one of Susannah's screams stunted an apple tree and caused another to stop bearing for several years—just why Susannah was screaming in an orchard, I have yet to find out. At any rate, her vocal range is inimitable, and therefore immediately identifiable.

I stuck my head outside the straw, and sure enough, there was Susannah, screaming her head off. Her back was turned to me, but she was draped in the familiar yards of filmy fabric, her only wrap the polyester leopard-skin cape that was sheer enough to strain chicken soup. On her feet were those ridiculous clog sandals. That I could see her was due to the fact that there was now light coming through the hole in the roof. It also appeared that the snow had stopped.

Susannah was the only person I could see, but I couldn't

just materialize out of a hay pile and say howdy, or could I? Once I came home late from a church youth conference, just aching to hit the sack, and when I pulled back my covers, there was Susannah pretending to be my pillows. Everything I'd learned that weekend about love and forgiveness went immediately out the window. Susannah would have followed, except that Mama just happened to be walking by my door.

I waited patiently for the screams to subside, and when, after a reasonable length of time, they didn't, I gently tapped her on the shoulder. Of course I had to wait again.

"Put a sock in it, dear," I said kindly, after all other attempts to calm her had failed. You wouldn't believe the severity of my headache.

"How could you?" she screamed. Actually she screamed it several times, but only the last time was decipherable.

"How could I what? How else was I supposed to get your attention? Tackle you?"

"How could you be a part of this?" she wheezed.

"A part of what?"

"Don't play coy, Mags. You're here, aren't you? How much did Marvin pay you to be part of his little kidnapping scheme? Or are you doing it for free, just because you hate me?"

That hurt. I do not hate my sister. In fact, I'm pretty sure I love her. She is, after all, my flesh and blood. Just because I'm not normally fond of her is no reason for her to feel unloved. Unfortunately, there were more important issues than our relationship to discuss just then.

"You mean Marvin Stoltzfus kidnapped you and brought you out here?"

"As if you didn't know."

"I didn't, dear. I was kidnapped myself. By Arnold Ledbetter. Stayrook was kidnapped too. We managed to escape and ended up here. Stayrook went for help in the blizzard, but hasn't come back yet. But I would expect him any minute now, now that the storm has passed."

"Ha! Tell me another, Mags. I suppose Danny Hern was kidnapped too."

I nodded. "Actually he was. He's sleeping there in the hay."

"Funny, I don't see him."

I pointed out the hay clinging to my dress. "We have a hideaway back there. In an old wagon bed. That's where we spent the night."

"Holy sh—!" I can read Susannah like a three-page book and was able to clamp my hand over her mouth just in time.

"Have you tried the door, dear?" I released my hand.

She nodded. But just to be sure, I tried it half a dozen times. It was just as stuck as it had been the night before.

Now that she had calmed down considerably, my adrenaline level was falling and I realized just how cold I was. My coat had made a wonderful pillow, and Danny and I, in our enclosed space, had produced more than enough body heat to keep us warm. The open barn, however, was another matter. If Susannah and I didn't hit the hay soon, we were going to end up as popsicles, and the PennDutch would end up as the property of a two-pound pooch, depending of course on who died first, Susannah or I.

"Come on, dear."

I grabbed her hand and pulled her into the hay pile.

"Holy cow!"

"Susannah, please! You know how I feel about swearing."

"What's with all these empty bottles? And what's with that smell?"

"The bottles were here when I got here, dear, and that smell is Danny Hern. Well, most of it. You wouldn't bother to get up in the middle of the night either if you were stuck in a barn."

She sniffed my face like a bloodhound hot on a trail. "Way to go, Mags! You've been drinking too, haven't you?"

I turned my head. "No, I haven't. I had a few sips of an elixir to help me sleep. That's all."

"Uh-huh." I might as well have told her I'd been dining with the Clintons.

"You can ask Danny," I said. "As soon as he wakes up." By the smell of things, Danny wasn't going to wake up until long after our conversation was forgotten.

We pushed the empty bottles aside, as well as Danny's legs, and settled in as best we could. Two people living in a small wagon bed is cozy. Three people and fifteen feet of fabric is a tight fit.

"So you and marvelous Marvin didn't sail off into the sunset after all?" I asked pleasantly.

"What are you talking about, Mags? Marvin is a world-class scumball."

"I see. Well, what I heard was that you and Marvin flew off to Aruba to get married. This, by the way, I got straight from the horse's mouth—his secretary. Or would she be the jockey?"

There was a moment of silence, which, in a dark, moldy hay pile, can last forever. "Ha! I wouldn't have married Marvin Stoltzfus if he was the last man alive. I was in love with Danny, remember?"

"You've been known to turn on a dime before, dear," I said gently. "Besides, the last thing I saw, the two of you were headed for each other like moths to a flame."

"You are so dense!" Susannah screamed. Fortunately, hay tends to muffle things a bit. "I was only trying to get back at Danny for dumping me."

"Was that all?"

"Well, Aruba would have been nice, but we were barely in the airport. We never made it to the plane."

"Oh?"

"We picked up the tickets all right, but then Marvin turned around and gave them away to total strangers. He only wanted it to look like we'd taken the flight. He had no intention of ever getting on the plane."

"Why am I not surprised? Then what?"

"Then he dragged me off to some cheap motel—"

"Please, dear, I've had a long night."

Susannah undoubtedly meant to clobber me with her clogs. I denied her the satisfaction of crying out.

"This isn't funny, Mags. That's when Marvin began interrogating me."

"He what?"

"He asked me a billion questions. Most of them about you, incidentally."

"Like what?"

"Like what were you really doing in Farmersburg. Who did you work for. How well did you know Danny Hern. That kind of thing."

"And?"

"I told him the truth. Not that it did any good. He suspects you of something, Mags. What did you do? And why did Arnold kidnap you?"

Silence is golden as Mama said ad nauseam. I tried to follow her example.

"Well?"

I told Susannah everything I knew about the deaths of Levi and Yost. Even as I was telling her I could hear just how silly some of the information sounded. Sometimes we need to think our thoughts aloud. Chances are we'll change directions half the time.

"Wow! Now it all makes perfect sense to me," Susannah said.

"It does?"

"Sure. Marvy—I mean Marvin—was real nervous about you staying in Farmersburg so long. He even called the

Pennsylvania Department of Transportation to see if the turnpike was really closed. He said he didn't like outsiders coming in and acting like elected officials."

"Somebody has to do the job."

"He called you a busybody, you know. He accused you of harassing everybody, from the town's largest employer right down to the man on the street."

"In this case, field," I corrected her.

"He got real mad when I told him about your date with Danny Hern."

"He was your date, dear. I was just the chauffeur, remember?"

"Wow, Mags. You don't suppose he's covering up something about our cousin's murder, do you? Even worse, could I have been dating a murderer?"

"You can ask him yourself, dear, when he wakes up. Personally, I think Danny hasn't seen enough daylight in the last two years to be dangerous to anyone but himself. At least not intentionally."

The clogs connected with one of my ankles, and I yelped delicately.

"I'm not talking about Danny, you idiot! I'm talking about Marvin." She gasped. "Do you think that's why he dropped me off here? Do you think he plans to get rid of me?"

"Could be, dear. This seems to be the holding bin for undesirables."

Hay can only muffle so much. I wouldn't be surprised if Susannah's screams—once she hits her stride—could wake the dead. I will certainly make it a point not to visit a cemetery again when she's along. Poor Danny Hern, who may well have been dead, sat up as abruptly as Lazarus.

"Coming, Mama," he groaned.

I pushed him gently back down, and at the risk of obliterating my lifeline, put a hand over Susannah's mouth.

"Don't you worry, dear. I'll get you out of this alive. If I have to rip open the walls of this barn with my hands—"

Susannah ripped my hand away from her mouth. "I'm not worried about *me*, Mags. I'm worried about *him*!"

Who says mercy doesn't run in our family? "Why, that's very generous of you. Spoken like a true Mennonite. Frankly, I'm not sure I can forgive Marvin, and I'm certainly not ready to start worrying about his future."

The clogs beat a furious tattoo on my ankles. The tap lessons Mama had allowed Susannah, but denied me, were finally paying off.

"I'm not worried about Marvin, either. I'm worried about Shnookums!"

"Shnookums?"

"Marvin's got him," she wailed. "Marvin's got my baby!"

I suppressed my rendition of the Hallelujah Chorus. "What on earth do you mean? That thing is never less than six inches from you at all times. Did you check your other cup?"

Between sobs of joy I got Susannah to tell me the whole tragic story. When she was done, we were both sobbing, but for different reasons.

"Do you remember the name of the kennel you dropped him off at on your way to the airport?"

"Paws and Claws. It couldn't have been more than a mile or two away. I remember I heard planes landing."

"There, you see? As soon as we get out of here and get to a phone, we'll give them a call. I'm sure Marvin only wanted to make it seem like you were really leaving the country. I don't think he meant the little dear any harm." I patted her knee reassuringly.

"A little higher would be nicer," Danny said. What a difference darkness makes.

Just to show I am a good sport I obliged him. I patted harder, as well as higher.

"Eyow! Take it easy, babe."

"Time to sober up, dear. We need to break out of this joint and make a run for it."

"But I thought you said your Amish friend, Stayrook, was coming back with help."

"So I did. Unfortunately, it's beginning to look like something might have happened to him. If Marvin and Arnold really are in cahoots, no telling how many guys they have working for them. I think our best bet is to get out and make a run for it while we can. Who knows how soon someone will be back?"

"I know," Susannah said.

"Did Marvin say?" I asked. Leave it to my sister to sit on lifesaving details.

"No. I know because I just heard Marvin's car pull up outside."

There was only a slim chance Susannah was wrong. Susannah's ears have been trained since puberty to hear the sound of approaching cars, and distinguish them by their horsepower. Once she predicted, based solely on the sound of backfire over a mile away, that Pete Parmalee, her tenth-grade beau, was on his way to see her in a 1965 Chevy pickup with a sticky valve. The boy had just bought the truck that day and had yet to tell any of his friends. Go figure.

"Time to pray," I said seriously.

We waited, like three frightened rabbits trapped in their burrow while the weasel, and maybe the fox, dug them out.

It turned out to be neither.

Thirty-two

"Stayrook?"

"Yah, it's me, Magdalena. You can come out now."

"But I'm sure I heard a car," Susannah said.

"Thank heavens, you didn't," I said charitably. "Now at least we have a chance to get away."

We scrambled out of the hay pile and clambered around our deliverer, who was holding an armful of clothes.

"Ach, there's three of you!"

"Danny was already here," I began. "And Susannah—"

"No time," Stayrook said with surprising curtness. "Put these clothes on. They'll disguise you."

They were Amish winter clothes, thick blue dresses, black aprons, and black bonnets. Black wool capes finished the ensemble. For some strange reason there was a set for each of us.

Stayrook glanced down at my feet. "Couldn't find any shoes large enough for those."

I took the outfit he handed me. "Thanks," I said dryly.

Susannah was less charitable. "Yuck. You wouldn't catch me dead in that stuff."

"You could be dead without it, dear."

"All right then! But what about Danny? What's he supposed to wear?"

Danny waved his breakfast in a bottle. "Yeah, what about me?"

"You and I will switch clothes," Stayrook said.

"Where do we change?"

The nerve of Susannah. Despite Danny's claims to the contrary, that woman has undressed in front of more men than has your average male recruit. Only in her case, "unraveled" is probably a better term.

Using Susannah for a shield, I managed to slip into my costume before Danny could get his eyes to focus. Susannah, of course, took her own sweet time, and completed dressing only when the goose bumps on her arms began to lay eggs, answering that age-old riddle about which came first.

I must say, given the fact that I don't wear makeup, and had on sensible black shoes to begin with, that I looked quite passable as an Amish woman. Susannah, on the other hand, required a slight stretch of imagination. Of course, her clogs didn't cut it, but it was the purple and green eye shadow, and what remained of her blood-red lipstick, that were the biggest tip-offs. Imitating Mama, I was able to remove most of it with a handkerchief and spit. But it was after I got her to remove the six-inch iridescent fish-skeleton earrings that things really fell into place.

Danny, despite a three-day growth of beard, simply did not look like an Amish man.

"Lose the bottle, dear," I suggested.

That helped a little, but not much.

"Hey, since I had to remove my earrings, why doesn't he have to remove his?" Susannah complained.

Fair is fair, and when Danny was done shedding several

pounds of gold chains and bracelets as well, he might even have passed for a Yoder.

So there we were, three fairly convincing Amish and one Englisher with a full beard, but no mustache.

Something suddenly occurred to me. "Stayrook, dear, this isn't going to work. Amish families don't generally have English chauffeurs. And I don't think the rest of us know how to drive a horse and buggy. Do we?"

"I can play the horses. Let me try," Danny offered generously.

"Thanks, but no thanks, dear. Maybe we—"

I was rudely interrupted by the sound of the barn door sliding open. We all turned to see Arnold Ledbetter step inside. Several of us gasped.

"What the hell is taking so damn long?" Arnold asked, proving that he was not only crude but crazy.

"I don't see a gun," I whispered to my comrades. "You two guys tackle him and hold him down, and Susannah and I will tie him up with her dress."

"But it's out-of-stock chiffon all the way from Pittsburgh," Susannah wailed. "I'll never be able to find another bolt like that again."

"Is that a promise?" Hope sometimes springs forth in the most surprising circumstances.

"Just shut up, Yoder," Arnold said.

A gun had magically appeared in his grubby little hand, and he had it pointed straight at me.

Never trust an Amish man and a drunken playboy to tackle the bad guy for you when you can do it yourself. A well-aimed pocket book, followed by a couple of hard kicks, and Arnie would have been down for the count. Now it was the second hand on my clock that was ticking, and just when life had never been better. The thought of breathing my last just when my Pooky Bear had given me a reason to breathe made me incredibly angry. Perhaps a little incautious as well.

"Shoot if you must this old gray head," I said, "but then you'll have to shoot three more. Right, guys?"

"My head is *not* gray," Susannah said. "Come to think of it, yours isn't really either. Except for that one small patch—"

"Danny, dear, are you ready to stand up and be counted?"

"Ninety-nine bottles of beer on the wall, ninety-nine bottles of beer—"

"Stayrook, dear, you, of all people, are not afraid to die for truth and justice, are you?"

"Actually, the truth is that I'm on his side," Stayrook said.

"I beg your pardon?"

Stayrook ignored me and turned to Arnold. "Where's Marvin?"

"Damned bastard is chickening out on us. Says he's done too much for us already. Doesn't want to be part of anything else."

"Ach, I was afraid of this. What do we do now? With them?"

"Can we sit down?" Danny whined. "My feet are killing me."

"Try walking a mile in my shoes," Susannah snapped.

Without waiting for permission, I sat down, but first I scraped my jaw off the floor. I will confess to being just as shocked as you must be. I, of all people, should have known that the Amish, like any group, have both their saints and their sinners. Still, that an Amish man, a minister even, could be involved in multiple murders stretched even my imagination. One thing that wasn't hard to imagine was the speed at which Stayrook's mama was spinning in her grave.

Finally, thanks to Stayrook Gerber, my mother would be shamed into retirement.

"On your feet, Yoder!"

I reluctantly obeyed. When a man with upside-down glasses waves a gun at you, it is probably best to appease him. After all, I still had a sore spot on my ear to remind me he meant business.

"Now listen up, everybody. You're going to be taking a little trip. Anybody here in the mood to visit the pearly gates?"

"Ach! You aren't going to shoot them, are you?" The concern in Stayrook's voice suddenly gave me hope.

"Nah, got something better in mind this time, Stay. Especially for the good-looking one in the funny shoes. You"—he pointed the gun at Susannah—"sashay on over here and give Big Daddy a closer look at the goods."

"Please, Arnold, you promised there would be no more violence."

"I said get over here!"

My dear sweet sister tottered bravely over to the gunman. "Good cop, bad cop," she said solemnly.

"What?" The gun swayed in her general direction.

"Stayrook is playing good cop, and you the bad. Saw it once on a TV show. But it isn't working, you know. You're both rotten to the core. And so is Marvin Stoltzfus. Anybody who would separate a mother and baby deserves to fry right along with the two of you."

Arnold seemed surprised. "Thought you two were sisters. Oh, what the hell, the old one can strut her stuff too if it will make her daughter happy."

I don't think I've ever been so insulted. At least that time when Eugenia Rupp, our church secretary, refused to include my picture in the church directory on the grounds it might scare away prospective members, she did so privately over the phone. You can bet I would have given Arnold a good chunk of my mind if Susannah hadn't come to my defense.

"Oh, you are just too stupid," my brave sister said. "Do you think she looks like a dog? I mean, a small dog? Besides, Shnookums wouldn't be caught dead with hair like that!"

"*Et tu*, Brutus?"

In the event that we survived, Susannah's allowance was in for a major downward readjustment.

"Was that little animal you had a dog?" Danny demanded. "I thought sure it was a rat. It had teeth like—"

"Shut up, all of you!"

I don't think Arnold had just cause to fire his gun then, but even so, a gentleman would have aimed at the hole in the roof. The avalanche of dust that followed made Susannah's comment about my hair prophetic—Shnookums probably wouldn't be caught dead with a mop like that. As for the rest of us, it's a wonder none of us died from fright.

I would like to say that none of us screamed at the resounding crack, but who would I be fooling? A gunshot in an enclosed space would turn even Margaret Thatcher into a quivering bowl of jelly. At least I can say Danny Hern screamed the loudest. Susannah, of course, screamed the highest. As for me, just because I screamed the longest does not necessarily mean I am any more of a coward than the rest. You would scream too if a 180-pound Amish man, having fallen into a dead faint, was lying across your arches.

After that, Arnold Ledbetter turned nasty. He whipped that little gun around like a flashlight in the hands of an overzealous parking-lot attendant. He called us names that made even Susannah blush and left Danny asking for explanations. Then he ordered us to pick up Stayrook and carry him outside.

"Hey, that's my car," I said. "That's stealing, you know."

He laughed cruelly. "As I recall, you abandoned it along

the road last night. Finders keepers, Yoder. Anyway, your car has front-wheel drive, unlike mine. And now your car has some first-rate scratches and dings, unlike mine. This barn is not the most accessible spot, you know." He had the nerve to laugh again.

"Well, never mind," I said charitably. "Hop in and we'll all go get some breakfast."

"Excellent idea," Arnold agreed. "About you three hopping in. Stayrook and I will stay right here."

"You sure? Pauline makes a mean stack of pancakes, although you do have to ride her on the bacon. Tends to make it too crispy for my taste. Sausage is always good though."

I'm not a total idiot. Of course I knew something was wrong with his offer—I was just stalling for time. There was always a chance—albeit a slim one—that my Pooky Bear would come riding up over the white horizon in a sleigh. There was even a slimmer chance that either Susannah or Danny would come up with a brighter idea of their own. They didn't.

"Shut up, Yoder." He jangled my keys wickedly and then flung them out over the snow. "Now the three of you push that car up against the barn."

We did what we were told.

"*Now* hop in."

"Knock the snow off your feet first," I told the others sternly.

"Wait! What are you doing?'

It was Stayrook, come back to life. Apparently a dead faint is hard to feign when you're lying facedown in the snow.

"Well, well, well. Sleeping beauty finally wake up from her nap? Just in time, Stayrook, to watch these three take a final ride up to those pearly gates we were talking about."

"Ach! You promised no more violence, Arnold, remember?"

"I promised not to shoot them, and I won't. Not if they behave. But is it my fault the old one accidentally drove her car into the side of a barn and it caught on fire?"

"You can't kill me," Danny said, hiccuping between words.

"Says who?"

"She says so."

All eyes turned to me. All except Danny's were focused.

"Hey, it's true," I hastened to explain. "You can't kill Danny Hern until he signs the deed handing over Daisybell Dairies. Right?"

"Wrong!" Arnold was as gleeful as Rudy Trump was when he stole that shiny red apple out of my lunch box in the fourth grade. What Rudy didn't know—until he took a big bite—was that the apple was wax.

"I'm not wrong. If you kill Danny now, you'll be killing the goose that lays your golden eggs."

"Not a goose," Danny slurred.

"You were, but your laying days are over," Arnold said cruelly. He turned to me. "Penmanship was always my best subject. All it took was a little practice, and now even Danny boy can't tell mine from his. You care to see a sample?"

It was time to switch tactics. "No one is going to believe it was an accident if I'm found dead wearing Amish clothes."

"That's right," Stayrook said. "We had them dress that way so we could drive them over to the border and dump them in the Ohio River. Next to where you had me hide that buggy."

I shook a finger at the only real Amish there. "Why, Stayrook Gerber, I am ashamed of you. And you said no more violence."

"Well, at least no more violence in Farmersburg County," he said, with a whine in his voice. "I plan to keep living here, you know."

"Shut up! All of you. No one's going to tell what they're wearing when I get through with them. They'll be burned to a crisp, like Pauline's bacon. Won't be able to tell one from another."

I took a deep breath and steadied myself against the car. "Well, so long, sis. It's been an experience knowing you. And I do love you, I hope you know that. Even if I wasn't always as patient as I might have been."

Susannah had the decency to burst into tears. "You were right, Mags, there is a God after all. At least my little Shnookums doesn't have to die."

"Mind if I have just one more drink?" Danny asked politely. "There's still a bottle of good scotch back there in the hay that I'd hate to see wasted."

Arnold smiled broadly. "Damn good idea. Bring all the bottles. Wouldn't hurt for them to find the car filled with the stuff." He waved Danny into the barn.

"Must be a dozen bottles in there," I said quickly. "I'll give him a hand."

I darted in after Danny before Arnold could fire a shot. I finally had a plan.

Thirty-three

I might have left my car keys behind when I fled, but I didn't leave my purse. There isn't an American woman over forty who can step outside without her purse. It is, of course, a political legacy that dates back to the beginning of our country. Whereas our founding fathers claimed the right to bear arms, our founding mothers claimed the right to bear purses. So entrenched did this idea become that at the height of McCarthyism, or so I'm told, a woman outdoors without a bag on her arm was immediately branded a Communist. Some intensely patriotic women, like Mama, go so far as to be buried with their purses.

This anti-Communist gesture has spread to other Western nations. Now even the Queen of England carries a purse, although what she puts in it is anybody's guess. The British tabloids have told us everything there is to know about the insides of the royal bedrooms, but nothing about the insides of the royal pocket books. Susannah insists that the Queen carries a pooch in her purse. Who knows, she may be on to something. Some of the pocket books I've seen that grande dame toting lately could accommodate a small corgi. On the other hand, they might simply be filled with tissues, given the sad state of her family's affairs.

At any rate, my purse was still in the bar, and in it was an extra set of car keys. Although I had my doubts that Arnold would let me back out of the barn toting my bag, there was no way he could stop me from smuggling out my keys. Thanks to Susannah, I knew that bras made excellent substitute purses (which leads me to conclude that some of the bra-burners back in the sixties might indeed have been Communists).

We emerged from the barn with our arms full of bottles and dumped them into the back of the car. Arnold had Stayrook frisk us both, which is kind of like what I would imagine sex was like between my parents. My bra went undisturbed.

"Now line up, folks," Arnold said, pulling a syringe from his coat pocket and handing it to Stayrook. "Time for those flu shots."

"I already had mine, dear."

"Not one like this, you haven't. Thanks to my comrade here, today's selection includes the finest in cattle tranquilizers. We originally intended it to sedate you while you took the big swim. But as you see, I'm flexible."

"I hate needles," Susannah said. "I think I'll pass as well."

Arnold clicked the safety off. "Actually, the shots are not optional. How else am I going to keep you in a burning car? So it's either a nice, relatively painless shot, or a bullet to the head. What will it be?"

Susannah calmly took off her bonnet and patted her hair. "I'll take the bullet then. I told you I can't stand needles."

Stayrook was obviously distressed. "The injection will hardly hurt at all," he said. "I give them all the time."

Susannah held her head high. "Yes, to cows. But I'm not

a cow. And anyway, I don't know where that needle has been. What about AIDS? Go ahead and shoot, Arnie."

I was horrified. My plan did not call for Susannah to throw in the towel so quickly.

"She doesn't mean it, Arnold." I winked at Susannah. "She would really rather have the shot."

"I would not!"

"You would so."

"Would not, and what's wrong with your eye, Mags?"

"Piece of hay, dear." I moved closer to Susannah so I could whisper to her, if not kick her.

Arnold was no fool. "Get back, Yoder, or you buy the farm now. Kinda make your choice easy for you."

I had been thinking the whole time, and now I started praying as well.

"I'll take the first injection," I said. "If it doesn't hurt too bad, promise me you'll take it, Susannah."

My sister rolled her eyes, possibly for the last time. It was a strangely touching sight.

"All right. If you take the shot, I'll take it. But I'm warning you, I might faint."

"Good girl. All right, buster," I said to Stayrook, "sock it to me."

It was hard to tell that Stayrook had ever injected a cow by the way he handled that syringe. He was almost as incompetent as old Nurse Schrock, before Doc Gingerich made her retire. Of course, both nurse and doctor are dead now, but a generation of Hernians, Susannah included, have left arms that look like they have been pressed up against miniature waffle irons. Arnold had to do a lot of stabbing before he got the blunt needle to penetrate my clothes.

Of course the injection hurt. A cattle syringe is just barely smaller than a pastry funnel. At least it felt that way. But even though my teeth drew blood, I kept my mouth shut.

"Next!"

Dear Danny was obviously in his cups, and he responded as if Arnold were passing out free drinks. Fortunately for him, his inebriety was in his favor, because he seemed to feel nothing.

"Piece of cake," he said, and wobbled aside.

Susannah screamed. This was not one of her run-of-the-mill screams intended to attract attention or sympathy. This was a scream generated by pain and abject terror. My heart went out to her.

Even Stayrook, criminal that he was, appeared moved. He dropped the syringe like a hot potato and steadied Susannah with both hands.

Arnold, however, had the heart of Satan. "Now get in the car, suckers," he said with a wave of the gun.

"Ach, Arnold, please. Two deaths are enough. At first you said nobody had to die."

"Those two dying was their own fault. I never pushed Levi from his damned silo, and I sure as hell didn't hold Yost under in his milk tank."

"But the drugs—"

"The LSD was your idea, remember? Something you picked up from watching those hippies camped out on that farm next to yours."

"Annie Stutzman's place?" I asked. After all, why die ignorant?

Stayrook glanced at me and then down at his feet. "Yah. When they took that stuff they acted crazy. Like they were possessed. I wanted Yost and Levi to act like that, not to kill themselves."

"Drugs kill, Stayrook. Or haven't you seen those commercials on TV?" Arnold laughed wickedly.

"You bought the stuff," Stayrook said, a catch in his voice. "I only saw to it that they took it."

"So you're blaming the apple on Eve, are you, Rev?"

"Ach, but Arnold—"

"Then get in the damned car with them, if that's how you feel. What's it going to be, Gerber? You want to live and own the largest dairy farm east of the Mississippi, or do you want to start your eternal roast a little bit early?"

"Come on, Arnold, I have a wife and kids. You know that." Despite a temperature hovering around zero, Arnold's face looked like Niagara Falls.

"I'm sure they'll be very proud of you, whatever you choose," I said meanly.

"Well, if we're going to die, let's get it over with," Susannah said sensibly. "This cold air is chapping my face."

We three pseudo-Amish climbed into the car. I, of course, climbed behind the wheel, since it would make more sense to find my remains there. Danny, of course, climbed into the backseat, where most of the bottles had been dumped. Susannah, as my sister, should have claimed her rightful place at my side, but I cannot fault her choosing to die in the backseat. People facing death often reach out for the familiar.

While Stayrook made one last pitiable plea for mercy, I fished out my car keys and slipped the appropriate one into the ignition. Not even Susannah, who was still conscious, saw what I had done.

My detractors would claim that I am far from being a saint. I would have you know, however, that I counted slowly to ten just before I pumped the gas and turned over the ignition. Just as the engine caught, the front door flew open and Stayrook jumped in.

I shifted into reverse and pressed the pedal to the metal.

Thirty-four

My vehicle might have front-wheel drive, but on the snowy lane that led from the barn to the highway, it performed with about as much accuracy as a carnival bumper car. But it was the very erraticism of my driving that made it impossible for Arnold Ledbetter to hit his mark. That and prayer.

Farmersburg County does not generally plow its minor roads, but Highway 5 had been cleared, and once on it we had smooth sailing. The only question was where.

"Keep going east," Stayrook said. "We're only eight miles from the county line. We can ask the sheriff there for help."

I stifled nothing. "Ha! Right, like we should trust you? For all I know this is another trap." I began looking for a spot to turn the car around.

"Yah, I don't blame you for not trusting me. I shouldn't have said anything."

"What? That's it? No argument?"

"No argument."

That did it. I stomped on the brakes, but even with the road cleared, we skidded fifty feet farther than I'd intended.

Stayrook was playing mind games again. Undoubtedly Marvin, or some other criminal crony, was just down the road lying in wait. Stayrook wanted me to doubt him, and then feel guilty for it, and second-guess my better judgment. Of course, Stayrook knew I was smarter than that, and had gone one step further in his thinking. Being a stubborn Yoder, he reasoned, I would overcome my guilt and do the opposite of what he suggested anyway. Then he would have me in his trap. Boy, did he think wrong.

"Don't you think you've fooled me for a minute," I snapped. "We're headed east, and that's that. You don't like it, you can jump out."

"Yah, east is good."

I covered my right ear with my right hand. "I can't hear you! I can't hear you! I can't hear you!"

A mile or two down the road I glanced over at Stayrook. He was sitting silently, tears streaming down his cheeks.

I removed my hand from my ear. "Nice touch, dear, but I don't believe it for a second. Save your tears for the next sucker."

He said nothing, and his silence was deafening.

"Susannah, dear," I called, "how you doing back there?"

Neither my sister nor Danny had uttered as much as one word since our escape. In both their cases it was close to a record.

"I think they're asleep," Stayrook said quietly.

"Asleep?" I snarled. "You mean zonked out with the tranquilizer. Come to think of it, I'm starting to feel kind of funny too."

"Magdalena, there's something—"

"I can't hear you. I can't hear you!"

Stayrook covered his face with his hands. It was a shame well deserved.

I fought the tranquilizer as long as I could. Despite my rather large frame, and the quaint way I sometimes chew my food, I am not a cow. Undoubtedly the drug worked a lot faster on me than it did on its bovine victims. The numbness began in my feet and spread upward through my body, and I had trouble feeling both accelerator pedal and the steering wheel. My eyelids must have become numb too, because they kept drooping and obscuring my vision. Each time they drooped they became hard to open, and I was convinced that in a minute or two I would be out like a light. Still, I had to get across the county line.

I was weaving badly, fading off into the twilight zone, when I saw the store up ahead on the right. Tacked on a post just in front of the store was a new county sign. I breathed a prayer of thanks, took my foot off the pedal, and coasted into safety.

"Not here!" Stayrook said sharply. "It's too close."

"It's here or nowhere," I said. I unbuckled my seat belt, laid my seat as far back as it would go, and settled down for a long winter's nap. At that point I was so far under that ten Arnolds and all the guns in the world wouldn't have roused me from my slumber.

Stayrook certainly tried. "Wake up, Magdalena. Wake up!" He shook me, like I used to have to shake Susannah every school morning.

"Go away, Stay, and stay away."

"Magdalena, there's something I have to tell you."

"Tell me anything you want, dear, just let me go back to sleep."

"Magdalena, that wasn't tranquilizer in the syringe."

I smiled. Intense drowsiness breeds benevolence. "Yes it was, dear. It was cow tranquilizer. You put it in there yourself, and then you gave it to me. Right here, in the arm. Moo."

"It was water, Magdalena. I couldn't go through with it."

"What?"

"Arnold wanted you sedated before he threw you into

the river—his original plan—but I couldn't go through with it. You would have drowned. That was his point. And I would have been a part of it."

I began to wake up. "Water? There was nothing but water in that syringe?"

"Yah. Clean water. I boiled it first."

I was wide awake. "Then why am I asleep? I mean, was."

"Ach, that must be just stress. I'm very sorry, Magdalena. I really am."

I put my seat back into its upright position. "Well, I had you fooled now, Stayrook, didn't I? I knew it was water the whole time."

"Yah," he said kindly. "You had me fooled."

"Don't you take that tone with me, buster. You're still going to be in a heap of trouble, you know."

"I know."

I started to open the door, but he grabbed my arm. "This really isn't such a good place, Magdalena. I know the owners. They buy from the dairy. Friends of Arnold, I think. There is a better place just down the road, once you cross the interstate highway. A busy place, lots of customers. You can call the sheriff from there."

"Tough cookies, toots," I said. What good is having a younger sister if you can't borrow a phrase from her now and then?

I should have gotten right out of the car, but I guess I really am a sucker. Either that, or too proud to stop trusting my instincts. So even though I knew that Stayrook Gerber was a Judas and a snake, I let the sound of his voice and the hurt in his eyes give him one more chance.

There was indeed a very popular spot just east of I-77. The twelve-foot-high black concrete pot with the words "Dutch Kettle" painted in white on it must have been easy to see from the interstate, because the parking lot was jammed. A smaller sign advertising "authentic Amish cooking" was held rigidly in place over the door by two very tall wooden Amish figures, one male, one female.

"Cigar-store Indians," I said.

"Ach, the English will do anything for a dollar."

"Do I hear the pot calling the kettle black?"

Stayrook blushed a pleasing shade of red.

We had to circle the parking lot three times before a van of Canadian tourists, their funny vowels trailing them, left me a spot right next to the front door with its two behemoth guardians. The fact that it was a handicapped space does not make me feel guilty one whit. If a middle-aged Mennonite in an Amish costume, with an arm full of water, who is running for her life from a diabolical dairyman does not qualify as handicapped, then who does?

I insisted that we leave Susannah and Danny sleeping peacefully in the backseat. In case it was a trap, it was better that we split up. Although just what the two of them could do to protect themselves was anybody's guess. Throwing Molotov cocktails is a learned, not an instinctive, behavior.

Just inside the door a massive woman, no doubt the inspiration for the figures outside, stopped me with an outstretched arm. Like me, and the statue, she was supposed to look Amish.

"You my replacement?"

"Pardon me?"

"You're seven minutes late, dearie. Being late your first day as hostess is definitely not cool. Thelma's gonna stick you back in the kitchen if this happens again."

I glared up at her. "I am not a hostess. I just want to use your phone."

"The phone is for customers only, dearie."

"Then I'm a customer. Where's the phone?"

"Ah, a customer. You have reservations?"

"For breakfast? You've got to be kidding!"

"Big Bertha doesn't kid, dearie. You don't have reservations, then scram. And take him with you. This here is a very popular place."

I tried to push gently past her, but Bertha the Hun wouldn't budge.

"You want me to throw you out myself, dearie?"

"No dear, certainly not. Call the police instead."

The crabby colossus wouldn't cooperate. "All right, dearie, it's out on your ear, if that's the way you want it."

I folded my arms across my meager chest and puffed it out as much as I could. "You wouldn't dare throw out the entertainment, would you?"

"Huh? What kind of entertainment? I don't know anything about any entertainment, and I've been working here going on four years."

"We're Amish folk singers, dear. Hired just last night."

Brunhild grunted and eyed Stayrook suspiciously. "He don't look *Aymish* to me."

I smiled patiently. "He's a Mennonite, dear. You can tell by the nose."

"Funny, but the owners didn't say nothing to me about no folk singers. You sure this is for real?"

"See for yourself, dear. These folks have come for miles around just to soak in the atmosphere. That's why Johnny, here, and I have been hired. We're your breakfast duet. In fact, you were supposed to help us set up."

"Ach!" I had the feeling Stayrook would rather be staring down the barrel of Arnold's gun.

"Who hired you?"

I pointed to a mean-looking woman in a gray business suit that I had observed slip behind the register counter several times to harangue the cashier.

"Mrs. Wilson?"

"Herself. Can we get started now?"

" 'Spose so. Where would you like me to set up?"

"Drag a couple of chairs over by the breakfast buffet,"

I said. "*Now* may I use the phone? I need to call our manager."

"After you perform, dearie."

I was just about to tell Goliath's mother what she could do with her phone—in a ladylike manner, of course—when the door opened and in walked Arnold and Marvin.

Thirty-five

Ohio River-Bottom Sludge Cake

◆

1 cup pastry flour
⅔ cup sugar
3 tablespoons cocoa
2 teaspoons baking powder
½ teaspoon salt
½ cup milk
3 tablespoons melted butter
1 teaspoon vanilla

Topping:

½ cup brown sugar
¼ cup white sugar
3 tablespoons cocoa

1 teaspoon vanilla

¼ teaspoon salt

1¼ cups boiling water

Preheat oven to 350 degrees. Sift dry ingredients in the first list together. Add liquid items in first list and blend well. Pour mixture into an 8-inch-square greased glass baking dish. Combine ingredients in second list and sprinkle evenly over the "cake" mixture. Pour the boiling water over this but do not stir. Bake for 40 minutes. A fudge crust will form on top, with a thick sauce underneath. Allow to stand for 15 minutes before serving. Delicious served warm or cold, with or without whipped cream or ice cream.

Thirty-six

Stayrook didn't even know the words to "Kumbayah," so I gave him a half-filled water glass and a greasy spoon and told him to tap out a rhythm. Any rhythm. He looked at me like a lost puppy, so I patted him on the head and told him to hop on his chair.

I hopped up on mine. "Velkommen to de Deutsche Kettle," I said in my best fake German accent. "Dis morning vee haf—"

"Mama, who's the weird lady in the black clothes?" an obnoxious urchin asked. Even Miss Progel, my high school gym teacher, didn't have a voice that loud.

"Hush, Jamie. I think she's Aymish."

"Are they like witches?" The wicked boy made a face at me.

"No, dear. I think they're very poor, though." She handed her son a few coins. "Go ahead and give them to her."

I glared at them. "Dis morning I veel be singing zee traditional songs of my people. Hit it," I said to Stayrook.

He looked like a sheep who'd been asked an algebra question.

"Tap on your glass."

The boy was in front of me then with his sticky handful of quarters. Since it is a sin to reject charity, I reached for the money. The boy, true to type, dropped all the coins at my feet except one. "Better fork it all over, buster, or you'll find out firsthand why it is that chickens have no lips." Please understand that it was the stress talking. I'm usually far more creative.

"Mama!" The little devil ran back to his mother.

At the same moment I saw the mean-looking woman in gray threading her way to me through the packed tables with Brunhild hot on her heels. Coming at me from a slightly different direction were the Farmersburg fiends. Marvin, ever the coward, was not wearing his uniform.

It was then or never.

"Oh give me a home,
Where the pacifists roam,
Where the Amish and Mennonites play.
Where seldom is heard—"

My pursuers were closing in too fast. It was time to switch songs.

"De Camptown races five miles long, dooda, dooda,
Dial nine one one all morning long, oh dooda day.
Dial nine one one, dial nine one one,
Some bad guys are after us with a gun,
Dial nine one one."

The mean-looking lady in gray was the first to reach me. "Get off that chair right now!"

I obliged her. "Where's the back exit?"

"Oh, no you don't. Not so fast." Brunhild had me by the arm.

"Ach! Ach!"

Stayrook was flailing around helplessly on his chair, clearly immobilized by genetics. Or was he? After all, his ancestors had only recently adopted the pacifist creed. Perhaps his repressed instincts could still be tapped. I am not one to advocate violence, mind you, but surely a display of fisticuffs would inspire someone to call for help.

"Punch out the big one, Stay. I'll take care of the mean one."

That's all it took to undo just one generation of genetics. Not that Stayrook could bring himself to hit the woman, but he did the next-best thing. He leaped into the air like a cougar and landed on the giant bison's back. I once saw a still-life display of the same scene at the Carnegie Museum in Pittsburgh.

The bison bellowed and bucked, but the brave cougar clung on tightly.

"Call the sheriff!" I screamed. "Somebody call the sheriff!"

"I am the sheriff!" Marvin had the audacity to pull a badge out of his coat pocket and wave it pompously at the patrons. "Everyone stand back now."

"Eeeeeyah!"

My ninety-pound sister came sailing out of nowhere to land on Marvin's back, and like a proper she-cat dug her claws into his scalp. Marvin moaned before collapsing, the first victim of the hunt.

The second victim to fall was Arnold Ledbetter. A well-placed whack across the kneecaps with an empty bottle was all one could expect from Danny Hern, given his condition, but he performed well. Although judging by the sounds Arnie made as he went down, the acoustics in the Dutch Kettle left much to be desired. The mean-looking lady in gray was going to have to do some major remodeling if she expected me to come back and give a serious performance.

Fortunately, Stayrook was able to cling to the bison long enough for me to convince the owner, who really wasn't as mean as she looked, that we were the real victims, and that the fellows on the floor were the felons. The sheriff was immediately summoned, and justice prevailed.

Of course, it was a tremendous relief to finally be safe and sound, but nothing could match the relief I felt when I saw Aaron Miller come through that door, just minutes after the sheriff. My Pooky Bear still loved me.

Thirty-seven

"**A**ch, everyone knows that Amish farms produce the richest milk," Freni said from the backseat.

"Flirting with pride, aren't we, dear?" I chided gently.

"Pride, shmide, it's true. That dairy was going out of business. It needed Amish milk. Imagine that! One of the largest dairies in the country, and it couldn't exist without Amish milk."

"It needed milk from local farms, but not necessarily Amish. It's the soil and climate of Farmersburg County that make the local milk special, not the religion of the farmers."

"Ach, that's practically sacrilegious! And you a Mennonite yet. I would have expected such a comment from Susannah, but not you, Magdalena."

"Leave me out of this, please." Susannah, with Shnookums safely returned to her bosom, was acting alarmingly mellow. If she didn't perk up by the time we got home, I was going to insist that she see a doctor.

"I suppose you think that Stayrook is innocent just because he's Amish."

"Your words, not mine."

"Stayrook was greedy, that's all there was to it, dear. He was the one who gave envelopes with LSD in the glue to Levi and Yost. Envelopes that perfectly matched the cooperative's stationery."

"Yah, but it was that Ledbetter fellow who gave Stayrook the envelopes. And it was Ledbetter who put the idea in Stayrook's head about buying up all the farms."

I was fit to be tied. Ledbetter was quite possibly the devil himself in upside-down glasses, but Stayrook was certainly no angel.

"What is this, blame-it-on-the-English day?"

"If the shoe fits," Freni said smugly.

"No one forced Stayrook to do what he did, Freni. We are all responsible for our own choices."

"Yah, and that English—what was his name? You know, Susannah's boyfriend?"

Susannah groaned. "His name is Danny Hern, and he isn't my boyfriend."

"Yah, anyway, he chose to be drunk all the time, which is why Ledbetter was able to take over the business. A big business too, worth millions of dollars, they say."

"Was, dear. Though maybe if Danny dries out the Amish will start supplying him again."

"Ach, the English and their alcohol," Freni said sanctimoniously.

"Ha! There you go again. The English this, the English that. Marvin Stoltzfus took a bribe to look the other way, which makes him just as guilty as Arnold Ledbetter. Maybe even more so, because Marvin was sworn to uphold the law."

"So?"

"So, Marvin Stoltzfus shares enough of your genes to practically be your son. He even looks like you."

"Why, I never!"

"If the shoe fits, dear. And one more thing, Freni.

Stayrook knew that Arnold, not Danny, was harassing Elsie Bontrager. But he didn't say anything, did he? He didn't even say anything when Arnold got Elsie to sample some LSD in a slice of cheese, just so she would appear crazy. If that doesn't make Stayrook guilty, then I don't know what does! In my opinion the guilty parties should be strung up by their thumbs and pelted to death with cheese balls. And that includes Stayrook!"

"*Ach du Heimer!* How you talk. Your mama—"

"Leave Mama out of this!"

"Ladies, please," Aaron said patiently.

To please my Pooky Bear I bit my tongue and pretended to be interested in the snow-covered hills of western Pennsylvania. In less than two hours I would be home, back at the PennDutch Inn, empress of my domain. I had a lot to be thankful for. Just hours before I had almost bought the farm, on a farm, and now I was seated next to the person I loved most in the whole wide world, with the two people I loved next sitting right behind. I could afford to be generous.

"I love you, Susannah," I said impulsively.

"Huh?"

"I love you, dear."

"Yeah, right. Same here."

"I love you, Freni."

"Ach!"

"Do you love me?"

"Ach!"

"I'll take that as a 'yes.'" I turned to Aaron, who was driving my car. "I love you, Aaron."

Aaron carefully pulled the car over and parked it under a sign that read BEWARE OF FALLING ROCKS.

"I love you too, Magdalena Portulaca Yoder. Will you marry me?" Without waiting for an answer, my emperor pulled me to him and kissed me hard and full on the mouth.

"Yuck, gross," Susannah had the nerve to say.

Freni held her tongue, but I knew she was watching us with intense interest, no doubt thinking about her Mose.

Oh, for the record, I said, "Yes."